JUSTICE

**A Novel
In
Three Parts**

By Michael L. Rea

Other Works by this Author:

The Raven Stone-A Novel

Connected: Remaining Human in a Networked World (Non-Fiction)

Other Works by Workshop For Writers:

Old Bones- A Mystery by Greg Picard and Wendy Picard Gorham

Christ at the Center: What Christians Should Know by Janet E. Rea (Non-Fiction)

Coming Fall of 2014:

This Side of Reality by Michael L. Rea, (sequel to *Justice*)

All Things in Christ: What Christians Should Understand by Janet E. Rea

www.workshopforwriters.com

Contents

Justice

KNOWING

Part I

Justice

The mind is its own place, and in itself
Can make a heav'n of hell, a hell of heav'n.
John Milton, *Paradise Lost*

For my students.

Justice

Chapter One

Garrett Adams stared out the front window, gazing deep into the mist. It was drizzling outside. It could barely be called rain, more like a falling mist, nothing new for Seattle. It seemed as if there was some sort of moisture falling from the sky three hundred days of the year. He was used to the rain, having lived here his whole life. Despite the gray, it was not going to dampen his spirits; not today.

He turned and looked down into the crib next to him. Emily was sleeping quietly; unaware that daylight had already announced itself. She was now nine months old, named after Garrett's grandmother and the spitting image of her mother. He was still growing used to the idea of being a father. Every day seemed like a new adventure as he watched her grow and change.

He still remembered the day he first held her in his arms. He had been in awe when he had held her close and felt her breathing. She was a miracle, a new life, both exciting and a complete mystery at the same time. She occupied every moment of his every day, as if everything else in the world had been reduced in its importance. He felt a sort of pride, not the pride of selfish arrogance, but the sense of being a part of something more meaningful, something of purpose. It changed him, changed the way he saw himself, and the way he saw the world. He wanted to be a good father. He wanted to make a difference in her life.

He sat down in the chair next to the bed. Stephanie was still sleeping. She had gotten up in the middle of the night to care for Emily and he did not want to wake her now. He just sat watching her sleep. She was his best friend. From the first moment they had met, he had fallen in love with her. Even as she slept, he could only see her for how beautiful she was. She was his wife and this too amazed him. What she ever saw in this tall, gangly scientist, he would never understand, but, whatever it was, he was glad for it.

He felt perfectly at peace, content, as if all things were as they should be. Right here in this room was everything he could ever hope for, an Eden of sorts, perfect in every way. He turned and looked out the window again, it was still gray and dark, as it had been before, but he no longer noticed or perhaps it no longer mattered.

"Good morning," he heard a gentle voice whisper. It was Stephanie, she had awakened. "What are you doing?"

"Nothing, just enjoying the quiet of the morning, I suppose." He answered in a hushed tone, careful not to wake his sleeping daughter.

"This is a big day for you, isn't it?" she said.

"I guess so, we'll see," somehow his enthusiasm for his work had waned a bit, forgotten in the moment.

"You guess so," she sat up. "You haven't been able to talk about anything else for the past two weeks and now all you have to say is, 'you guess so'. Are you having second thoughts?"

"No, I'm still excited. In fact I should be getting on my way."

"Do you want me to make you some breakfast?"

"No, no. Don't get up, you had a long night. I'll be fine. I'll get a muffin and some Starbuck's on the way. You don't have to get up." He stood up, bent over and gave her a kiss, and then placed a kiss on Emily's forehead, before starting for the bedroom door.

"I'll try and come home for lunch; that is, if everything goes smoothly. I'll give you a call." As he stepped through the door, he glanced over his shoulder. Stephanie was already out of bed and slipping on her robe.

"Goodbye, Garret, I hope everything goes well," he could hear her say as he left.

He skipped down the steps, umbrella in one hand and his satchel strung over his other shoulder. They lived in a small, second story, two bedroom apartment on Queen Ann Hill. They had moved there right after they were married. It had been conveniently located, in close proximity to the University of Washington where he had received his Ph.D. in neurobiology. When they discovered that Stephanie was pregnant with Emily, they had talked about moving to a bigger place, but as of yet they hadn't found anything they really liked.

He got to the bus stop just as the bus arrived. He had stopped driving to work during the first week. Parking in downtown Seattle was sparse and it turned out that the bus was actually a cheaper and easier alternative. As he plopped down on an empty seat, he began thinking about work.

Stephanie was right, today was a big day. He was about to try something that if successful would have far reaching implications for all of society. He mused that there might even be a promotion or, even more importantly, a significant increase in salary, as a result.

He worked at the Institute for Enhanced Artificial Thought, or the IEAT. (No one had particularly liked the acronym, but it had stuck just the same.) It was a relatively new company and most of the researchers were very young, much like him, recently hired, and right out of graduate school. The goal of the company was to find new ways to enhance the virtual world experience. VWE was quickly replacing the old antiquated 3D video games and would soon provide enthusiasts with the full artificial waking-dream experience.

As with any new form of technology, there had been many glitches, the most common one being that the technology had not fully bridged the experiential gap between the real world and the virtual. Although the participant was fully immersed in the virtual experience, almost in a dreamlike state, there was the constant threat of the individual's consciousness remaining connected to the real world, diluting the virtual experience. Then there was also the problem that the virtual experience remained dreamlike, not quite real, lacking a sharp focus, as if the images had blurred edges and the colors were either muted or too vibrant; it wasn't quite natural.

His research team had been working on trying to solve the problem of isolating the participant's conscious mind from the external surroundings. The real breakthrough came when Garrett had stumbled on an article in an obscure psychotherapy journal that mentioned the use of a drug that was being used in experiments with patients to enhance their ability to remember waking dreams. The drug was a derivative of a plant that grew in the Caribbean. At one time it had been used by those who practiced voodoo to place their victim's in a trance-like state. Despite the nefarious and superstitious nature of its origins, researchers believe the drug may actually work to block the neural pathways between consciousness and self-awareness.

Experiments with the drug allowed Garrett and his colleagues to isolate these pathways in the brain and to synthesize a similar drug which allowed them to enhance brain recognition of virtual stimuli without interference from sensory perception. There had been some concern early on because the original article had suggested that there was an unusual side effect when using the drug in which the victims claimed they had memories of a telepathic nature, being able to read other person's minds. Garrett took this to be merely a hallucinogenic experience and dismissed it. He had been a little leery of suggesting the use of an untried drug to his colleagues, especially something associated with the mystical vodoo, but in the end, the results ended up being almost staggering in terms of their promise.

The second breakthrough was even more astonishing because it happened by accident. His research partner, Raphael Seraph, had been working on a way to block the electrical impulses sent to the brain by the sensory neurons. He had come up with a way to send low intensity electromagnetic waves to interfere with these electrical signals, thus eliminating any connection to the outside world. The result was a completely enhanced virtual experience that mimicked the real world. However, the side effect was completely unexpected.

After several experiments with trial subjects from off the street, with mixed results, Garrett decided they needed a fresh approach. The problem with using untrained minds was that the subjects were not always able to articulate their entire experience and therefore it was difficult to know just how real the experience seemed to them. In the end he determined that the only way to solve the problem was to play the part of a subject himself.

Raphael had argued that this was far from being professional-the scientist getting too close to the science so to speak-but in the end he consented to doing one trial. Grudgingly, he placed the electrodes in position around Garret's cerebral cortex, and the shielded visor over his eyes. He then injected him with the drug cocktail. Garrett could still see his friend's concerned look as he slowly slipped into dreamlike state, from the real world to the virtual.

At first, Garrett found himself sitting on a beach on what seemed to be a deserted island; the programmed virtual experience. He could feel the breeze coming off the ocean against his skin and hear the gentle rhythmic sound of the waves as they fell on shore. It was quite peaceful and soothing, and completely real. The only thing that was disturbing was the lack of self-awareness. His sense of person was barely on the edge of his consciousness. It seemed to be working. Then the real fun began.

While Garrett was completely immersed in his virtual beach experience, Raphael was monitoring his vitals and playing with the dials of EM wave modulator, the whole time making sure the computers were recording every variance. At some point, without warning there was surge in the current of the electromagnetic pulse generator. To Raphael, the effect was unobserved, but for Garrett it was a completely different matter.

Without warning Garrett was transported from the beach and suddenly found himself standing on a street corner in downtown Seattle. He knew this, because he had been on this very corner several times before. It was kitty corner to the bus stop where he caught the bus home from work. The experience was real, in fact so real, that it wasn't until later, after he had left the virtual world, that he realized that it had not been real. The thing was, it was so real, that the longer it lasted, the more he became convinced it was real. It had been a success, he had been completely unaware of the lab bed he was laying on-the real world-in that moment, the virtual had become the real.

Then there was the twist. As he stood standing on the corner, watching the people and traffic flow by, the accident happened. Without warning, in a flash, the light changed, a man stepped out on to the crosswalk in front of him and a car came out of nowhere striking the man and sending him sprawling. Garrett heard the impact and it sent a chill through him. There, right in front of him, lay the man on the ground, blood flowing from his head. He was not moving, he was dead, killed instantly. Garrett felt the rush of adrenaline in his veins as his heart started to pound.

In the next moment he was awake, brought back to the real world by Raphael as soon as the technician had noticed his rapid heartbeat. Garrett literally sat up on the bed, causing some of the electrodes to fall from his head. The rapid change from one "reality" to another was too quick for his mind to absorb and brought a surge of nausea and dizziness. He turned and vomited onto the floor, soiling Raphael's shoes.

Raphael spent the next several minutes flooding him with questions as he tried to sort out what had happened. There was nothing in the programing of the virtual experience that should have allowed for his sudden change in location to downtown Seattle. After several days of pouring over data and checking every connection, they came to the conclusion that the current surge was merely an anomaly and that the whole virtual experience, including the accident, was nothing more than something manufactured by Garrett's subconscious.

They chalked it all up to a failed trial, that is, until something quite strange happened a few days later. Garrett had left work a little early on a Friday, still pondering what had gone wrong with the trial the week before. He was sitting on a bench, waiting for his bus ride home, trying to make sense of everything, when all of sudden something caught his attention out of the corner of his eye. The light at the intersection had changed and the cars closest to him had come to a halt, but on the other side a car continued into the intersection. He was about to jump up and shout a warning, but it was too late. The car slammed into a pedestrian who had just stepped onto the crosswalk. As he stood looking at the scene, he was beside himself with wonder. When he regained his composure, he ran across the street to where the victim was lying, blood already staining the pavement. It was the same person, he was sure of it. It was the very man he had seen struck by the car in his virtual experience. He looked up, there was a man standing on the curb, looking down at the victim, not moving, in shock. He was standing in the very spot where Garrett had been standing in his dream. 'It was a dream, right', he thought to himself, trying to convince himself that this was just déjà vu.

Garrett couldn't go home. He went back to the lab where Raphael was just cleaning up for the day. He slouched down in a chair in front of his friend. His mind was racing, trying to make sense of what he had seen. After regaining his composure, he told his friend what had happened and over the next several hours they tried to come up with an explanation.

There was only one possible conclusion they could reach that made any sense. Somehow, the electrical surge had resulted in some kind of premonition experience. Garrett had seen into the future, not only that, he had seen it through someone else's eyes.

Given the unlikeliness of this event, they spent the next several days examining the ramifications and every possible scenario. They checked and double checked the data. Finally, Garrett came to the realization that they needed some help, so he decided to enlist his friend, Michael DeAngelo.

Garrett had first met Michael at the University of Washington during a Saturday morning pick-up basketball game at the gym. Michael's three on three team was short a man and they invited Garrett to jump in. From that moment they became friends and played basketball together nearly every weekend. When they both graduated, they just kept on with the weekly appointment; it seemed natural, since both had taken jobs with local companies.

Michael was a theoretical physicist specializing in quantum singularities. His doctoral thesis had been on detection of micro-singularities generated by high frequency electromagnetic fields. Early theorists in space-time problems had proposed that time travel might best be accomplished by the use of wormholes. However, since finding a worm hole in space is a little bit like finding the proverbial needle in a haystack, and in a haystack the size of the sun, recent attempts at finding wormholes and been relegated to looking into the micro-world. Micro-wormholes were purely theoretical and essentially useless in the realm of time travel. Even so, if they could be detected, then they might provide a clue for finding larger ones in space.

When Michael first heard of the space-time problem encountered by Raphael and Garrett, he was more than intrigued. Instead of merely looking at the event as a premonition, he looked at it as a form of time travel. Was it possible that a singularity could be opened momentarily in space-time by an electromagnetic impulse combined with an enhanced telepathic brain wave just long enough for a person's consciousness to pass through or at least look through to the other side? Furthermore, since brain waves essentially take up no space, the size of the micro-worm hole would be inconsequential.

When Michael had first begun relating his theory to Raphael and Garrett, he had hardly been able to contain himself. The ramifications of this accidental discovery were far reaching. Although he never said it aloud, he could envision a Nobel Prize in it.

Garrett had always thought of telepathy as being from the realm of hokum. Despite this, he tried to remain open-minded. Michael's theory had some merit. If a person could read another person's mind, this could only be accomplished by some form of brain waves traveling from one person to another. Since brain activity was essentially electrical, and electricity could generate electromagnetic waves, it was not out of the realm of the possibility that these waves could travel from one mind to another. And since brain waves in the form electromagnetic signals take up very little space, it would be logical to think that they could pass through micro-fissures in the space-time fabric, regardless of how small.

Of course, this would mean they would have to test the theories with additional experiments. They would have to recreate the conditions and get reproducible evidence of seeing into the future. In addition, several questions needed to be answered. How long could the micro-worm holes be kept open? Could they have any control over where the other end of the worm hole opened; that is, could they look at a particular time into the future? If so, what were the limits? How far into the future could they look? And if they could look into the future, could they also look into the past?

For the next several weeks, they ran experiments with volunteer subjects. The records of the first event helped greatly in establishing the necessary conditions. With each experiment, Michael kept pouring over the data, trying to work out the quantum physics.

They were still faced with the problem of who to use for the subjects in the trials. To suggest to a trial subject that they were going to be sending them or at least their thoughts into the future seemed to be a little risky. In the end they decided to tell the subjects to simply report anything and everything unusual about their virtual experience, in hopes that they would reveal something that would suggest a future event. At first, this proved to be unsuccessful. Nothing the subjects related seemed to suggest that they had been successful and they began to worry that they had not been able to recreate the proper conditions.

Then, just when they had given up hope, one of their subjects came back. It was a young woman in her mid-twenties and right away Garrett could see that she was a little shook up. When he asked her what the problem was, or more specifically, whether she was experiencing any adverse side-affects from the trial, she simply asked if he believed in déjà vu. She then began to relate to him that she had recently relived her virtual reality, or least she thought she had. It had been strange. It was as if she was watching it happen from a different place.

Garrett assured her that it must have simply been a coincidence, a premonition, and sent her on her way. As soon as she had left the office, he and Raphael began jumping up and down. They had done it. Over the next several days they called in each subject for follow-up interviews. Two others also reported having similar déjà vu experiences. This was just enough data for Michael to start working out the parameters for a controlled experiment in which they could roughly pinpoint the moment of the opening on the other end of the worm hole. The only thing was, this time one of them would have to be the trial subject.

They had decided to try and leap forward to an event that they already knew was going to happen. In the end, they decided to choose the date of a seminar on Super String Theory that was being held by the University's Physics department. It would mean setting the parameters to open a worm hole twenty six days into the future and to ensure their success, they all planned to attend the seminar, and to sit at different locations and record everything to be able to check the accuracy of the trial. In this case, Michael would serve as the trial subject. Even though they had worked out the mathematics of the time jump, they were still unsure of how to determine the location in space.

To everyone's surprise, Michael's consciousness leaped directly into the auditorium where the seminar was being held. Garrett monitored every neurophysiological reaction, while Raphael monitored the electromagnetic pulse. They kept the connection open for two minutes, and then brought him back.

When Michael woke, he was able to confirm that he had been (or least his mind had been) at the seminar in the auditorium. Raphael captured his description of the event on video as Michael described everything that had happened in minute detail. It appeared they had been successful.

Twenty six days later the three of them sat in different locations in the auditorium. In the end they were able to isolate the location where Michael had transported to, or in other words the mind he had transported into. This was the last part of the mystery, why this person? What was it about him that made him receptive to the opening of the "neuro-field singularity" as they would come to call it? And also, why did he jump directly to the auditorium? The calculations didn't allow for that level of control of the space-time target on the other end of the micro-wormhole.

Chapter Two

Garrett stepped off the bus and made a bee line for the Starbucks on the corner. He ordered his regular grande vanilla roast and a blueberry scone. He took a sip of his coffee and tucked the bag containing the scone into his satchel and then walked the half a block to the building where the IEAT was housed.

The Institute occupied the entire sixth floor. It was unlikely that anybody in the city, other than IEAT employees, was even aware that the Institute existed, or if they did, they had no idea what it was for. For that matter, Garrett was a bit unsure of what research was being done in the Institute except for what was happening in his own department. The only other person he talked to besides Raphael and Michael, was his supervisor, whom he presented a written report to every month.

It had now been nearly five months since the first event and today they had planned to push the envelope a bit. It had been decided that an attempted leap several days into the future was not enough to be convincing to anyone. They would have to leap years into the future, maybe decades.

It was decided that, this time, they would attempt to open a singularity that would connect to a time and place twenty years into the future. After much debate, it was decided that Garrett would have to be the subject this time. The calculations for making a jump through this much time required Michael to remain on this side. They no longer thought of the event as a virtual reality, but instead as a bridge between two sides of reality. In order to determine the level of success, Garrett would have to find some evidence of the time marker in the future.

Garrett entered the lab to find Michael and Raphael hard at work making the final preparations. Garrett had been able to convince his boss to employ Michael full-time at the Institute, and Garrett was convinced that he was beginning to spend more time in the lab than either Raphael or himself.

"Good morning gentleman, how are we doing?"

"It's about time you got here," Michael greeted. "Where have you been? We were concerned that you might be having second thoughts."

"Speak for yourself," Raphael chimed in. "I wasn't thinking any such thing. I knew you would show up. Although I don't think I would blame you if you did back out."

"Sorry guys, I got up a little late. Emily was up, crying much of the night. What do you mean you wouldn't blame me if I decided to back out? What's that supposed to mean?" he directed at Raphael.

"It's just that sometimes I wonder if we should be doing this. You know. One shouldn't know too much about their future, space-time paradoxes and all that. Perhaps we should leave well enough alone."

"Come on. You can't be serious," Michael chided. "After all this work, you think we should leave it alone, and call it quits. Are you crazy? We're right on the verge of making the most significant breakthrough of the 21st century. If we're successful, it could open the door to possibilities that none of us could even imagine."

"It could also be dangerous!" Raphael insisted. "I don't think that it was meant for man to know the future. There are some things that we are just not supposed to know. The whole problem with knowing the future is that if you like what you see, you may try and make sure it happens and in the end change the outcome. Or, you may not like what you see, and do everything you can to change it, which in the end may be more disastrous. I think we need to be cautious. It might be better to leave it alone, to not know."

"Okay, Raphael, I think we all realize that we need to move cautiously. Just don't get paranoid on us. Besides I'm counting on you to bring me back, or I guess I mean to say wake me up, when the time is right." Garret realized he had made a little play on words. He was merely trying to lighten the moment, but he wasn't sure he was successful. Raphael still seemed a bit on edge.

"I think you were right the first time, I will be bringing you back." Raphael corrected. "It is important that everyone realizes that this is not a dream. It's not just a matter of waking you up. I will be pulling you back from one reality into this one. Your body may not be going anywhere, but everything suggests that this is an actual transportation of your conscious being to the other side. That's what I'm worried about. What if I can't get you back? What then?"

"I'm sure everything will be fine," Michael encouraged. "It's all about the physics, and I believe we can trust it. It hasn't let us down before."

"True, the physics does work, and although we have been able to roughly estimate the time on the other end of the micro-fissure in the space-time fabric, we have not collected enough data to allow us to control the location of the jump. Why for instance did you end up at the place of the accident in your first event, Garrett? Have you thought about that? Was it mere chance? What if we send you somewhere unsafe over which we have no control?"

"Really, Raphael, have you forgotten that his body will still be here under the strictest of conditions and your careful eye."

"No, I haven't forgotten, but I'm sure Garrett is well aware that the mind can be influenced to believe the danger is real, even if the body is safe."

"You're right of course, but the body will also show signs of stress, increased heart rate, adrenaline, etc. It is your job to watch these things carefully, and to yank me back at the least sign of a problem. I'm quite confident in your being able to handle this." Garrett was confident, but he had to admit to himself that he had at least a few reservations. Raphael was right to be concerned, but it was not enough to cause him to think they should abandon the trial.

"Well, after all, it's your neck on the line. I'm okay with it, as long as you know what you're getting into."

"Okay, then, let's get on with it," Michael insisted. "Everything is set, my calculations are completed and we are ready to begin. All we need now is a subject on the bed."

Garrett smiled. He knew that Michael wasn't throwing caution to the wind, it was not his style. He was just trying to bring a little levity to the situation. Michael was more than aware of the danger, but he was also weighing the potential reward. It would have been hard for him to give up on the dream of making such an incredible discovery.

He took off his jacket, unbuttoned the top few buttons on his shirt and then climbed onto the bed. Raphael began attaching a series of detectors to his chest, wrist and head, all of which were necessary to monitor his vitals during the entire exercise.

Michael then placed a cap on his head. The cap was attached by dozens of wires to an interface that was in turn connected to a computer. This would allow Michael to create a series of electromagnetic impulses that would open the micro-fissure while at the same time creating an interface for the human conscious to pass through space-time. Although Michael had several theories about how and why human brain waves could pass through a micro-wormhole, the reality was it was purely theoretical. The truth was that they really didn't know how it worked. The discovery had been completely accidental and they were merely reproducing the conditions that resulted in the first event. This was experimental science at the basest level. The cap was also connected to a visor and earphones that would enable them to completely eliminate any outside stimulus.

Raphael completed the preparations by placing an I.V. needle into Garret's right forearm. This would be the means to introduce the drug concoction that provided enhanced telepathic abilities. It would also be the means for giving a shot of stimulant should they need to revive the subject quickly.

Raphael spoke into a microphone so that Garret could hear him. "We're just about ready. Are you okay?"

"I'm as ready as I will ever be. Proceed." Garrett responded.

"Okay, starting the drip," Raphael's voice came through the earphones.

Garret began to feel the effects of the drugs almost immediately. It was a strange feeling, not entirely unpleasant. His eyes were closed, but the blackness soon turned to a kaleidoscope of colors. Strangely, he could actually tell when the electromagnetic stimulus began, it was as if he was watching a rapid slide show of images appear, as if little pockets of his mind were being opened up one after other, first memories, and then imaginations. Progressively they became more real, as if he were passing through a dense fog into the sunshine. Then without warning there was a bright flash.

When he opened his eyes he was sitting at a table outside a small cafe. He knew this place, he had been here before, he was sure he had. It was right at the edge of his mind, but he couldn't remember when. He looked down at the table. There was some sort of electronic tablet on the table. He picked it up and as if responding to his touch, the screen came to life. The image on the screen seemed to be some news item. In the upper left he noticed the words *The Times.* The headlines jumped off the page, *Gas Prices Reach New High of $95 Per Gallon,* he picked up the tablet and began reading the first few lines of the lead article...*Middle Eastern Coalition holds Americans hostage, oil supply cut-off. With American oil reserves dwindling, the Federal Department of Resource Management warns extreme shortages in the near future.* He looked at the date at the top of the paper...*June 6, 2048.*

It took a moment for it to register. He had leaped forward to the future, 34 years. It had worked. Although Michael's calculations had been a little off-by fourteen years to be exact-it was by far the largest jump they had ever been able to achieve.

He looked up from the device. There was something different, something wrong. There were no cars on the road, none. There were some vehicles parked along the street, some of which he recognized, others of which he had no idea of the make and model. All of them looked as if they hadn't been in use for some time.

Was it possible that things had really gotten so bad that no one used their cars anymore? There were people walking in the street, not across the street, but in the street, as if they were unconcerned about traffic.

While he was lost in thought, he heard the voice of a young boy. "Hey Mister, I think he might need your help." He looked to his left to find a boy of about ten looking up at him from beneath a well-worn baseball cap. "Hey Mister, did you hear me. It looks like he's thinking about jumping. Don't you think you should do something?"

"What? What do you mean, who needs my help." Garrett was a little surprised. In his previous jump, he had never interacted with anyone. This was a new and strange experience. His voice was not his own.

"Up there!" The boy pointed to the top floor of the five story building across the street. "I think it's a jumper, sure it is. I've seen it before, he's a jumper alright."

Garrett followed the line of the boy's pointing finger until he could see a young man standing on a ledge just outside one of the fifth story windows. The boy was right. It looked as if the young man was thinking about jumping to his death. It was disturbing to hear the boy say it so matter of fact, as if it was a common occurrence.

"What makes you think there's anything I can do about it?" Garrett was not about to get involved. He was still unsure how long he would remain in this time.

"It's your job ain't it? I mean, like ain't you a Blue. Ain't you supposed to try and stop such things?"

A Blue? What did that mean? Garret turned and looked into the window of the café. His image was reflected in the nearest window. He was wearing a uniform. He was a cop.

How could that be? How could he have jumped into the mind of a cop? Why a cop? He was supposed to be inconspicuous, invisible. He could hardly do that as a cop. He was going to have to do something. But what was he supposed to do? He knew the paradox problem of messing with the past, but, what about the future? Would he affect the space-time fabric if he changed the future? What was he supposed to do? He couldn't just sit there without doing anything, especially now that a crowd was gathering and there were now several adults joining in with the young boy, trying to encourage him to do something.

"Alright, alright, I'm going." Garrett stood to his feet. It felt a little weird as if his body were made of lead. He walked across the street, the whole time looking skyward at the young man on the ledge. He entered the building on the ground floor and soon found the stairs. He tried to climb the stairs quickly, but each step seemed awkward, uncertain. It was not until he reached the fifth floor that it felt as if he had his legs under him. He walked down the hall and stood in front of the door of the apartment he believed the young man was standing outside of. He tried the door, it was unlocked.

He opened the door, slightly. "Hey there! Is there anybody there?" He said cautiously.

"Go away. Don't come any closer. If you do…if you do, I'll jump. I swear I will."

"Easy young man, I'm not coming any closer. I just wanted to know if you were okay. I mean, I don't think you really want to jump, now just come on back in here." Garrett was trying to sound calm, but the truth was his heart was pounding in his chest (well not really *his* heart, that's what made the experience so weird. Even though it wasn't his body, he could still feel his physical surroundings). He moved a little closer to the window, but still remained out of sight of the young man.

"I mean it. Don't come any closer." There was a tremble in the young man's voice.

"Easy kid, I am not going to do anything. Just relax. I just thought you might want someone to talk to. By the way, what's your name?" Garrett figured he just needed to keep him talking.

"What d'you care what my name is? What different does it make? You don't know me. You don't care anything about me. You're just some Blue in the wrong place at the wrong time."

"I just thought it would be better if we knew each other's name. My name is Tom." He saw no point in giving his real name.

There was a silent pause, with neither saying anything until the young man spoke. "My name is David, David Adams."

Garrett thought it strange that the young man had the same last name as his own, but he dismissed it as coincidence. "Hey, David. Nice to meet you. Now why don't you tell me why you're out on the ledge? You can't really be serious about jumping. After all, you have your whole life ahead of you. What are you, about sixteen?"

"Seventeen, and I don't see what that has to do with anything. You want to know why I am on this ledge, it's because it's meaningless. Everything is meaningless. My life is meaningless."

"It can't be all that bad. Why don't you tell me what has you all worked up?" Garrett was stumbling over his words. He wanted to keep David talking, but he was trying to be careful not to irritate him any further.

"It's just meaningless that's all." David said this very softly, so soft that Garrett almost didn't hear it at all. There was another lengthy silence.

This time Garrett broke the silence. "Hey, David." He spoke very softly. "Do you think I could at least come to the window? You know, just so I can see your face while we're talking. I think it might be better if we could actually see each other."

There was another pause. "I suppose that would be alright, but keep your distance. Any attempt to get to me and I jump."

Garrett moved to the window slowly. He looked out the window and saw David sitting on the ledge about six to eight feet from the window. The young man looked very agitated, sweat was beading on his forehead. He looked so young. His hair was jet black, but from the looks of it, it was dyed. He wore earrings in both ears and he had a third ring piercing his lower lip. His left arm was covered in a tattoo that extended from the sleeve of his T-shirt all the way to his wrist. It looked like some sort of snake winding itself through some sort of vine. There was fear written in his eyes. It was weird. There was something strikingly familiar about him.

"Hey there David, why don't you tell me what you mean? Why is everything meaningless?"

"Do you believe in fate, Tom; that events are purposeful, or predetermined? Or is it all just about random chance, or perhaps coincidence?"

"Fate, I suppose." Garrett wasn't really sure. It was difficult for him to think things were just blind chance, especially since he was currently experiencing a sort of time travel.

"Not me," David replied. "I think it's all just meaningless, blind chance. I'm just the result of chance. In fact I'm not sure I'm supposed to be here at all. I'm the consequence of a series of bad choices, an accident."

"I'm sure your parents would disagree. I don't think they would think of you as an accident."

"You don't know anything about my parents."

"Why don't you tell me about them? I'm sure they love you and right now they would be horrified to see you like this."

"Love, ha! That's a laugh. I don't even know my father, never have. He disappeared from the scene before I was even born. As for my mom, she has never loved me, not really. She is too caught up with herself, bouncing from one boyfriend to the next, all strung out on drugs or booze or both." Tears started to well up in his eyes as he spoke. "I've never known anything of love," he almost whispered this last phrase.

Garrett was unsure how to respond to this. The kid had obviously had a rough upbringing. He wasn't sure there was anything he could do or say that would make a difference.

"Com'on David. It can't be all that bad. We're all here for a reason. You're still young. You have your whole life ahead of you. Certainly there has to be someone who has shown you love. What about a girlfriend? I'm sure a good looking kid like you must have a girlfriend."

"Did, would be more like it. She dumped me. I can't really blame her. I mean who could love this," pointing to himself. He paused, the tears began to flow. He put his head in his hands and started weeping. "It's all my fault. I didn't mean to hurt her, it was all an accident." There was another pause. "It doesn't really matter anymore," he was more composed. "It's all over for us, just as it should be. I should never have been born, and in short while it will be like I was never here."

"Easy, David," Garrett was starting to get a little nervous. "Don't do anything stupid. There will be other opportunities, other girls."

"You just don't get it. There is no future for me, because there never really should have been a past. I wasn't supposed to be here." He started to cry again. "Only, could you do me a favor."

"Sure, whatever I can do for you."

"Tell my grandfather goodbye for me. He was always a pretty good guy. His name is Garrett, Garrett Adams." He was sobbing again. "Tell him I'm sorry."

The next moment happened so quickly and unexpectedly, Garrett couldn't even react. Without warning, David pushed himself from the ledge and began to fall. Garrett tried to reach for him, but he was too far away. All he could do was scream. In the next moment he found himself looking down to the street below where David's lifeless body now lay. His heart was pounding, he wanted to scream again, but nothing came out. He couldn't breathe. What was happening?

Chapter Three

Garrett started to stir slightly. The visor and cap had already been removed. Raphael checked the I.V. to make sure that the drip was sufficient. He had learned from all the previous trials that it was best to bring the subject back to reality a little slowly. The last thing he wanted was for Garrett to vomit all over his shoes again.

Garrett had only been under for a couple of minutes before his heart rate had begun to race. Raphael was not about to put his friend at risk. Whether Garrett had been able to determine the time he had jumped into was of little importance if they were unable to get him back.

Garrett slowly began to open his eyes, he was still very groggy, but he was aware enough of his surroundings to realize he was back, that is, back to his own time. He could barely decipher the muddled voices of his friends. "Garrett, are you awake? Hey Garrett, are you in there? C'mon, open those eyes. You can do it. That's right. Talk to us. Were you able to determine the time and place?"

He closed his eyes again. Everything was so foggy. He could barely remember what he had seen. It was all on the edge of his memory. He opened his eyes in a jerk. He remembered, he could see the headline of the news article again, just as plain as day. They had been successful. Or sort of successful, they had missed their time projection by fourteen years, but he had jumped more than two decades into the future. "We did it," he struggled to speak. "We were a little off on the time, but we did it."

He could see the building across the street in his mind and the young man who was sitting on the ledge. He closed his eyes. The young man was not just anyone. It was *his grandson.* He had been a witness to his own grandson's suicide. Was this possible? Was it real? Maybe this was just his imagination playing tricks on him.

"Garrett, are you still with us?" it was Michael.

He opened his eyes a second time. "Yeah, I'm here." The fogginess was slowly dissipating. "I can hear you, just give me a second." He was all torn emotionally. He could still see David's face as he fell from the ledge. It was haunting. But was it real? How could he know?

"You said we were a little off. How far off?" Michael asked.

"Fourteen years too much; I ended up thirty four years into the future."

Michael looked stunned. "Thirty four years, are you sure? I don't understand it. How could I have been that far off in my calculations?"

"It was thirty four years, I tell ya. I'll explain the whole thing later. Right now I need a chance to recover, a chance to think."

"Sure thing. Why don't you take a moment to collect your thoughts?" Raphael said. "We can ask all these questions later. You go ahead and take your time. Just relax."

Garrett closed his eyes again. "How long was I under, uh, I mean gone?"

"Just under two minutes," Raphael answered.

This was strange. It had certainly been more than two minutes. It should have been closer to an hour. Was it possible that time passage on either side of the worm-hole was different? Still too many questions, and not enough answers. He kept his eyes closed for several minutes, trying to regain a sense of the present. It was unnerving, moving between two realities.

It was still difficult for him to believe that what he had experienced was in fact the future. Even more difficult, was to believe that he had actually been talking to his grandson. Was it really the future? Or perhaps it was merely one possible future. He remembered having a discussion with Michael about the possibility of parallel dimensions, each a consequence of different choices, different events. Was this really his future or was it just a possible future? If it was the real future, then what had driven this young man to take his own life? More importantly, was it possible to change the outcome. He could hear Raphael's words again, echoing in his mind, "When we know the future and we don't like it, then we try and change it."

He slowly regained his sense of the present again. When the dizziness was gone, he opened his eyes and sat up in the bed. He was fully back and once again in control of his faculties.

"It was the future, or at least it seemed to be. Who knows if any of this is really real?" he said aloud, continuing his thoughts.

"How do you know what year it was? How can you be sure?" Michael said skeptically, clearly still a little irritated by having missed the projected year.

"I saw a newspaper report that was dated June 6, 2048."

"A newspaper? Thirty four years into the future and they still have newspapers?" Raphael questioned.

"Well not a newspaper exactly. It was a news report on an electronic tablet, a sort of Ipad, only the case was more translucent and it was completely responsive to my touch. It was different than anything I've ever seen."

"Slow down a little, Garrett. I think it's important that we record this," Michael instructed as he placed a video camera on the table in front of Garrett. "Start from the beginning. Try and remember everything you saw and did; every detail."

Garrett related everything he could remember. He amazed himself with the level of detail and clarity. It was as if could still see everything in his mind. He shared everything up to the point when David leaped from the ledge, everything except for who the young man was. He saw no point to telling them that he thought it was his grandson, at least not until he had sorted it out in his own mind.

Michael and Raphael sat in utter disbelief during the entire discourse. "You're saying you were in the body of a policeman?" Raphael finally asked.

"It seems so. I guess it was just coincidence. It was very strange. I could actually feel what he was he was feeling, or what I was feeling. I mean what his body was feeling. I guess I really don't know what I mean, it was so weird. And what's even stranger, while it only took two minutes, it seemed to me to be at least an hour."

"Fascinating," Michael broke in. "The truest essence of time travel is leaving from and returning to the same point in time as if no time had passed. However, in this instance, some time passed. It means the opening of the quantum singularity shifted slightly in this time. I have to study this further. There must be an explanation. We need to get greater control."

"What about the fact that you were fourteen years off in your calculations? I would think this would be of greater concern," Raphael chided.

"It's true; I'm still confused by that. But then again, it was by far the largest jump forward we have ever attempted. I suppose we shouldn't have expected too much. I will double-check my calculations and then we will set it up to try again."

"Try again, what are you talking about?" Raphael said. "Don't you think we should step back from this moment and reevaluate? Don't you think this is getting a little dangerous? Garrett's heart rate was off the chart before I was able to bring him back. The next time he may not be so lucky. I mean, what do you think Garrett? Don't you think we should proceed a little more cautiously?"

"I think I need a little break from all of this," Garret responded. Truth was, he was tired and somewhat unsettled by the whole experience. He didn't really want to talk about it anymore. "If you guys don't mind, I think it might be best to pick this up again tomorrow. Maybe after a good night's sleep, I will be able to remember more. I just don't think we have to decide what we're going to do next, right now. Let's give it some time. In the meantime, Michael, you can work out the glitches."

"I guess you're right, Garrett," Raphael said. "Sorry, we were so excited. I guess we momentarily forgot that you've been through quite enough today. Why don't you go ahead on home? Michael and I can finish going over the data and reviewing the event. We can talk about it tomorrow."

"Yeah go ahead on home, Garrett," Michael agreed. "We can talk more tomorrow." It was clear that he was already distracted and working on some calculations. He hardly looked up from his papers when Garrett grabbed his jacket and said goodbye.

Raphael walked Garrett to the door. "Take care of yourself, Garrett. Get some rest; you have been through a lot today. We'll talk more tomorrow," he said, patting Garrett on the back.

"Goodbye, Raph, thanks," he sort of mumbled. The door closed behind him and he walked down the hall to the elevator.

His mind was racing all the way home. David was his grandson. Did that mean he was Emily's son, or did he and Stephanie have more children? He did the math in his head, if he was born in 2031, then Emily would have only been about 17 or 18. It was her son. But why was his last name Adams? Who was the father? What did he mean he never knew his dad? What had happened? Did he say that his mother was a drug addict? How was that possible? It couldn't be possible, it wasn't so.

What was he going to tell Stephanie? Would she understand? Could she understand? Would she even believe him? He wouldn't tell her; he couldn't tell her. He wasn't even sure it was true. How could he tell her? It would only serve to hurt her; there was nothing to be gained by it.

As he entered the front door of the apartment, he could see Stephanie sitting at the kitchen table with her back to him. Emily was in her high chair, her mother trying to feed her something green from a baby food jar.

"Is that you Garrett?" Stephanie looked over her shoulder. "You're home early. Is everything okay? Did your experiment work?"

"Yeah, everything is fine. I just decided to knock off a little early. The experiment went okay. We are going to go over the data in detail tomorrow. There was nothing more we could do today. I think I'm going to lie down for a bit. I have a bit of headache."

"Do you want some lunch?" Stephanie asked. "I could make a sandwich or something."

"No thanks, maybe a little later. I just need to lie down."

Garrett kicked off his shoes and left them at the foot of the bed. He draped his jacket over a nearby chair and then he just plopped down onto the bed. He closed his eyes. He could still see David, looking up at him as he fell toward the ground below. He couldn't get the image out of his mind. It had all been so real.

He felt horrible, a deep, undefinable, sorrow. He didn't really know the young man, but he still felt connected to him. It was his grandson, a grandson who had not been born yet, but he was still his flesh and blood. It was hard to imagine what would have driven him to such a desperate act. Why hadn't there been someone to stop him? Why hadn't he been there to stop him, not his time traveling conscious self, but his real self, Garrett Adams. He kept thinking about it, and then he drifted off to sleep.

He was at the corner café, looking up at the building across the street. A young man was sitting on a ledge and a police officer was leaning out a nearby window. They were talking. He could barely see the young man, but he looked familiar. He stepped out into the street. He wanted to shout up to the young man, *but he couldn't seem to speak. No matter how hard he tried, he couldn't make a sound. Then without warning the young man fell from the ledge. He cried out, "No!"*

"Garrett, are you all right?" It was Stephanie. He felt her hand on his shoulder. He opened his eyes. "You fell asleep. Did you have a bad dream? You were screaming."

"Sorry. Yeah I guess I was having a bad dream." He sat up.

"Are you hungry? I made you a sandwich."

"Yeah, I guess I should eat something. Sorry, I hope I didn't startle you, I guess I was a little tired."

"No, but I just put Emily down for her nap. I hope you didn't wake her." Stephanie left the bedroom.

Garrett stood up from the bed slowly. He was a little dizzy. It was almost as if he were having a bit of an out of body experience, as if everything wasn't connected. It must be because of the leap in time. It was a far different feeling than his first leap. It was possible that the side effects were more pronounced with longer leaps.

He sat down at the table and took a bite of his sandwich. It was weird, his dream, it was as if he were watching the whole thing all over again, but this time from ground level. He still felt the horror, it was hard to let go of it.

"You want to talk about it?" Stephanie asked as she sat down in the chair next to him.

He smiled, hoping to place her at ease. "No, I'm alright. It was just a strange dream."

"I wasn't' talking about the dream," she put her hand on his. "Raphael called while you were napping, to ask if you were alright. He wouldn't tell me what it was all about, but I could tell he sounded concerned."

"It's okay. It's just that the experiment proved to have some unexpected results and it kind of wore me out, nothing more." He was not about to tell Stephanie the details. For all she knew, he was simply trying to enhance virtual world experiences. He had never told her about the attempts to leap into the future. It was supposed to remain a secret. The only person, outside of his team who was aware of their research was his supervisor.

Justice

She smiled at him. "I can see that this is your story and you're sticking to it. You just better be careful."

Chapter Four

Raphael looked down at the half empty beer glass in front of him. It was clear he needed a moment to digest what he had just heard. "What do you mean it was your grandson? How could that possibly be true? For that matter, how could you even know that?"

"He told me." Garrett knew his friend would have a hard time believing him. He just couldn't keep it inside any longer. It had been eating at him for six months. He was still having dreams. He tried to forget, but he couldn't. Every time he looked at Emily, he thought about it. Regardless of what he had tried to do, he just couldn't put it out of his mind.

They had spent the last six months trying to figure out why they had been so inaccurate in their calculations. They decided to go back to using paid trial subjects, only this time they decided to do a more thorough job in the pre-interview. They not only asked questions about their past, but they asked the subject to describe any plans they had for the future. They used this as pretext for creating virtual events that mimicked their future plans. They were looking for any event that they could use as a target time.

In one instance, the subject said they were planning a trip to Mount Rainier in a month. Another said they were traveling to Hawaii in three months. These were perfect test cases for trying to pinpoint exact moments in time while at the same time using events that would appear as nothing more than virtual simulations. In each case, the trial subject believed themselves to have simply experienced a virtual dream. They were careful to make sure that there was nothing to suggest to the trial subjects that they had actually traveled into the future.

In six months they had run more than thirty trials, with a ninety percent success rate in pinpointing the right time. The level of success was so great, that Michael was convinced that the failed trials were only because the subject had made a change in their plans. With each day they grew more and more confident in their ability to control the opening of the worm-hole in another time.

"What do you mean he told you? How could he have told you? I guess I mean, why would he have told you?" Raphael still had a bit of a shocked look on his face.

"He told me. It wasn't as if he knew who I was. He thought he was talking to a cop. He simply told me to give a message to his grandfather, just before he jumped. He said that his grandfather's name was Garrett Adams. What do you think that means?"

Raphael shook his head in disbelief. "I don't know. I guess it is a little weird, too much so to be a coincidence. What was the message?"

"Tell him I'm sorry," Garrett paused, and swallowed before speaking. "And then he jumped. I can still see his face."

"No wonder your heart was racing," Raphael said. "You should have told us. I think we had a right to know."

"I'm telling you now. Besides, I had to sort it out in my own mind. It was unnerving. I mean, what would you do if you saw your grandchild jump to their death?"

"Me? I don't even have any children. I'm not even married."

"You know what I mean. It's why I have to go back. I have to find out what happened. I need to know why."

"I know what you're thinking," Raphael was clearly getting anxious. "This is exactly why I told you that we were playing with fire. We're not supposed to know too much about our future. We think by knowing we can control it. You think you can change it, but that's not true. The only thing you can change is the here and now."

"Okay, maybe I can't change it. Maybe you're right. But I need to know why. Why in the future is my grandson going to commit suicide? Does it have something to do with me? I just need to know? I've been a wreck ever since that moment, ever since I saw him die. I can't sleep at night. Every time I close my eyes, I see his face. I won't have any peace until I know why?"

"Maybe it's better if you don't know why. Have you thought of that? You are thinking that by knowing that you will have closure. Once again, you think by knowing that you are in control. That's just it, we are not in control; you are not in control. You are not God. Knowing is not going to change anything, least of all, it will not change you."

Garrett didn't respond. He didn't know what to say. He was starting to feel angry inside, not because he was mad at Raphael, but because his friend might actually be right. He wanted to know because he wanted to change the circumstances, he wanted to have control. The thing was, he couldn't let go of it. It was too late, once he had the knowledge of the future, the damage was done. It was consuming him.

"Look Garrett, I understand what you're going through, but you have to understand the risks. A leap of thirty four years in the future was obviously very taxing on your psyche. You were not the same for days afterward. Until we get a clearer picture of how it all works, I don't think the risk is worth it. I mean, you may not come back the next time. Think of Stephanie and Emily. The risk is too great."

"That's just it, Raph, I'm not thinking of making the same leap. I was thinking of something a little shorter, say seventeen or eighteen years. I need to go back in time from where I was, if I am going to find the answers I'm looking for. The reality is, I don't think I have a choice any longer. The cat is out of the bag, so to speak. I have to try."

Raphael looked at his watch. "It's getting a little late, I need to be going. We have a trial first thing in the morning."

"What time is it?"

"Ten thirty," Raphael replied.

"Ten thirty! I need to be getting home. Stephanie is going to be worried. I forgot to tell her I wouldn't be home for dinner." He left a five on the table as a tip and headed for the door. "See you tomorrow, Raph, we'll talk more then."

"Goodnight Garrett."

He stepped through the door and then tried to close it as quietly as he could. He figured Stephanie was probably sleeping. He slipped off his shoes and left them at the door. It wasn't until he turned around that he realized that Stephanie was sitting on the couch in the living room, in the dark.

"Where have you been?" she said, tension in her voice.

"Oh! Hi, Steph. I thought you'd be asleep. I stopped and had a pizza and a beer with Raphael. I guess the time sort of got away from us."

"You could have called, I have been worried sick."

"I know; I'm sorry. I meant to call, really. I just forgot."

"You forgot. Did you forget that you're married and you have a wife and daughter waiting for you at home?"

"Now Steph, don't over exaggerate it. I said I was sorry and I meant it. I just got caught up in the moment."

"It's not just this moment," she was clearly agitated. "I mean, what has gotten into you lately? For the past six months you have been working longer and longer hours. You're never home, and when you are, it's as if we're not even here. When was the last time you even played with your daughter? Emily started walking four months ago, but it was as if you hardly even noticed. I don't understand. It's as if you're afraid of her or something."

"That's crazy. I love Emily. Okay, maybe I haven't been quite myself lately, but that doesn't mean I don't love Emily, or for that matter you as well. I love you both, you are my whole life. I'm sorry I have been a little distracted. Things at work are really hopping. Besides why do you think I work so hard, if it's not for you and Emily? I do it for you, for both of you."

"Please, don't even suggest it. There's nothing that says you have to spend every waking hour at the lab. This is not about us at all. You're there, because you prefer there to here. What I don't understand is why. It's not like you. When Emily first came along you were such an attentive father. What changed? Is it something I did? Do you think I haven't noticed that you aren't sleeping? I can't tell if you're eating right, because we never eat together anymore. It's as if you don't really live here anymore. Just tell me what's wrong. What do I have to do to make it right?"

"You didn't do anything wrong." Garrett realized that Stephanie was absolutely right. It was the very thing he had been discussing with Raphael. He was in trouble and he knew it. He just didn't know how to fix it. "I can't really explain it Steph. It's not your fault, it's me. I've been troubled about some things at work and it has kind of had me distracted. I'm trying to work it out. I wish you could help, but you just can't. I just need a little more time." Even as he said it, it seemed using the word "time" carried with it a little irony.

"Why can't you tell me, Garrett? I'm your wife, if you can't tell me, then who?"

"You know what it's like at work. I'm not really supposed to tell you what we're doing. It's just the way it is, I wish I could tell you, but I just can't." It was only a half-truth.

"Then quit. We don't need it, not if it means that you can't be at home with your family. Just walk away. I'm sure you could find a job somewhere else. You don't have to work there. I'm afraid, Garrett. If you stay there, I'm afraid it's going to kill you. Right now it's killing all of us."

"Stephanie, I can't quit now, we are just about to make a breakthrough. Besides Michael and Raphael are depending upon me."

"I'm sure they will be fine without you. I'm telling you Garrett, we can't go on like this. I can't go on like this."

"Just give it a little more time, Steph. You'll see. It will be alright. I just need a little more time and then everything will calm down and we will be back to normal."

He paused a moment, reflecting, trying to come up with the right words to say. He knew she was confused. He wanted to ease her pain, but he just couldn't tell her about David. How could he?

"I love you and Emily, more than anything in the world. I would never do anything to hurt you. You just have to trust me."

Stephanie stood up and placed her arms around his waist, her head against his shoulder. As she hugged him she whispered in his ear, "I just don't want to lose you. Promise me things will get better. I need you here."

"I promise," he whispered back. "You'll see, everything will be back to normal before you know it. Now let's get to bed, I think we all need our rest. Things will look better tomorrow."

Chapter Five

Michael bent down over Garrett and checked each of the connections of the circuits attached to the cap. "Everything looks ready to go. How are you feeling?"

Truth was, Garrett was a little frightened, but he wasn't about to let on. "Everything is fine, I'm fine. Just make sure to get me to the right time."

"Don't worry, I've got this down. Just sit back and relax and let me be your guide into the future, future, futu…"

"Stop messing around Michael," Raphael interrupted. "I wish you would take this a little more seriously. If Garrett is putting himself at risk, the least we can do is make sure we get him back."

"Easy there Raph. It will be alright. He will be alright. You'll make sure of that."

"Are you sure you want to do this?" Raphael asked, directing the question toward Garrett.

"Yes, not only do I want to do this, but I have to do it. Now let's get on with it. I don't know why we have to go through all this discussion every time we are about to try something new."

Michael had reworked the data a hundred times, and with the number of new trials he was able to determine the patterns necessary to make a fairly accurate prediction of the parameters for any length jump. He was confident that he could pinpoint a date with about ninety six percent accuracy, which for a jump of seventeen years would be accurate to within seven or eight months. This was good enough for Garrett.

He closed his eyes. Everything was the same as it was before, the swirling colors and then all of a sudden a brilliant flash of light. He opened his eyes. He was standing in what seemed to be the hallway of a hospital. He looked down, he was wearing scrubs and a white coat; a stethoscope hung around his neck. He was a doctor.

"Can I see her now doctor?" A familiar voice spoke. He raised his eyes, the initial shock of seeing the person in front of him almost caused him to faint. It was Michael. Where was he? Had he failed to make the leap? Wait, it was different somehow, he was different somehow. There was a little gray hair at his temples, and a slight wrinkle at the corner of each eye. It was Michael, but he was older. He had leaped, and now he was standing in front of his old friend. He was about to say "Hey, Michael, don't you recognize me", when he stopped himself, realizing that he couldn't reveal who he was, not if he was to find the answers he was looking for.

"Doctor, did you hear me? Can I see her now?"

"Ah, yeah, of course…" Garrett was not sure what to do. He was holding a clipboard in his hands. At the top of the sheet was a room number-Examination 407. He looked up and down the hall; there were room numbers on every door. "Right this way, er, a, follow me."

He found the examination room without any difficulty and then opened the door, allowing Michael to pass through in front of him. Inside, sitting back in a bed, wearing a hospital smock, was a young girl of about eighteen.

"Hi Uncle Mike, thanks for coming," she said, reddening a little in the cheeks. I'm sorry you had to come all the way down here.

"Nonsense, glad to do it," Michael assured. "Are you alright?"

"She'll be fine." A nurse interrupted them. She was standing at the bedside, taking the young girl's blood pressure. "She just had a dizzy spell, nothing more, pretty normal."

"Dizzy spell, what from? What happened?"

"Oh Uncle Mike," the girl put her hands in her face and started to sob. "I've been so stupid," she hesitated. "I'm pregnant! I don't know what I'm going to do."

By this time Michael was sitting on the edge of the bed. He placed his arm on the girl's shoulder. "There, there, Emily, everything will be okay. You'll see. It will be okay." At this point, the girl buried her head in Michael's chest, and let the tears flow.

When Garrett first heard Michael say the name Emily, he almost stopped breathing. His eyes scanned the chart in front of him. The name at the top was Emily Adams. He scanned down to where it said Father and Mother's name-Garrett and Stephanie Adams. This was Emily, his Emily, all grown up. He could hardly believe it. It was all he could do to keep from running to her and taking her in his arms, letting her know that he was there, that it would be okay.

Emily regained control again of her emotions and sat up, wiping the tears from her cheeks with the back of her forearms. "I guess I am being a little silly. Crying isn't going to get me anywhere."

"It's okay Em, cry as much as you want. Only I don't understand. Why did you call me? Why aren't your parents here?"

This was the same question that had come into Garrett's mind. Why did she call Michael, and not him, or Stephanie?

"Oh, Uncle Mike, I just couldn't call them. You know what it has been like between us lately. I just couldn't face them. I can see their glowering faces now, passing judgment, telling me 'I told you so'. I wouldn't be able to stand it. They have no right to criticize me, they have no right. They gave that up long ago. They gave up their right to tell me what to do when they broke their promise to me."

"What do you mean?" Michael asked. "What promise?"

"The promise to love each other, you know, that 'til death do us part' crap. They made a promise to each other, and when they did, they made the same promise to me, even if I wasn't born yet. When they broke their promise to each other, they broke their promise to me. They have no right to judge, not them, but they will. The moment they find out they'll come down on me. They have no right, I tell ya, no right." She started to cry again.

What broken promise? What did she mean? What had happened? Were he and Stephanie separated? That's impossible. It couldn't be true. Garrett's mind was racing a mile a minute trying to sort it all out.

"Easy there, Em. I think you're being just a little too hard on them. They both love you very much. Don't jump to any conclusions. They might just surprise you. The last thing they wanted to do was hurt you."

"The last thing, hah, that's a laugh. They never once gave one thought about me. It was never about me, it was always about them. In fact that was what they were always saying. 'Darling this is not about you. Sometimes grown-ups just grow apart. This is between us. We both still love you, and we would never do anything to hurt you.' What a load of crap. The truth is they did hurt me, and no matter how they painted it, it was about me as well. They made a promise, a promise to love and care for one another for the rest of their lives and in so doing, to love and care for me as well, together.

If it was the last thing they wanted to do, to hurt me, then why didn't they make the first thing they should have done was to love each other? Daddy was always spending so many long hours at work, day after day and night after night, mom sitting at home, wondering when he would be there. You know what I mean, he was completely consumed with it, it was an addiction, still is."

"Your father works very hard, and it's true, he is sometimes distracted, but it doesn't mean he doesn't love you. I can't count the number of times he has told me how proud he is of you, how much you mean to him." Michael was doing the best he could to break through her anger.

"Well he has a strange way of showing it. He was always buying me presents as if that made up for abandoning me, and for abandoning Mom. And don't get me started on my mother, always nitpicking me and Daddy, never satisfied with anything either of us ever did. Instead of criticizing so much, she might have done well to look in the mirror, to realize she was not perfect. Instead of fighting for Daddy, instead of putting aside her own selfish pettiness, and just loving him for who he was, she had to go out and find herself, to discover her own personal fulfillment. Meanwhile, I just got swept into the background."

"She loves you, Emily. There is no doubt. It would pain her to think that you thought otherwise."

"Doesn't she know that the best way for her to love me was to love Daddy? Was that too much to ask?" She was sobbing again.

Garrett's emotions were all churned up. It was hard for him to sit and listen to all he was hearing. What had gone wrong? He couldn't imagine not loving Stephanie. She was the only woman he had ever loved. It couldn't be true, how could they have separated? This young girl was his daughter Emily, who he watched first enter the world with her big eyes staring up at him. In that moment he could not have imagined that anything would have been more important to him than her. What happened?

Emily looked his way and noticed the painful expression on his face. "I'm sorry Doctor, I guess I shouldn't bore you with my story. I didn't mean to go on and on like this. Is there any chance that I can get out of here soon? I mean, is it alright if my Uncle Mike takes me home?"

Garrett didn't know what to say. He looked down at the chart. There didn't seem to be any indication that she was hurt or anything. He guessed she could leave. He tried to remember back to when he and Stephanie first went to the doctor, when she was pregnant with Emily. The very thought of it caused his emotions to come to the surface again.

"I will get the nurse to provide you with some prenatal vitamins and you should make an appointment to see your personal physician as soon as you can." He wasn't a doctor, but it seemed the right thing to say.

He looked down at the chart again. "Miss, I noticed that your chart doesn't show the father's name."

"His name is Jesse Jacobson. I call him Jess, not that it really matters, the rat."

"What do you mean, Em?" Michael asked.

"I kept trying to tell him that I didn't want to have sex. He kept pressuring me. Telling me that he wasn't really sure that I loved him and that it would be a way that I could really show him how I felt. Then when I told him I was pregnant, the jerk had the nerve to suggest that it wasn't his baby. He basically told me that he didn't want to ever see me again."

"I'm sorry Emily. He does sound like a bit of jerk." Michael said.

"Yeah, and you can bet my parents will never let me hear the end of it. Mom never liked him from the start. She kept saying that there was just something about him, like he couldn't be trusted or something. It is one more chance for her to remind me of how stupid I am. The thing is, down deep, Jesse was actually a nice guy. I really did like him, the jerk." Tears started to trickle down her cheeks again. "Uncle Mike, do you think we could just get out of here? Can you take me home? And...maybe you could be there when I tell my Mom, you know, for a little moral support."

"Sure, kid, I'd be glad to. Go ahead and get dressed. We'll get you home and then you'll see; everything will be okay."

Garrett followed Michael into the hallway. "Seems like she's had had it a little rough," Garrett offered. It still seemed a bit weird that he was talking to Michael and yet his friend had no idea of who he was.

"Yeah, poor kid. Her parents got divorced when she was only six. She has never gotten over it. I think they always thought that she would be resilient and adjust. I don't think they had any idea how much it hurt her. Now, she constantly feels their disapproval, and I am sure she is afraid that this will send them over the edge."

"But I'm sure her parents must love her. I mean, parents never stop loving their kids." Garrett was still getting over the shock of the word divorce ringing in his ears.

"Oh sure they love her, but sometimes their pride and perhaps a little of their guilt gets in the way. The reality is that they love her enough to try and keep her from making mistakes, while all the time not allowing her to know that their love is unconditional, that even if she makes a mistake, they will still love and accept her. Right now, I'm not sure she is feeling that. It's not always just feeling love for a child, but how you demonstrate that love in the most difficult of circumstances."

Garrett was trying to figure out where Michael had gained such wisdom. He had never heard him talk like this before. It made him wonder if he was married. Did he have any children of his own? The door behind them opened and Emily stepped out wearing jeans and t-shirt with the word 'Freedom' in bold letters printed across the chest.

The nurse appeared out of nowhere and handed a bag to Emily. Michael shook his hand, "Thanks Doc, we appreciate everything. C'mon Em, let's get you home."

"You're welcome," is all Garrett could manage to say. Then as the two walked down the hallway toward the elevator, he whispered "Goodbye Emily, I do love you and I'm sorry."

Garrett went back into the examination room and sat down on the bed. He had insisted on coming to this time, to find out the answers to the questions, and the pain of what had been revealed to him was more than he could bear. This was the circumstance in which David had been born. An unwanted pregnancy for a young mother who did not feel she had the love and support of her own parents. David would grow up never knowing his father, and his mother, Emily would continue on a path to self-destruction, and he, Garrett, was responsible. It was he who had abandoned his wife and child. He had let something so meaningless as his work to distract him from his first priority, his first and most important love. Right now he wished he had never started this project and that he had never stumbled upon time travel. He began to weep, his heart felt so heavy, he didn't think he would recover. Raphael had been right. It was better, not knowing.

Chapter Six

Garrett found it a little difficult to focus on the menu in front of him. He rubbed his eyes gently to clear the fog. Traveling to and from the future was beginning to wear on him. There were these lingering moments of fuzziness, as if his mind was not fully connected to his body.

He was sitting in a booth next to a large window facing the street. The top of the menu read Johnny's Café. It was one of his favorite places to eat. He was particularly fond of the French dip sandwich piled high with tri-tip and smothered in Swiss cheese. He looked out the window. It was one of those strange and surprising sunny days in Seattle. He could barely remember what day it was, a sure sign he had been working too hard.

Stephanie appeared at the front door of the café. She was wearing that blue dress he loved so much. It was something about the way in which it was cut, flattering her feminine form and the color brought out the blue in her eyes. She was stunning. He waved at her so she could see where he was seated. As she approached the table he stood and gave her a kiss on the cheek.

"I hope you haven't been waiting long," she said as she slid into the seat opposite him.

"No, not long," he replied, a sort of half-truth since he really did not remember how long he'd been waiting.

The waitress arrived and placed a couple of glasses of water in front of them. "Are you ready to order?"

"I'll have the French dip and a Pepsi. Stephanie, do you know what you want?"

"I'll just have the Caesar salad."

"Where's Emily?" Garrett asked.

"I left her with my Mom, we have the entire afternoon free, that is, if you don't have to return to work."

"No, I'm free." He couldn't remember the last time he had taken time out from work. "You're looking quite beautiful today. Did you do something different to your hair?"

"Yeah, I bet you say that to all the girls." She laughed slightly as she said it.

"No, really Stephanie, you should never have to grow tired of hearing how beautiful you are, I mean it." He did mean it too. She was every bit as beautiful as the first day they had met.

"Thanks, it is nice to hear it from time to time. Ever since Emily came along, I felt like I have been losing myself. I love her and all, but she can be a little demanding. It's nice to take a little time off for myself, you know, to stop being Mom for a brief moment."

The waitress delivered their food and they sat quietly eating their lunch without interruption.

Stephanie finally broke the silence. "Have you ever felt like there was more to life, that perhaps you were missing something?"

It seemed a bit of a strange question, but Garrett played along. "I suppose everyone has thoughts like that. Everyone has dreams and aspirations, many of which don't come true, I suppose this leads to a certain kind of disappointment. What about you? Do you have dreams that have gone unrealized?"

"No, that's not exactly what I mean. I'm not naïve, I know that not all of our dreams come true. It's just that sometimes I feel like my life is out of control. I just wish it could feel different. I wish I could feel more in control."

"I see, it sounds like you would like to be able to know the future. That is really the only way to have control." Garrett thought this was a little ironic, given that he had never told Stephanie about the experiments at IEAT.

"What do you mean?" Stephanie seemed genuinely intrigued. She was looking at him as if she was hanging on every word. It sort of reminded him of when they were dating. It made him feel good.

"When you say you want to be in control, you really are saying that you want to know what will happen next. By knowing what will happen next, you may have the ability to control the outcome by making different choices now. The interesting thing is, the choices you make now do, in fact, affect the outcome of future events. In that sense you have control of the future already. You have complete control of your will. The key is you need to stop thinking about the future. What you have control of is the present. If you want to feel in control think in the present, make your choice now, that's when you have control."

"You make it sound so easy," Stephanie said.

"It is that easy. Take advantage of every moment, by making the choice. Don't let the choice be made for you. What is it that you want?" Garrett could hardly believe what he was saying. The words were coming out of his mouth, but did he really believe it. Did he think he really had any control? And what about the consequences, weren't there always consequences to every choice?

"Well, right now, I just want to enjoy a quiet afternoon, just the two of us." She smiled.

"There you go, you made a choice."

Garrett didn't usually order desert, but Stephanie seemed to have her heart set on some ice cream. As they finished up, she started talking about an art exhibit that was coming to the Seattle Center next month. She really wanted to go see it. Art was not really his thing, but he agreed to take her when the time came.

As they left the café, he looked up at the building across the street. It was a five story apartment building that had just recently been refurbished. There was a huge "Now Renting" sign out front. A bit of a chill went down his spine. He was having a sort of déjà vu moment, but couldn't really tell why. It was eerie.

As they started down the street, he reached down and took her hand. It had been awhile since they had actually walked hand in hand, he wasn't sure why. They were in walking distance from the apartment. There was a little park on the way and they stopped for a moment to look back at the city. They could see the Space Needle and the downtown beyond.

Garrett was reminded of when he and Stephanie had first met. It had been at the reception of the wedding of two of their friends, she had been a friend of the bride and he was friend of the groom. He had noticed her the first time he saw her. The reception was held in a pretty little park on the east side. When she wandered off from the rest of her party, he followed her and found her standing on a bridge over-looking a small pond. As he approached her, he noticed she was looking at her own reflection in the water. He thought she was the most beautiful creature he had ever seen. He had hesitated at first, but he had to speak, he could not let the moment pass without saying something to her.

"What do you see?" He asked.

She was startled at first, but then recognized that he was one of the guests at the wedding. "I'm not sure what I see. A girl who knows me, but I am not sure I know her."

"Then she is a mystery to you. Perhaps the reflection is not very clear."

"She is a mystery and perhaps a little vain for having looked so long."

"Then maybe you should look here instead. What do you see?"

Stephanie turned and looked at Garrett. "I see kindness."

"Look harder, look at my eyes. What do you see?"

She looked for a moment, and then a smile crossed her face. "I'm sorry, I'm not sure I see anything. What should I be looking for?"

"If you look closely, you will see beauty and grace reflected there, because that is what I see."

She smiled again. "Oh now I think I see. I see charity."

It was in that moment, standing on the bridge in the middle of a little park that they had fallen in love. Garrett had never really believed in love at first sight until that moment. He knew then that Stephanie was meant for him and there would never be anybody else like her.

Now walking with her, holding her hand, he felt good. It felt good, the love he had for her and she for him. Nothing else really mattered.

As they entered the apartment, Stephanie didn't let go of his hand. She led him to the bedroom. It was an invitation and he didn't resist, he couldn't resist. As she let go of his hand, he sat down gingerly on the end of the bed. She walked over to the bedroom window and carefully, gently pulled down on the chord, closing the curtains. It was still daylight and the late afternoon sun filtered in through the openings at the edges.

Stephanie turned and faced him. She just stood there, not moving, as if she were contemplating her next move. Then with subtlety and grace, she unfastened the buttons on her dress and let it fall to the floor. She delayed coming to him, it was both coy and amorous. She was unashamed, but in a way that demonstrated a modest pride.

She was yielding to him in complete submission. She was giving of herself, not as if she could be possessed, for she was not merely an object of affection. It was a willful subjection, a choice that stemmed from an inner confidence and strength. She belonged to him and he belonged to her. Both were masters and both were servants. Neither was the master, and neither was the servant. He loved her for it, more than he knew how to express. He wondered if she really knew how it made him feel. In that moment he was whole, content, and unafraid.

Without warning the bedroom door swung open and a man entered the room. Garrett stood up from the bed not initially knowing how to respond. He didn't understand what was happening. It was as if everything moved in slow motion. Stephanie had horror stricken across her face. She was trying to cover herself with her arms. He continued to stare in disbelief. At first he couldn't understand what he was seeing. The intruder was not a stranger, far from it. It was him. He was looking at himself.

He turned and caught a glimpse of his own face in the mirror. It was not his face. It was that of a stranger. What did this mean? Could it be that none of this was real, that he was in some sort of dream? No this was not a dream, it was...this was his future. The realization was more than he could bear.

"No!" he cried out, but it was not his voice. It had never been his voice.

He could not breathe. He fell to his knees, and then everything went black.

Chapter Seven

He woke in a darkened room. He was lying on a bed in the middle of a large room. There was no other furniture in the room. There was too little light in the room for him to be able discern any color. Everywhere he looked it was gray. At the far end of the room there was a door. Around the edges of the door he could detect a soft glow of blue light.

He placed his feet on the floor and carefully, with great effort, stood to his feet. It was not as if he was sore or in any kind of pain. It was just that his limbs did not seem to be responding to his will. It was as if the connections between his brain and body were not fully engaged.

He walked toward the door. It seemed an eternity before he finally reached it. He reached out his hand to the door knob. He stopped. He wanted to open it, he needed to open it, but something was stopping him. It was as if his will was not his own. He let go of the knob.

Why was he here? Where was here? He closed his eyes. He was trying to remember. How did he get here? The strain of trying to remember made him weary. He turned and looked around the room again. There were no clues. Nothing that would help him determine why he was here?

It wasn't as if he was afraid. Then he realized he didn't really feel anything. He was not happy. He was not sad. Was he dreaming? He pinched himself. He could feel the pinch, but it didn't hurt, there was no pain. What did this mean?

There was a large window on the wall across from the bed. He walked to it, very slowly. It appeared to be dusk. The sky was overcast and like the interior of the room, everything outside was gray. There were buildings, but there were no lights, no sign of people. Deep shadows cast a dark gray over everything. He could not see any plants, no trees, no grass. It was as if there was nothing alive.

Was he alone? Was there anybody else here? He sat down on the bed, staring at the door. Should he open it? What was on the other side? Maybe it was better to leave it alone. He wasn't in any pain. He was perfectly okay where he was. He didn't need to know what was on the side of the door. He could stay here, and wait. Why did he have to go anywhere?

He sat back in the bed. He closed his eyes. Maybe someone would come for him. That's right; he could wait here until someone came for him. He was fine for now. That's what he would do. He would just wait. When they wanted to, they would come. He would hear them. Their footsteps would sound their coming. He would wait until then.

When they came they would knock on the door and then they would enter. They would look at him and he at them. They would call his name...

His name, he didn't know his name. He had a name, he knew that. It was right on the edge of his mind, but he could not remember it.

It's not the worst thing, not remembering. Memories can be pleasing, but they can also be painful. Why did he need to remember? Was it really worth the risk? What if his memories were painful? He was perfectly content. He didn't really need his memories, good or bad. He would just wait here until someone came for him.

Did he really need a name? After all, there was nobody else here. What would be the point? We have names to identify us to other people, but there is no one else here. He did not really need a name. Who would call him by it? He would just sit here and wait. Waiting was good. Waiting meant no pain.

Maybe no one would ever come. That would be okay to. After all, if someone came, he might have to leave this room. He might have to go through the door. He didn't really want to go through the door. They couldn't make him go through the door, could they? He was fine with the way things were. He would wait.

Maybe he never had a name. Perhaps he was all there was. Why did he think that there was anybody else? There was no evidence that anybody else even existed. If no one else existed, then no one was coming. This was okay with him. He would wait. After all, what was wrong with waiting? At least here there was no pain.

He closed his eyes.

"Garrett, wake up."

He opened his eyes, nothing but grayness. "Is someone there? Who was Garrett? Was that his name? He couldn't be sure. He couldn't remember." There was no one there. He closed his eyes again. He didn't fall asleep. He didn't really feel tired. He didn't feel anything.

"Why are you here? Why don't you come back with me?" There it was again, the voice. He opened his eyes. There was someone there he could sense it. He could just make out someone deep within shadows, in the corner of the room.

"Don't you want to come back?" The voice seemed familiar.

"Who are you?" He asked.

"Don't you recognize me? It's me, Michael? Don't you remember?" The figure stepped out of the shadow.

"Michael? I'm not sure if I know you, I don't seem to remember anything."

"Sure you do, I'm your best friend. Come on, it's time for you to go home. It's safe now. All you have to do is walk through that door. Then you'll remember everything."

"I don't think I want to go with you. I'm not sure I want to know what's on the other side of that door. I tried to go through it earlier, but then I stopped. I was afraid. I don't want to feel like that again. It's safer here. Here I don't have to feel."

"What are you talking about? You can't stay here. Don't you see? There is nothing here. Besides, what about Stephanie and Emily, don't you want to see them?"

He'd heard those names before. They were there on the edge of memory. Why did he know them? He closed his eyes again. He was starting to remember. He then opened his eyes. "No! He shouted. Don't you understand? I can't leave here. Pain! I don't want to feel the pain."

"I see. You don't want to remember. Then you will have to remain here, and you will never know joy."

"What do you mean?"

"It's true that if you walk through that door you will remember and those memories may bring some pain, but they may also bring some joy. Here you will never know either, but here you are not really alive. There, on the other side of the door is life. With life you will know both pain and joy. That's how it works. This is death. Come with me, now."

"I don't know if I can. I'm afraid."

"I know you're afraid, but you can't stay here. You just can't. Take my hand, I will guide you. You'll see. Whatever is on the other side, I will be there with you. I will help you." The stranger held out his hand. "Come on Garrett. Come with me."

He remained on the bed. There was something familiar in the stranger's voice. He was sure he knew it. It was kind and he wanted to trust him. But he was still afraid.

He stood to his feet. It took a great deal of effort. His body was not responding to his mind. It felt so heavy. "Okay, I'll go with you he said." He took the strangers hand. He wasn't sure why? It was just something about that voice. He felt as if he could trust him.

Together they walked to the door. "Go ahead, open it." The stranger called Michael said.

"Can't you do it?" He asked.

"No, you have to do it. Go ahead, I'll be right by your side, but you must open it. I can't do it for you."

He reached down and touched the door knob. His hand let go again as if repulsed. He hesitated a moment and then tried again. This time he was able to turn the knob. He pulled the door open. There was a flash of light.

He opened his eyes. He was in the lab. Raphael was hovering over him. To his left lying on a second bed, electrodes attached to his head, was Michael, his eyes open as well.

"What happened? Where am I?" He tried to see past the fog in his mind. "How long have I been out?"

"Welcome back, Garrett. We thought we had lost you." Raphael replied. "Just relax a bit, Garrett. You've been through a lot. Take your time."

Garrett sat up in bed. He was trying to remember what happened. The last thing he could remember was Raphael counting backward as the trial began. He was being sent to the future. Did it work? He couldn't remember anything.

"How long was the trial? How long was I out?" He asked again.

"Nearly two hours, the longest of any trial," Raphael explained. "Two minutes in, your heart rate started to climb and then just as we were about to stop the trial and bring you back, you calmed down again. Then another two minutes and your vitals went off the chart. I tried to stop the trial, but nothing worked. It seemed you had slipped into some kind of coma. We thought we'd lost you all together. Then Michael got the bright idea that he could follow you, that he could somehow connect to your mind. I guess he was right, because here you are again, back to reality."

Garrett looked over at Michael, who, by this time had disconnected himself and was sitting up. "You came in after me?" He asked. "But how?"

"It seemed the right thing to do at the time. Although, I have to admit, I was skeptical whether it would work or not. But desperate situations require desperate measures. Besides, if we didn't bring you back, there would have been hell to pay with Stephanie."

As soon as he heard her name, the memories came flooding back all at once. He remembered everything, every painful detail. It was overwhelming. "Agh!" He cried out. "Why?" He buried his face in his hands. "Stephanie. I didn't want to remember. Can't you understand? It would have been better had I not come back."

Both Michael and Raphael jumped when Garrett cried out. They looked at each other quizzically. "Why, what happened, Garrett? What did you see?"

Garrett looked up at Raphael, anger and frustration written across his face. "You were right all along, Raph. We should never know our future. I wish we would have never created this contraption. We were all fools, and I was the biggest fool of all." He got up off the bed. His legs wobbled slightly, but he was able to regain his balance. He bolted for the door.

"Garrett, wait! Where are you going?" Michael shouted after him.

"I don't know, anywhere, but here," he shouted back. "Anytime, but here," he whispered as he passed through the door.

He stumbled aimlessly down the street. His mind was racing a mile a minute. Tears were filling his eyes. Why had she betrayed him? How could she do that to him? It was all her fault. He bumped into a man who was passing by on the sidewalk. "Sorry Mister," he apologized. He stopped and looked around. There was an Irish Pub on the next corner, he needed a drink.

Chapter Eight

Michael knocked on the door. It opened almost immediately, Stephanie waiting on the other side. She was obviously distressed, fear in her eyes.

"Thanks, for coming Mike," she said as he entered. "I didn't know what else to do. I've never seen him like this. He's drunk. He's never been drunk before, never, not in all the time I have known him." She began to sob. "He came home in a fit of rage. I don't know what's got into him. He has never said a cross word to me, not really." More sobs. "He kept going on about how I betrayed him. When I tried to ask him what he meant, he flew into a rage, throwing things against the wall and turning over furniture. I was afraid. I didn't know what to do. I took Emily into the bathroom and locked the door."

"Where is he now?" Michael asked.

"He is sitting on the floor of our bedroom, crying. He's crying. I've never seen him like this. Mike I'm so afraid. What happened to him?"

"He's had a rough time of it, Steph, an experiment gone wrong," Michael tried to explain. "It's a little complicated. He's not really himself."

"I don't think I can stay here. I'm not sure what he might do next. I'm taking Emily and I'm going to spend the night at my mom's. Can you help? Can you stay with him?"

"Sure Steph, you go ahead. I've got this. I'll sober him up. I know what to do. You'll see, I'll have him back to normal tomorrow."

Emily was sleeping, already packed into her car seat. Michael helped Stephanie carry her to the car. "Don't worry Steph, it will be alright. I'll call you in the morning," he assured. He stood on the sidewalk watching as mother and daughter drove away.

Despite his assurances, Michael actually had no idea what he was going to do. He still didn't understand what had sent Garrett over the edge. What happened during his leap into the future?

He found Garrett sitting against one wall of the bedroom. He was no longer crying, but clearly still despondent. "Hey Garrett, how ya doin' bud. Gosh, you look like hell."

"I feel...well let's just stay it's pretty close to hell." His speech was slurred. He paused a moment as if he were deep in thought. "Say, where'd you come from? Where's Steph?"

"She left Garrett, went to her mom's. You have her pretty shook up."

"Just as well, she might as well leave. She doesn't belong here anymore."

"Com'on Garrett, you don't mean that. Here let me help you up. I think maybe we need to get some coffee in you." He pulled Garrett to his feet and led him into the kitchen, where he promptly slumped down in a chair. Michael found the coffee in one of cupboards and poured a healthy amount into the top of the coffee maker. He then went into the bathroom and soaked some washcloths in hot water. After getting some coffee in Garrett and cleaning him up a bit, he sat down in the chair next to his friend. Garrett was still hunched over, alert, but still despondent.

"You want to tell me about it," Michael began. "What happened to you? What did you see?"

"I don't know if I can talk about, Mike. It was hard enough, without reliving it all over again."

"Look, Raphael told me about your first jump, that you met your grandson and how you were there when he committed suicide. You should've told me. I should have known why you wanted to go back."

"Raph was giving me enough grief. The last thing I needed was for you to get involved. It wasn't like I had a choice. I needed to know. He was my grandson. I needed to know what would have brought him to the place to take his own life."

"And did you? Did you find out the reason?"

"Perhaps, or at least a part of it." Garrett hesitated before continuing. "I saw Emily, as an adult. She had just found out she was pregnant. You were there."

"I was there?"

"Yeah, it was a little weird. You were there, because she didn't want to see me; or Stephanie for that matter. She was angry at us. She didn't want anything to do with us." Garrett went on to share as much of the conversation between Emily and Michael as he could remember. Michael listened intently.

"I suppose Raphael was right," Michael said after having heard everything. "Perhaps we shouldn't know too much about our future."

"I suppose, but maybe it is better I found out now and not later."

"What do you mean?"

"I haven't told you everything. You see I know why Stephanie and I got a divorce. I leaped a second time. This time I saw Stephanie." He didn't want to go on. The memory of it was more than he could bear. "I saw Steph...I saw her with another man. She was having an affair."

"Oh, I see," Michael now understood. He understood why Garrett had remained in the gray place. Why he hadn't wanted to return and what he meant by the pain. "I'm sorry Garrett."

"I don't understand. How could she do that to me? Why, doesn't she love me? Did she ever love me? Poor Emily."

"Yes, poor Emily and poor Stephanie, as well."

"Poor Stephanie, what do you mean? She betrayed me. It's all her fault. She doesn't deserve pity. I'm the one that feels the pain of what she did. Our child and our grandchild are the ones that paid the price, not her. She needs to feel the pain. She needs to know the consequences of her choice."

"Easy Garrett, you're not thinking straight. You're talking in the present tense as if this has already happened. You want to punish her for something that has not even happened yet, for something that may never happen. I think you need to step back from the situation and reflect a bit. It might not be too late. Who's to say things can't change?"

"Yeah, maybe things can change, but does it even matter? Do I really know who she is? I don't understand how she could have done this to me; not if she ever loved me."

"I think your being a little too hard on Steph for something she hasn't even done yet, perhaps hasn't even ever considered. We don't know or understand the circumstances? Do you remember what Emily said? She was angry at you because you had neglected her. You were spending too much time at work, too preoccupied. Is it possible that Stephanie will someday have these same feelings of neglect?"

Garrett sat up straight. "Are you saying this is all my fault?"

"No, I am not saying it's all your fault. I am merely suggesting that maybe you have to share in the culpability of the situation. It may not have been all Stephanie's fault, either. You know as well as any that when couples are in trouble, it usually means that both can share the responsibility. You make bad choices and she makes bad choices; shared culpability. It doesn't do any good in such situations for one to blame the other."

Garrett was finding it hard to think about this. He was tired. He rested his elbows on the table in front of him and placed his head in his hands.

"Maybe you should get some sleep. It is getting pretty late," Michael offered.

"Yeah, I am feeling a little tired." Garrett got up from the table and without looking back walked into the bedroom and plopped down onto the bed.

"I'll just crash here on the couch," Michael said. "I'll be right here if you need anything." Garrett didn't hear anything else, he drifted off to sleep.

The sun peeked through the window. Garrett could see blue sky in the opening between the curtains. He just lay there. He had a horrible headache, a reminder to him that the previous night's activities had not been a dream. He couldn't remember everything, but he knew he had behaved badly.

Michael had been right of course. He was angry over something that had not even happened yet. It was difficult to separate the virtual future from the reality of the present. It had all seemed so real, too real.

He had wondered whether there were possible paradoxes when traveling into the future. He thought back about what Raphael had said. "When we know the future and we don't like what we see, we try to change it and we end up doing more damage." He had been preoccupied. He had been so determined to find the answers to his questions, he had neglected Stephanie and Emily. And now, as a result of his behavior the previous night, he had further pushed them away.

Michael had been right. He was at least in part responsible, or would be if he continued on the same path. It was all too confusing.

He had seen the bitterness in his daughter's heart. He had seen the death of his grandchild. He was horrified by the thought that he might be partly to blame.

He slid out of bed and took a shower. The hot water eased a little of his headache and removed some of the fog. As he entered the kitchen he found Michael standing over the stove, frying some eggs.

"I figured you would probably need something to eat," Michael said as Garrett sat down at the table. "How'd you sleep?"

"I don't really remember. Gosh, I was such an ass last night. I don't know what got into me."

"Yeah, you were pretty hellish. Poor Stephanie, you really had her shook up." Michael smiled. "Don't worry I think you'll both survive."

"Oh my gosh, Stephanie. I can't imagine what she must think. She must've thought I had completely lost my mind. Do you think she can ever forgive me?"

"Knowing her, she already has. Look, I told her that I would call her first thing this morning, let her know how you were doing, but maybe it would be better if you called. You owe her an apology and the sooner the better."

"It's so confusing, looking into the future. It frightens me. I am afraid there's nothing I can do. It's as if everything is out of control. I just don't know what to do, what to think."

Michael placed a plate with some eggs and toast in front of Garrett and then sat down next to him. "Look, Garrett, I know you've had a traumatic experience, you know, this looking into the future and all, but you don't have to let it paralyze you. I don't know if we have the ability to change the future, but I do think we can correct the past. You screwed up last night, big time. You hurt the very person you promised to love and cherish. Right now you have to make a choice. Are you going to continue to love her or hurt her? Regardless of what happens in the future, you are still in control of the choices you make today. What are going to do?"

"You're right. I know you're right. I love Stephanie, and I have behaved stupidly. Perhaps there is still time. Maybe it's not too late. I can still be the husband and father I need to be.

Chapter Nine

The three of them walked hand in hand down the path that led to Second Beach, Emily in the middle, Stephanie and Garrett on either side. They were taking their time, given that Emily's little legs were still a little unsure. They had stayed at the Three Rivers Resort the previous night. It was one of their favorite vacation spots on the Olympic Peninsula.

Garrett had taken a leave of absence from work. He needed some time away to sort some things out and to bring a little healing to his family. Raphael and Michael kept calling it a vacation, but Garrett was not so sure. He wasn't sure he ever wanted to return to the Institute.

When they got to the end of the path, he picked up Emily in one arm so he could carry her down the steps that led to the beach. He loved this spot. There were huge haystack rocks in the water less than a hundred yards off shore. The beach stretched for two miles in either direction, beautiful golden sand, a bit of an anomaly on the Washington coastline. They found a secluded drift log and laid out their blanket right up to its edge. Garrett looked up and down the beach. There couldn't have been more than a dozen people within shouting distance, another appeal of Second Beach.

It was a beautiful summer day. Most people think of Washington as a place where it is always gray and cloudy, however, moments like this were almost heavenly. He needed it. He had already been too close to hell.

He watched as Stephanie and Emily played at the edge of the water. The waves were very calm, and Emily kept running back and forth trying to avoid the white foam as it approached and receded. It was nice to see them enjoying the day, enjoying each other, at peace.

He was still haunted by his visions of the future. He had long gotten over being angry with Stephanie. It was unreasonable to punish her for something that hadn't even happened yet. The problem with only having glimpses of the future is that you are blind to the circumstances of the events. He wasn't sure if he could do anything to change the future, but he was determined to do all he could to demonstrate his love to his wife and child. They were his first priority and would be, from this moment forward.

Stephanie had been more than understanding about his little temper tantrum. The first moment she saw him she simply hugged him, holding on to him for the longest time. When she finally let go she simply said, "I love you. I will always love you, no matter what." She didn't wait for an apology, she didn't ask for an explanation. There were no pretenses. She just wanted him to know her love and acceptance. She had not lost faith in him. She was remaining true to her promise of love.

He understood what (the older) Emily had meant. He had made a covenant with Stephanie when they were married and that covenant was extended to Emily and to any other children they were to have.

He knew that he was going to have to tell Stephanie about his experiences. He needed for her to know, if only in part, what he had been through. He could not carry the burden of pre-knowledge alone. He had waited, not knowing just how to begin.

Stephanie and Emily returned to the blanket and they all enjoyed a leisurely lunch. The combination of the warm sun and food in her stomach had its natural effect on Emily and it wasn't long before she had fallen asleep.

"Steph, I know I have apologized for my poor behavior these past six months on more than one occasion," he began, "but I think we still need to talk about it."

"It's okay, Garrett," she looked at him quizzically. "I've already told you that I forgive you. You don't need to say anymore. Really, I'm fine. It's in the past."

"I know, you've been really gracious to me, and you haven't ever asked me to give you an explanation, but I have thought about it, and I think I owe you one. Even more importantly, I have to tell you what happened to me, you know the day I sort of flipped out."

"Okay, if you think you need to."

"I have to start by telling you that some of what I'm about to tell you is going to be a little shocking, even disturbing. It won't be easy. If I thought I could keep it from you, I would. The last thing I want to do is bring you any pain." He was still not sure how to start and already he could sense the tension in her countenance.

"Hurt me, what do mean? I don't understand." Stephanie was clearly getting a little anxious.

"A moment ago, you said it is all in the past. Well that is not entirely true. You see, it has to do with the experiments we have been running in the lab for the past year."

"You mean your virtual world machine." Stephanie interrupted.

"Yeah, but you see, it's not really a virtual world creator. We, that is to say, Raphael, Michael and myself were able to create a new sort of technology for looking into the future. Well not exactly just looking into the future, but actually traveling into the future."

"What? I don't understand. How could you possibly travel into the future? I thought that was impossible."

"Well to be more exact, it was not like we actually traveled to the future, it was just our mind. It's kind of like having our consciousness leap forward in time and it lands in the mind of another person. To be honest we're not entirely sure how it works, but just the same, it works."

"But how do you know what you were seeing was the future. How can you be sure?" As expected Stephanie was still skeptical.

"We tested it over and over again, first with test subjects traveling very short distances or I guess I mean to say short times. Then Michael and I put ourselves on the machine and began traveling forward in greater and greater increments."

"Wait, are you saying you have been to the future. How far? What was it like?"

"Yes, I have. It was weird, so real. It took me awhile before I was convinced that it actually worked. Strange thing is, it wasn't totally random. It seems that every time I traveled forward, I always ran in to someone I knew or someone I had a connection to."

"What do you mean, connection to?"

"This is where it gets a little weird, even a bit horrifying. I have seen Emily in the future. I have also seen our grandson, her son." He stopped, realizing that Stephanie would need a moment to process.

All the blood drained out of Stephanie's face. She just sat there, as if not sure what to think or ask. "Are you sure? I mean, how could it be possible? I don't understand. Our grandson, you saw our grandson?"

"Yes. But there was a problem. It seems we should be very careful looking into the future. It turned out, some of what I learned left me disturbed and looking for answers. I was frustrated and hurt. It was all I could think about, it was all consuming. This is why I was so distracted, why I was working such long hours, and in the end it was why I totally lost it."

"I don't understand, what was so disturbing. Why were you so hurt?"

"Our grandson was in trouble." He had already decided not to tell her about the suicide. It would serve no real purpose. "From what I could gather, this was because he had been abandoned by both his father and his mother. Emily had neglected him."

"Neglected him, why?" She looked down at the napping Emily as she asked it.

"I was able to travel to the time just after Emily had learned that she was pregnant. It seems her child was conceived out of wedlock and the father had abandoned her from the beginning. This is where it gets difficult. She was a very angry and hurt seventeen year old girl. It seems this was because we had divorced when she was young. How young, I'm not exactly sure; I think when she was about six." He waited again letting the sting of what he said sink in.

"Divorced, I don't understand. Why would we have divorced? How could this be? It can't be true." Stephanie was obviously shaken.

"Here's the thing. It doesn't mean that this has to be the future. It was just one possible future that I saw. The way Michael describes it, there are a variety of futures, depending on a number of variables, sort of parallel universes, if you know what I mean. Just because this is what I saw, it doesn't mean that it has to be true. At least I believe there is still a chance to change it."

"But why, why would we get divorced?"

"As near as I could figure it out, it was my fault. It was because I had become so distracted at work that I had neglected both you and Emily." He would say no more. He was no longer in the place where he wanted to blame Stephanie for the failure of his future marriage. It was time for him to take ownership. Once again, he didn't believe it would serve any purpose to accuse her of a sin she hadn't yet committed. "This is why I am telling you all of this. At first I was afraid to, partly because I felt guilty and partly because I didn't want to burden you with the future. It's a difficult burden to carry. But, I need your help. I love you. I have always loved you. I don't want to take you or Emily for granted. I need for you to hold me accountable. I need you to remind me of this, when I start to stray from the path. You are the most important thing to me, both of you. I don't want to grow old and look back on my life and know that I didn't do all I could to show you both just how much I love you."

The whole time he was talking, Stephanie had moved across the blanket and was now perched so there faces were just inches away from each other. When he stopped talking she leaned forward and hugged him. "I love you Garrett. Nothing can stop me from loving you. I don't believe the future you saw was true. Till death do us part; that was the promise."

"That was the promise, till death do us part."

The two of them sat quietly, both deep in thought. Garrett realized that he had given Stephanie a lot to absorb. He let her deal with it in her own way. She was strong and courageous.

Even though it would be difficult to come to terms with the knowledge she had been given, it would not defeat her.

"Hold on to the hope, Steph,"he finally broke the silence. "We still have the ability to make our own choices."

"I know, but it's still strange, to think we can change the future, or that there might be more than one possible future." She said. "I'm bothered by something that just doesn't make sense to me."

"What is it?"

"You said that Emily was hurt and troubled because of our divorce. As a result she had rebelled and ended up having this relationship that lead to her unwanted pregnancy. If we have the ability to change the future, or at least some of the future, is it possible that Emily will make different choices? And if she makes different choices, then she doesn't become pregnant by this young man, and if she doesn't become pregnant, then this young man that you met, our grandson, is never born."

Garret had never considered this. Was it true? Could knowing the future and therefore trying to change it actually mean certain individuals would not be born? This was more than disturbing. Where did fate or determination enter into it? Were people born as a result of a series of random events, random choices? Or was every birth the consequence of predetermined events, even supernatural events?

Chapter Ten

Garrett hesitated a moment before opening the door of the lab. He didn't want to go in. There was still some lingering pain. It had been a month since his last visit here. He pushed the door open. Michael and Raphael were sitting at their stations, occupied by whatever was on their respective computer screens.

Michael looked up first, "Hey Garrett, welcome back. How was your vacation?"

"Great. Really great. It was good to get away and spend some time with Steph and Emily."

"It's good to have you back," Raphael added. "Are you ready to come back to work?"

"I don't know yet. I'm not sure I want to be connected to this project anymore. I'm still very unsettled."

"Completely understandable," Michael seemed sincere. "We weren't exactly sure how to proceed. We almost lost you, and we certainly don't want to make the same mistake. We've postponed all trials at this point. There are still too many questions. In the meantime, I've been trying to work out the actual dynamics of the micro-worm holes. It is still unclear whether we can control the worm holes. You know whether we can pinpoint the exact time and location of the opening on the other end."

Garrett sat down. He didn't comment and just listened as the other two dialogued about their findings.

Raphael interjected. "I agree, gaining control of the worm hole is important, but I have been looking at it the other way around. Instead of controlling the exit of the worm hole, I was wondering why the subjects have leaped forward to the particular place and time. I 've been looking over the interviews while you've been on vacation, I have invited some of the subjects back and interviewed them again, trying to find a pattern."

"What do mean pattern? How could there be a pattern?"

"That's just it. We have never considered a pattern before, because it would imply a factor beyond the electromagnetic impulses and drugs. The weird thing is, I think I've found something. At the least, it doesn't appear that the leaps forward are merely random."

"I'm still thinking Raph here is being a little too naïve. I don't see how the events on the end of the singularities could be somehow determined," Michael said. "The mathematics just doesn't allow for it."

"I'm not sure math has anything to do with it," Raphael replied. "It may have something to do with brain signatures."

"Brain signatures? What are brain signatures?" Michael asked.

"Brain signatures have to do with the electromagnetic patterns in the human brain. They may be genetic or having something to do with the conscious mind, but there is research that suggests that they do exist," Garrett chimed in. He suddenly found himself intrigued. "But what are these patterns you've been talking about?"

"Well, I knew it seemed a little improbable at first," Raphael began. "But I was surprised to discover that each of your jumps into the future resulted in contact with someone you were close to, first your grandson, then your daughter and then Stephanie. Three events, three outcomes with similar results; I think even Michael here would agree that it couldn't have been mere coincidence. That's when I started looking at the rest of the data for the other subjects.

"It turns out there was ample evidence to suggest a pattern. Keep in mind, not all of the subjects had experiences that we could confirm as leaps forward in time. However, of those that we did confirm, all but one resulted in leaps to a place and time they were personally connected to."

"All but one," Michael repeated. "That's weird. The probabilities of such an outcome of random events would be too impossible to even conceive."

"Wait, you're saying all but one," Garret said. "That is intriguing, but are you sure you didn't miss something with that one trial? Which one was it?"

"The first one, your first leap; I've not been able to make any connection between you and the car accident you saw during that first leap."

"That's weird," Michael interjected again. "The data would suggest there is a connection, but how is that possible."

"Yeah, how is that possible?" Garrett said almost in a whisper. He reflected for a moment back to that first event. It was what started this whole mess. He could still feel the revulsion he had felt standing over the body of the dead man lying in the street. Could it be there was a connection? Raphael's analysis of the situation was right on. If all of the other events were not random, that they were always connected in some way to the subjects, then this event could not be any different. In some way, Garrett was connected to the young man who had been killed, or perhaps one of the other witnesses at the scene.

"Raph, were you ever able to find anything out about the accident itself; anything about the victim, maybe the driver, or maybe one of the witnesses?"

"The only thing I've found at this point was a newspaper article reporting the incident. Here, let me pull it up on my computer. Here it is."

Husband and Father Killed by a Drunk Driver

Joseph Jacobson, husband and father of a one year old boy was struck and killed by a drunk driver yesterday afternoon. Witnesses at the scene stated that the car came out of nowhere, just after the light had changed. Two other bystanders narrowly missed the same fate as the car passed just in front of them. The **Times** *has been able to confirm that the driver had a blood alcohol level of .160, twice the legal limit. The name of the driver has not been released, pending the completion of the police investigation. Jacobson was employed at Boeing as an engineer. He is survived by his wife Rachel Jacobson and their one year old son Jesse.*

Garret was stunned when he read the last sentence and saw the name Jesse. He fell back in his chair, his mind swimming in confusion, his heart pounding in his chest. "I don't believe it. It's not possible"

"What? What's not possible?" Michael and Raphael both exclaimed nearly in unison.

"The victim's son, his name is Jesse, Jesse Jacobson. That is what Emily called the boy..." he stopped a moment.

"What boy?" Raphael asked.

"The boy that Emily said was the father of her baby, the father of your grandson," Michael completed the thought.

Garrett shook his head yes. "Is it possible? I don't understand. I thought I was through with all of this."

Both Michael and Raphael just sat in disbelief. Even for them it was difficult to contemplate the implications. Michael, always the mathematician knew that the probability calculations could never allow for such an event to happen randomly. It meant that some other causality was involved, something beyond any natural outcomes, perhaps something supernatural.

Raphael was growing more and more convinced of the evidence supporting unique brain signatures, but even this was not enough to offer a complete explanation. It would suggest that brain signatures were more a product of a person's soul, for lack of a better word, and not genetics, since Jesse was not directly connected to Garret by genetics.

"So what do we do now?" Raphael finally broke the silence.

"What do you mean, what do we do now? What is there to do?" Garrett was growing more and more uneasy by the moment.

"Raph's right, Garrett," Michael said. "It seems the only thing to do is to look up this woman, what's her name again, Rachel and her son. We should find out more about them, to see how they're doing. After all, this baby Jesse, is one day going to be the father of your grandchild."

"We don't know that for sure. Maybe things will change. Maybe Emily never meets this young man." Garrett knew in his heart he didn't believe this to be true.

"You do realize what you're saying, don't you?" Michael asked. "This means your grandson is never born."

"I don't think that's the way it works," Raphael said. "I'm beginning to think that the one thing we do not control is who is born and who dies. Perhaps the only thing we can do is change the circumstance, and maybe the time and place. Of course, that's if we can change anything at all. One of the problems with knowing too much about the future is that we suddenly begin to think that we have the ability to play God. That, I think, is a very dangerous proposition."

"But aren't you both suggesting that very thing? By finding out more about this mother and child, you're both thinking that we might somehow change the future." Garrett stated emphatically.

"Maybe you're right, but now that we have the knowledge, we can't simply ignore it. We all still have the ability to make choices. Maybe we can't change the future, I don't know. Regardless, we can make right choices or wrong choices. We don't know where this might lead, but you have to be curious. What harm could it do to check it out?" Michael offered. "Do you have an address for this woman, Raph?"

"Uh, yeah, I looked it up, just in case anything came of it."

"Wait a second, guys. What are you proposing? We just go over there and knock on the door, and say 'Hi ma'm, we just wanted to check on Jesse, he might one day be the father of my grandson'. Are you both out of your minds? Besides it's been almost a year, she might not even be living in the same place."

"Look, Garrett, you can stay here if you want," Michael said. "She might not even open the door for us. I just don't think it would hurt for us to go see how she is doing. I mean, she just lost her husband a year ago, and now she's trying to raise her son on her own. What about you Raph, are you with me?"

"Sure, I'm as curious as the next guy," Raphael replied. "Come on Garret, what will it hurt? We don't have to tell her anything. We can just make something up, like we knew her husband from work or something. Look here, it said he worked at Boeing. There are a few thousand employees there. She would never be the wiser. And look here, her address is on Queen Anne Hill, not far from your place. That's probably how he and Emily meet, at school or something."

Raphael and Michael were already on their feet, removing their lab coats.

"Come on Garrett, you don't want to miss this," Michael said.

Garrett stood to his feet. "Alright, I guess I can't let you guys go alone. You'll probably make fools of yourselves if I do. I still think this is a mistake."

Rachel Jacobson lived in a small duplex. The outside looked a little neglected; the front yard hadn't been mowed in a while and there were vines that were starting to invade the porch area. They walked up to the door a little hesitantly as if no one wanted to take the lead.

"Okay, this is what we say. We had just been thinking about poor Joe given that it was coming up on the anniversary of the accident and all, and we just thought it would be a good idea to come by and check on you to see how you were doing." Michael said it as if he had been rehearsing it in his mind the entire car ride from the Institute. "We'll just play it by ear after that."

All three stepped up on the porch. Raphael pushed the doorbell, but it didn't sound like anything happened. He then knocked on the screen door. The door rattled, as he knocked. There was no response.

"Maybe there's no one home," Garret said with a little hope in his voice.

"Wait a second," Michael said, "Do you guys hear something? It sounds like a baby crying or something."

Raphael walked over to the front picture window. Shielding the light from his eyes with his hands, he peered inside. There were no lights on in the room, but he immediately found the source of the noise. There was a small toddler, a boy, standing, holding on to a couch, and he was crying. Lying on the couch was a woman and she was not moving, unresponsive to the child's cries.

"Guys, I think we have a problem here," Raphael said with concern.

Michael and Garrett both went to the window. Raphael swung open the screen door, and tried the door knob. It was unlocked. He looked at the other two for just a moment, as if asking whether they should go in or not. Before they could even say anything, he was through the door, Michael right behind him.

They both were at the couch before Garrett had even entered the room; Raphael was checking the woman for a pulse. Michael held up an open medicine bottle that was sitting on the table.

"Anti-depressants, it's empty."

"She's still alive, but her pulse is weak and her breathing shallow, Michael call 911."

Garrett picked up the little boy and bounced him in his arms. "Hey little guy, you're gonna be okay," he tried to reassure him.

"Mommy's sick."

"Yes she is, but we are going to help her get better," Garrett felt tears gathering at the edges of his eyes. This little boy had lost his father a year ago, and now he was in danger of losing his mother.

It seemed like forever for the paramedics to arrive. Fortunately Raphael had EMT training and he did what could be done to stabilize the young woman. After the paramedics had transferred the patient into the ambulance, Michael handed Garrett a note written in the woman's hand.

Please don't judge me too harshly. After Joe died, I tried to go on. God, knows how hard I've tried, if not for myself, for Jesse. I was fired from my job last month and now they are saying they are going to take Jesse away from me. I can't bear it any more, the pain is too great. Take care of my Baby. Tell him that Mommy loves him.
Rachel

Michael sat at Rachel's bedside, little Jesse on his lap. She was very fortunate, had they been an hour or two later, she wouldn't have survived. Garrett and Raphael stood at the door of the hospital room speaking quietly so as not to disturb the patient.

"Penny for your thoughts," Raphael said, a smile on his face.

"I don't know what to think, it's all a little crazy," Garrett responded.

"I suppose you are beginning to finally see that things happen for a reason, that maybe there's a reason for everything."

"What do you mean?" Garrett asked.

"You might think it would have been better if you had never looked into the future and you might be right. Remember, I was the skeptic. I was the one who kept saying stop. In the end, as a result of the choice to go forward, to try and obtain knowledge of the future-knowledge you were not meant to have- you had to experience tremendous pain. However, despite this failure to understand the danger, we still went forward. We couldn't go back. In a sense, we had to pay the price for our sin, or more specifically you did. But, there were still choices to be made, because not all was lost. Those choices led us to this moment. If we hadn't been there today, that young woman over there would have died and the little boy would have been orphaned. I don't think that was random chance, do you?"

"Maybe, maybe not," Garrett said. "If not chance, then what do we call it."

"I call it providence," Raphael put his hand on his friends shoulder. "Providence and grace, my friend."

Rachel opened her eyes. Michael smiled, "Welcome back."

"I don't understand. Where am I?" she asked.

"You're in the hospital," Michael replied. "You had a pretty close call, but you're going to be okay. Everything will be okay now, you'll see."

"But, I don't understand. Who are you?" She nodded to Garrett and Raphael as she said it. "Do I know you? Where did you come from?"

Michael thought for a moment before responding, then smiled, "I guess we're your, uh... your guardian angels."

Epilogue

Garrett looked up at Emily, she looked so beautiful, all dressed in white. He was so proud of her. He took Stephanie's hand and gave it a gentle squeeze. She, in turn, leaned over and kissed his cheek. There were tears in her eyes, not of sorrow, but tears of joy.

Jesse stood next to Emily. He had grown into a fine young man. The two of them would both be enrolled in graduate school in the fall. They had much to look forward to. Garrett looked across the aisle at Rachel and Michael. Michael returned his glance and smiled; proud parents.

He felt a gentle touch on his shoulder. He turned and looked back at Raphael who was sitting in the row behind. His friend was smiling from ear to ear. Then he saw him mouth the word, "Providence."

Providence

Part II

Justice

He that takes truth as his guide, and duty for his end,
may safely trust God's Providence to lead him aright.
Blaise Pascal, *Pensees*

Chapter One

Life is something both mysterious and miraculous. Every birth is a miracle, preordained, not a random chance happening or a simple biological product of nature. What was not alive has now become life, and in the case of a human birth, a new soul has been created, a thinking, believing soul, free to act with volition and purpose.

Garrett glanced out of the window. The sun was just beginning to peak over the Cascades in the distance. A yellow glow rising low in the sky and to the south he could see the outline of Mount Rainier standing out against the light like a sentinel waiting the coming of the new day. It was going to be a beautiful summer day; as it should be. It was August 30th, 2032, the birthday of his grandson, David.

He looked back to where Emily lay in the hospital bed, holding her newborn son. She was exhausted, but glowing, tears of joy wetting her cheeks. On one side of the bed sat Jesse, looking as if he could hardly believe what he was seeing as he smiled at his young son. On the other side of the bed sat Stephanie, no longer looking at her daughter and grandchild, but instead looking back at Garrett. There was pride in her eyes and love as well; love for him, he could see it there. She no longer had to tell him what she was thinking, he knew, he always knew.

He was in awe of the moment; he couldn't be happier for Emily and Jesse. They obviously loved each other very much, and they were going to make great parents. Despite his joy, there was something nagging at the back of his mind. Something he couldn't let go of. What if? What if he had never looked into the future? What if he had not realized his own failures? What if he had continued to blame Stephanie? Would any of this come to be? Was any of this real, or was it only one of many realities? There were still so many questions.

From the first moment, when he, and his two friends, had rescued Jesse's mother, Rachel, from an attempted suicide, he had wondered whether he had actually changed the future and if so how much? When Michael and Rachel ended up getting married and the families began spending time together, he began to question the validity of every moment. Was any of it real?

Jesse and Emily grew up together, and when they decided to get married it was not a surprise to anyone, it seemed natural; as if they were predestined to be together. But was that really true? It was all so confusing.

Then when Emily announced that she was pregnant, it seemed one more natural state of events for everyone. That is everyone except Garrett. Then, a few months later, when Emily discovered the child was going to be a boy, and that she and Jesse had decided to name him David, Garrett found himself wrestling with his own emotions. It was a paradox. He was torn between being excited for his new grandson, while at the same time concerned that he may not have really changed the future at all. Or had he? Emily and Jesse were married, and in this *reality* David would grow up in a stable loving family. It would be different. It would have to be, he would make sure of it.

His phone started to vibrate in his pocket and he pulled it out and touched the screen in the center. It immediately came to life and the image of a young woman appeared. Her hair was mussed and she was in a bathrobe; she had obviously just gotten out of bed.

"Hey Dad," the voice rang out so everyone in the room could hear. It was Katie, Emily's younger sister by four years. She was enrolled as a freshman at Gonzaga University, on the other side of the state. "Any news yet?"

"Hi, Katie. You have a new nephew, born 5:32 AM, mother and son both doing well," Garrett responded as he walked toward the bed. "Here, let me show you." He held the phone so that everyone on the bed could see Katie's image on the screen.

"Hey everyone," Katie's voice rang out. "Hey sis, how are you doing?

"Hey Katie, wish you were here. I'm a little tired and sore, but we're both doing okay." Emily held up the baby in her arms a little higher toward the phone.

"Dad, move me closer, I want to see my nephew."

Garrett obliged. He was not particular fond of video phones, but this was one time when he was glad he had one. "There, how's that."

"Great. Oh, Em, he's beautiful. Man, I wish I could be there with you. If only he could have come a week earlier."

"How was everything your first week? Are you liking college?" Stephanie chimed in.

"Yeah, everything is great, Mom. College is great. Only, I'm coming home next weekend to see the baby, so I can tell you everything then. I'm going to have to go, I have an eight o'clock. Give David a kiss for me, Em. Love ya all, see you soon."

"Bye Katie," everyone said at once as her picture disappeared from the phone.

Just as the phone went dead, a nurse stepped into the room. She promptly walked over to the bed and took the sleeping baby from Emily's arms and then placed him in a basinet next to her bed. "Come on folks, it time to go home now, baby and mom need some sleep."

"I think that's our signal, Steph; we had better let this new mommy get some rest."

"Okay, I'm coming," Stephanie said with a little disdain in her voice. "Goodbye, Em. Jesse, you call us if you need anything. We'll come back later today, after you have had your rest."

Garrett and Stephanie walked to the elevator. As they stepped in, Stephanie grabbed Garrett's arm and then put her head against his shoulder. She was beaming.

"Come on grandma, let's get you home." He said with a little bit of a mocking tone.

As they left the elevator, Garrett's phone buzzed again, "Who could that be?" he said as he reached into his pocket.

The image on the screen was Raphael. "Hey, Raph, what's up? A little early to be calling, isn't it?" He chided.

"Sorry, Garrett," Raphael apologized. "I just had to talk to you. Something has come up. Something horrible; oh man, I am so sorry. I blew it, I really blew it."

"Easy buddy, what do you mean you blew it? Calm down, what are you so excited about?" Garrett could see by the expression on his friend's face, that he was really worried, perhaps even frightened. "Why don't you tell me what the problem is? I'm sure together we can figure it out."

"I can't, not over the phone." We need to meet, right away, and you need to bring Michael along, as well. Can we meet at the Starbuck's on 5th, say, in about a half an hour?"

"I can try, but I'm at the hospital right now, it may take a while. And I still have to call Michael."

"Oh, yeah, I forgot about the baby and all. Well...well just do the best you can. I'll be waiting."

"Okay, I'll be there as soon as I can. Only what is the problem? I don't understand. Why all the cloak and dagger?"

"Just be there, we need to talk! And...one other thing...if something should happen to me, I sent you a bunch of files. Keep them safe. Don't trust anybody."

"Don't trust anybody, what are you talking about? You're talking crazy. What's this all about?"

"Can't talk now, I think someone is coming." Raphael looked back over his shoulders. "See ya in a few. Don't be late."

The phone turned off, disconnected on the other end. Garrett just stood there looking at the phone, not sure what to think.

The elevator door opened and they stepped into the parking garage. Fifty feet away, walking toward them, were Michael and Rachel.

"What was that all about?" Stephanie asked.

"I'm not sure," I've never seen him like that. He was afraid, really afraid."

"Hey you two, how's our grandchild?" Rachel sang out as they drew close.

"He's doing great and so is Emily, but you're a little late. They just put them both to bed." Stephanie replied.

"Oh, and I was so looking forward to seeing them," the disappointment etched on Rachel's face. She turned and punched Michael in the arm. "I told you we should have gotten up earlier."

"Mike, I just got a strange call from Raph. He's in some sort of trouble and needs our help. He wants us to meet him downtown, right now," Garrett said before Michael had a chance to respond to Rachel.

"Right now, can't it wait? Doesn't he know we have a new grandson?"

"It sounded pretty serious. Something has him pretty shook up. I think we should go," Garrett said. "Rachel, do you mind giving Steph a lift?"

"No, no problem." Rachel replied.

"Come on, Rach, let's get some breakfast and then we can come back. I didn't really want to go home anyway. I figure David will be awake for a feeding in a couple of hours anyway. If we time it right, we'll back just in time."

"Sounds great," Rachel said as she grabbed Stephanie's arm and the two started for the car. "Call me later, Garrett. Let me know how it goes with Raphael.

"Come on Mike, I'll fill you in on the way." Garrett said as they watched the ladies leave.

Garrett couldn't imagine what had gotten into Raphael to make him so upset, although, admittedly, he had not seen him for a couple of months. When he'd first taken the teaching job at the University, he tried to keep in touch, but the occasional lunch meetings just became less frequent over time until they nearly stopped all together.

Michael left IEAT shortly after Garrett did. After marrying Rachel, he decided to start his own consulting firm and never looked back. Owning his own business had allowed him to set his own hours, which was particularly well-suited to Michael's ambitions in caring for his family, given, that with his marriage to Rachel, he had inherited a young son to take care of. Michael and Rachel never had any more children, and Michael spent most of his free time doting on his adopted son.

Jesse benefited from his stepfather's attentions and had grown into a fine young man. He had just recently completed his

Master's degree in English Literature and was now teaching English at King's High School, just across the canal from Queen Anne, where he and Emily had grown up.

The three friends, Garrett, Raphael and Michael had all agreed to leave their work on QT behind (as they had grown to call it-Quantum Transference of Brain Waves through Micro-Wormholes, to be exact). Despite the discoveries they had made concerning the control of quantum micro-singularities and telepathic brain wave response, they felt the risks far outweighed the rewards, and therefore they abandoned all thoughts of publishing their results or continuing their research. Their journals and data were filed away and the equipment was locked away in a closet.

Raphael had stayed with IEAT and had continued to work on enhancements for virtual experience technology in 3D. He had had some promising results and the word on the street was that a brand new holographic virtual experience program was just about to be launched and made available to the public. It was hard for Garrett to believe that Raphael was mixed up in anything underhanded or dangerous, but he couldn't help feel a little uneasy. His friend had seemed really frightened, it wasn't like him.

Garrett turned down Dearborn Street and then a few blocks later turned onto 5th Avenue. The traffic was a mess, not unusual for eight thirty in the morning, but a little more congested than usual. There was police car with its lights on a few blocks ahead and traffic was barely a crawl.

"There's a parking place," Michael said pointing to the right. "We can walk from here. It's only another three or four blocks and at this pace, I think walking would be faster."

Garrett agreed, and swung his car into the spot. He didn't really like to plug parking meters, but they were going to be a little late as it was. As anxious as Raphael had sounded, the last thing he wanted to do was make him wait.

Chapter Two

As Michael and Garrett drew near the coffee shop, they noticed a crowd had gathered and it looked as if there were some policemen who were attempting to restrain everyone. Clearly, there was something in the street that had everyone's attention.

"What's going on?" Michael asked the nearest person to him, standing too far back to actually see anything.

"An accident I think," the lady closest at hand said over her shoulder. "It looks like a hit and run. A man's lying in the street. I think he's dead. It's a crying shame. He was just crossing the street and this car came out of nowhere and just plowed right into him, a real shame. Who would do such a thing? And then just take off like that."

Garrett got a sinking feeling in his stomach. He pushed his way through the crowd with Michael close on his heels. When he got to the front, he could hardly believe his eyes. There in the middle of the street, sprawled in a pool of blood, was his friend. It was Raphael, dead. He turned away in disbelief and then looked at his friend who was standing next to him, just staring straight ahead.

"I don't believe it. It's…it's Raph," was all Michael could utter.

Garrett noticed a police officer, speaking to someone in a long trench coat just a dozen feet away. "Officer," can I speak to you for just a moment, he shouted above the murmur of the crowd.

"Just stay back, sir. Please everyone just stay back behind the tape," the police officer replied.

"But officer, I know this man, he's a friend of mine," Garrett tried again.

This caught the attention of the man in the trench coat who promptly walked over to where Garrett and Michael were standing.

"You know the deceased," the man said with such coldness, that Garrett couldn't help but grimace.

"Yes, his name is Raphael Seraph. He's an old friend. Michael, here, and I were supposed to meet him for coffee at the Starbuck's there (pointing). What happened?" Garrett tried to sound calm, but his heart was pounding and his voice was wavering with every attempt at speech.

"Could the two of you step over here and answer a few questions, that is, if you don't mind?"

Garrett and Michael both nodded and bent beneath the tape and followed the man to a place not far from the body. Garrett had the urge to bend down and touch his friend, to determine for himself that he was really dead, but he resisted.

"I'm detective Eli Beck," the man said, flashing a badge so quickly that neither of them actually saw it. "Condolences on your friend, I'm afraid I have to ask you a few questions." He paused as he fumbled with a small notebook. "How long have you known the deceased?"

"A little more than twenty years, we used to work together." Garrett responded, not comfortable with the detective's manner.

"And where was that?" Detective Beck asked.

"The Institute for Enhanced Artificial Thought, just down the street from here." Garrett answered. Out of the corner of his eye he could see Michael staring at the body, a tear trickling down his cheek.

"And you don't work together anymore?"

"No, we're just friends. Raphael still works there, or what I mean to say, did, but Michael and I moved on to other things several years ago."

"And today, what was the purpose of the meeting?"

"Not a meeting really, we were just getting together over coffee. Michael and I are celebrating the birth of our first grandchild and Raphael said he wanted to get together and talk. He wanted to share something with us, but he wouldn't tell me over the phone." Garrett was holding back a little, he wasn't sure how much he wanted to tell this detective.

"Do you know anybody who would want to kill your friend?" the detective said without emotion.

"That's crazy," Michael finally chimed in. "Who would want to kill poor Raph? He was one of the nicest guys around. It's crazy just to think it."

"Do you think someone did this intentionally?" Garrett asked. He was feeling that pit in his stomach again.

"No, it was probably an accident. Just a simple hit and run, nothing more, but we have to cover all the bases. You know, we wouldn't want to miss anything. Was Mr. Seraph married?"

"No, never has been, a confirmed bachelor. Too much time in the lab I suppose." Garrett couldn't help but notice that the detective had stopped referring to his friend as the deceased.

"Was Mr. Seraph seeing anyone, you know dating; someone we should notify?"

Garrett looked at Michael. His friend just shrugged his shoulders in return. "Not that we know of, but I'm afraid I haven't see him for a couple of months. There might be someone, I don't know."

"Well that should be enough for now. Could I call on you later, if I have any more questions?"

"Sure no problem," The two friends said in unison.

"Hey detective," Michael interjected as Beck was about to leave. "What actually happened?"

"It seems a black sedan came careening around the corner and hit your friend as he stood in the crosswalk. It then kept right on going, never stopped. Witnesses said it was kind of old and beat up, no plates. Sadly it was probably just some kids out for a joy ride; wrong place, wrong time I imagine." The detective turned and started to walk away, and then as an afterthought turned back again, "Sorry again, about your friend and all. Just dumb luck I guess."

"Nice fellow," Michael said as he and Garrett turned to face each other.

Garrett cringed as he heard the paramedics pull the zipper closed on the bag that now contained Raphael's body. "Where are you guys taking him?" he asked, and then added, "I'm a friend."

"I'm afraid he will have to go to the city morgue until the investigation is over. You can let his family know that they will be notified as soon as the body is released for burial," one of paramedics explained.

Garrett realized that Raphael didn't have any family. His parents had both died and he had never married, never had any children. He remembered a brother mentioned, living in Southern California or something, but Raph hardly ever talked about him. It was sad. In a moment, his life was gone. What was it all for?

He could still hear Raphael's words echoing in his ears. "If anything happens to me..." Could he have been murdered? It seemed unlikely, but Raphael seemed scared. Why couldn't he talk on the phone? What was he so worried about? What was he involved in?

Michael didn't say a word as they walked backed to the car. When the car doors were closed, Garrett spoke for the first time. "We have to go back to my place, Mike. Raphael said that he sent me some files that I need to take a look at."

"What? What are you talking about? What files?" Michael was clearly agitated.

"He was in some kind of trouble. He said not to trust anybody. He said that he was sending the files to me in case anything happened to him."

"Happened to him? Why didn't you tell the detective this? Are you saying this wasn't an accident at all? I don't understand," Michael was trying to get his head around it.

"I'm not saying anything. I'm not sure of anything. It seems that the only way to find out is to look at the files. This accident may be nothing more than a bad coincidence, but we won't know for sure until we look at the files. I couldn't tell the detective any more until I know more about what is going on."

"But he's the detective, not you. He's the one that is supposed to figure it out. I don't see how you could have withheld information, information that might have been crucial in finding out who killed poor old Raph. I don't believe this. What's happening here?"

Garrett paused before his next response. It was hard for him to believe what he was about to say. "Don't you see, Michael? It's just possible that this may have something to do with our work with Quantum Transference, and until I find out,

I'm not about to begin releasing too much information to that idiot detective. It won't hurt for us to take a look into it first, and then if we discover it was something else entirely, we can call up Detective Beck and lay it all out for him."

"QT? You think it might have something to do with QT? That was years ago. It's been under lock and key ever since. Raphael would never have opened that *Pandora's Box* again. He was always the one that was insistent about stopping the project in the first place."

"I hope you're right," Garrett affirmed. "In any case, we're about to find out."

They remained quiet for the remainder of the drive. They passed by the Seattle Center with the Space Needle towering above and then started up the hill. After Katie was born, Garrett and Stephanie bought a small three bedroom home, just down the street from their old apartment. They had thought about moving out of the city, one of the suburbs like Bellevue or Issaquah, but in the end they decided to stay. They liked the neighborhood and it was relatively close to the University.

It was an older home, with a basement, a perfect place for Garrett to carve out a work space. He pulled on the string attached to the single light bulb that hung just above his head and the room was filled with light. He had always talked about putting some recessed lighting in the ceiling, but like most of his projects, there never seemed to be enough time. He walked over to his desk, touched the desk lamp on top and immediately it came to life. He then sat down at his computer and opened his email, Michael peering over his shoulder.

There it was, an email from Raphael, with two attachments. Both files were compressed and securely locked. The first was a video file. Garrett clicked on it, and a password window promptly appeared. He looked at Michael at exactly the same moment they said, "Asimov". Raphael had always been a huge sci-fi enthusiastic and Asimov was his favorite author. It worked. The video opened and began playing.

It was Raphael, looking a little more haggard than usual. "Garrett, if you're watching this, it must mean something has happened to me..." Raphael looked around before continuing.

"It's four in the morning, I have been working all night...trying to make sense of it all. I hardly know where to begin. I've been an idiot." He wiped tears from his eyes. "About six months ago I was approached by Mr. Benson. He wanted to reopen the QT project. At first, I tried to convince him of the dangers of the project and that I had no interest in being involved with it, ever. You know how I had always been cautious from the very beginning.

Then, he began going on about how we could do so much good. He suggested that we could look into the future and perhaps bring back information that would revolutionize the medical field, perhaps even find a cure for cancer. We could bring medical treatments to those in need, twenty, maybe forty years in advance of their discoveries. He kept going on and on about how many lives we could save. Before long, he had me convinced. As a result, I began helping him to set up trials.

He brought in this assistant, a young quantum physicist, a bit of whiz kid. He worked through Michael's calculations and even suggested some improvements.

At first, it seemed all so innocent. I would send Benson into the future and with each leap forward he would bring back important information that he would pass onto our medical tech facility. I was so stupid, so trusting...

I didn't realize that something was wrong until he began suggesting the need for us to go back to the past. I explained to him that we had never had any success with traveling to the past, but he kept insisting, so we kept trying, little jumps at first and then slightly longer. He kept saying that he had discovered a scientist who had been on the verge of some major breakthroughs, who had been killed in a senseless accident. He thought we could actually change the past.

It wasn't until I started running the numbers and looking at the dates that I began to have a suspicion that something else was going on. It turned out that he wasn't trying to find medical cures at all. He was leaping to the future to steal technology; technology that he would profit from, the bastard..." Raphael paused again, rubbing his eyes, looking for the courage to go on.

"We were successful. He was able to go to the past, but there was evil in his intent. I should have seen it coming, but I was blinded by my own innocence. It had been so long, I didn't recognize the date that he had returned to, at first. I should have, but I didn't. When I went over the numbers, I realized what day it was. It was the day of your first jump, Garrett. The day you witnessed the accident; the accident that was not an accident. I went to the police station and had them pull up the transcript for the investigation of the accident. I should have known...

The driver, he was said to be drunk, but when they interviewed him, he had said he couldn't remember anything. He had stopped for a drink with some friends, one drink, and then everything went blank. He woke up after the accident, not knowing what had happened, having no idea that he had killed someone.

I don't think it was him at all. I think that Benson had jumped into his mind and the he had intended on killing

Jacobsen. At first, I couldn't figure out why, but now I think it has something to do with David. When I confronted Benson, he just laughed it off, said I was imagining things. But I know I'm right. I could see it in his eyes. He's an evil man, and he's capable of doing anything to get what he wants.

I'm afraid. You have to stop him Garrett, you and Michael. I know you can figure it out, you know, what to do. I'm afraid it's too late for me, but you must find a way to protect David. I'm not sure why Benson has it in for him, but it must be something important. You have to stop him, you must stop him.

I'm so sorry. Tell Michael I'm sorry, I should have told you what I was doing. Now I know it was wrong.

I have attached all my notes and files. You have to figure out what he was up to. I've included the project dates for every one of his jumps into the future. I don't know what he was after, but it had something to do with David, I'm sure of it. Be careful, he's a dangerous man. There's no telling what he's capable of."

The video ended. Garrett sat back in his chair, still trying to sort out what he had just watched. He looked up at Michael.

"Unbelievable," was all that Michael could say. "It seems so crazy. Mr. Benson? I don't get it. Why would he do such thing? He always seemed like a nice enough guy. I don't get it. I find it hard to believe that he's capable of murder.

"I agree," Garrett said. "It seems so unlikely. However, Raphael is not prone to exaggeration. And here we are, Raphael is dead, and it is looking more and more like it wasn't an accident."

"We need to go to the police," Michael said. "Detective Beck needs to see this."

"Don't you understand, Michael, we can't go to the police; at least, not yet. We have no proof."

"No proof, what do you mean, we have this video, and all of Raphael's notes. Isn't that enough?"

"Enough for us, maybe," Garrett said, "but not enough for the police. Remember, we already know that QT works. The police have never heard of it. All it would serve would be to open a can of worms, something I'm not sure we are ready to deal with. Don't you see? Benson, as unlikely as it may seem, has found the way to commit the perfect murder. There is no better way to take yourself out of the list of suspects than to have someone else commit the murder, at a time and place when you could not possibly have been involved."

"So what are we going to do?" Michael asked.

"We're going to have to figure out what is going on? We have to find out why Benson was traveling to the future, and why David has anything to do with it? I suggest that we split up these files, go through them with a fine tooth comb and see if we can find out what Benson was up to." Garrett looked at his watch. "It's almost noon. I have a one o'clock class. Can I drop you somewhere?"

"Yeah, maybe you can drop me at work. I suppose I should check in. Then maybe we can meet up with our wives at the hospital later this afternoon. I'm sure they'll not wander far from their grandson anytime soon."

"Oh my gosh, Steph," Garrett said. "I was supposed to call her. How am I going to tell her that Raphael is dead?"

Chapter Three

Garrett let the water run over his head and shoulders as he stood in the shower. The hot water was soothing, bringing comfort to his body, but not his mind. He'd been up late the night before pouring over Raphael's notes. They revealed no more clues, nothing that would explain what Benson was up to. The only thing he was able to determine was the time lengths of the jumps. There were a total of ten; two to the past, five to the near future and three that were twenty years into the future. There was nothing to explain why he had chosen those particular dates in time.

Stephanie had spent a good part of the evening crying. She couldn't come to grips with the death of Raphael. She had always liked him and considered him part of the family. She kept lamenting over the fact that they hadn't seen him in a while. She was feeling guilty, even though there was no way they could ever anticipated his death.

He could hear the phone ring as he stepped out of the shower. A moment later, Stephanie appeared at the bathroom door. "It's for you," she said, "a Detective Beck? He seems rather insistent."

Garrett wrapped himself in his towel and took the phone. "Hello, Detective Beck. What can I do for you?" He tried to sound cheerful.

"Hello, Mr. Adams. Sorry to disturb you so early and all. I was wondering if you could meet me at your friend's apartment. There's something I need to show you."

Garrett didn't like the tenor in Beck's voice. "Sure. Raph's apartment. No problem. In, say, half an hour okay?"

"That'll be just fine," Beck returned. "And maybe you might want to invite your friend to join us. What was his name, DeAngelo?"

"Michael, sure, no problem, we'll see you there." Garrett didn't like the way the Detective sounded. It was if he were inferring something. He felt a chill.

———

Garrett sat in his car for a few minutes, waiting for Michael to arrive. He wasn't about to take on Beck all by himself.

When his friend finally arrived, he looked at Garrett quizzically, "What's up?" Michael asked

"I'm not sure. He just said he wanted to show us something." They walked up the stairs to Raphael's apartment together.

As they entered the apartment, they knew immediately why Beck had called. The apartment was a mess. Everything strewn all over the floor, and much of the furniture had been turned over. Garrett peered through the bedroom door; even the bed had been turned on its side.

"Hello gentlemen," Beck greeted them. "Thanks for coming."

"What happened here?" Michael asked.

"Yeah, I was hoping you could help me with that," Beck replied. "It seems someone broke into your friend's place here, and turned it upside down. They were clearly looking for something. I was hoping you might be able to help. Do you have any idea what they were looking for?"

"Can't imagine," Garrett returned. "Like we said before, we hadn't talked to Raph in a couple of months. I can't imagine why anybody would do this. Raph was the nicest guy in the world. What could they have been looking for? It doesn't make any sense."

"Do you know what your friend was working on?" Beck asked.

"No, we haven't really had any contact with institute for several years. I suggest you go to the source. Go ask them."

"I intend to…I will do just that." Beck said. He seemed to be pondering something.

"Detective, do you think that Raphael was murdered," Michael asked.

"Well it certainly seems a possibility," Beck answered. "That's what we're going to find out. So the two of you have no idea what this is about?"

"Not a bit," Garrett said. He had never thought of himself as much of a liar. He tried to stay calm. "It just doesn't make any sense. Who would want to kill Raphael?"

"Yeah, who would want to kill Raph?" Michael added.

"Well, okay. If the two of you think of anything, I would sure appreciate you letting me know. In any case, thanks for coming by. We'll stay in touch."

Garrett and Michael stood on the sidewalk, looking back at the door of Raphael's apartment building. "You'll still think we should keep quiet about Raph's work?" Michael asked.

"I don't really think we have any choice. Not until we know what this is all about." Garrett remained insistent, although in the back of his mind he still doubted if they were doing the right thing.

"Well, where do we go from here?" Michael asked.

"I think we have to go see Mr. Benson." Garrett answered.

"What do you mean, to confront him? Don't you think that's a little risky?"

"No, not confront him exactly. I think it would be a mistake for us to let on that we know anything at this point. Detective Beck has given us the perfect opportunity. We can say that we were surprised about the investigation, and then that will open the door for us to begin asking questions. If we're subtle enough, we might be able to get Benson to let down his guard. Anyway, it's worth a try. What do you say we meet at the Institute later this afternoon, just before the end of the work day?"

"Okay, I'll be there." Michael said and then as an afterthought, "I hope you know what you're doing, Garrett."

So do I, Mike. So do I."

——

The secretary was young and pretty, Garrett had never seen her before. She pushed some buttons on her phone and then spoke aloud, "A Mr. Adams and a Mr. DeAngelo, to see you sir."

"Really, what a surprise, send them on in, Sandy. Send them in." Even though they hadn't spoken to each other in years, Garrett recognized the high pitched voice of Mr. Benson at once.

"You can go on in gentlemen." The secretary motioned with her hand.

"Thanks, Sandy," Garrett said.

Sam Benson was a bald round little man, with an infectious smile. Garrett was immediately reminded why he found it difficult to believe this man could be involved in a conspiracy that included murder. It just didn't seem in his character. He was such a likeable guy.

"Garrett, Michael, what a surprise," Mr. Benson greeted. "How long has it been, ten years, maybe more? Wow has it really been that long? I can hardly believe it. Please have seat. What can I do for you? Hey, how'd you like my new secretary? Quite a looker isn't she? Ha!"

Garrett and Michael shook his hand and then took seats opposite Mr. Benson's desk. He was the same jovial boss they had always remembered. He never had a cross word to say about anybody and was always friendly to everyone.

"It's good to see you Sam, it's been too long," Michael started. "We came to see you about Raphael. I'm sure you heard what happened."

"Of course, why else would you be here?" Mr. Benson replied. "Poor shame. It's hard to believe. I always liked Raphael. He gave his heart and soul to this company. It's just a crying shame, that's what it is. We will miss him." He seemed genuinely sincere.

"He was a good friend," Michael added. "We will all miss him."

"We were wondering," Garrett started a little hesitantly, "did a Detective Beck stop by to see you?"

"Yes, as a matter fact he did. Said something about someone breaking into Raphael's apartment; said that there might be more to Raphael's death than a simple accident. I don't understand it. Who would want to harm Raphael?"

"That's exactly what we were wondering," Garrett continued. "Do you know what Raphael was working on, maybe something someone would like to get their hands on?"

"Well, let's see, for the past few months he has been working on this new technology for integrating holographic imaging with our virtual devices. We've been making tremendous strides, but I don't see why anybody would go after Raphael for that. There are at least a half a dozen individuals who were more intimately involved with the project than he was. It seems unlikely that this would be the reason."

"We were wondering if Raph might have reopened the Quantum Transference Project, y'know, try to resurrect it, so to speak?" Garrett saw his opening and so he took it.

"Not that I know of," Benson responded. "As far as I know the equipment is still locked up in the closet where you left it. When you told me that the project had no real promise and that you were giving up, that was enough for me, so we set it aside; that was the end of it."

Garrett was watching Benson's every move, every expression, seeing if there was any way he could detect a lie, but he seemed to be telling the truth. Either Benson was a tremendous poker player, or he was innocent. "Are you sure? Maybe he was working on it after hours." He pressed a little harder.

"I suppose it's possible. Why? Do you think that is what this is all about?" Benson asked.

"We don't really know," Michael interjected. "I suppose we're just grasping for straws, you know, trying to make sense of it all. It was probably just an unfortunate accident, nothing more, but we had to ask."

"Yeah, that's right," Garrett offered. "I guess we're just trying to get closure. I mean, after all, who would ever want to hurt Raph, it's just a little crazy."

"I agree," Benson said. "I must admit that when the Detective showed up this morning, it got me to thinking, but I just couldn't bring myself to believe anyone would intentionally hurt Raphael. It's a shame, a crying shame, that's all." There was a pause as if Benson was trying to find the words, to provide some kind of assurance. He continued, "By the way, we are having a little gathering at my place on Friday night, a sort of memorial service. I would sure love it if the two of you and your lovely wives would join us. I know it would mean a lot to everyone."

"Uh, sure, we would be happy to come, wouldn't we Mike," Garrett said, somewhat surprised at the invitation.

"Sure, we wouldn't miss it, Mr. Benson," Michael added.

"In the mean-time, I'll ask around, see if anyone else has heard of Raphael working on anything else. If nothing else, it might put your minds at ease." Mr. Benson stood to his feet. "I hate to rush you out like this, but I have a Board of Directors meeting in just a few minutes."

"Sure, we understand," Garrett said as he stood to his feet. He shook Mr. Benson's hand. "Thank you for seeing us. We appreciate the time."

"Yes, thank you Mr. Benson," Michael said.

"See Sandy on your way out and she will give you directions for Friday night. Thanks again for stopping by. It was really good to see you again."

Michael turned to Garrett once they were in the elevator. "What'd you think?"

"I don't get it. He was very convincing. I mean, it sounded like he was telling the truth. If I didn't know better, I would have said that Raphael got it wrong, or that he was making it up. At this point, I don't think we're any closer to finding out the truth."

"Yeah, I know. Did you see how he reacted when you brought up the QT project? He seemed genuinely bewildered, almost as if he hadn't even thought about it in years. It was weird, not a flinch."

"I know, I thought for sure that would touch a nerve, but there was nothing. Either he's telling the truth or he's a complete sociopath." Michael added.

"He's just so damn likeable. It's, like, how could he even hurt a flea. I don't get it."

"Me neither," Michael added. Neither said another word during the entire trip to the hospital.

Chapter Four

The Benson home was a three story mansion in a gated community bordering the local country club. The back yard had a hundred chairs, or so, set up in front of a gazebo that backed up against the golf course. After greeting the few employees who they actually recognized, Michael, Rachel, Garrett and Stephanie took their seats down front. There was music playing softly, a small string ensemble that Benson had hired for the occasion.

The service was a little surreal. Several employees stepped to the microphone and shared their favorite memories of Raphael. There was the appropriate shedding of tears and the common reference to the tragedy of someone dying so young and how much he would be missed. There was nothing religious, not that Garrett really expected it. The scientific community had grown more and more skeptical about anything connected to the spiritual.

Garrett had always been a bit of a skeptic himself, but his experience with QT had changed all of that. A day did not go by when he didn't think about causality or purpose. It just didn't make sense to him that everything was just a product of random chance. He had grown convinced that there just had to be more to life. There had to be purpose and meaning, otherwise, what was it all for. It was strange to hear people talk about the death of a friend without any reference to the "what happens next." Is that it? A man lives his life, gives everything to his work, and then dies and it's over; nothing to show for it, but a few pleasant memories shared by friends over his grave. What's the point?

Some people think it has to do with how much wealth you accumulate, or what kind of mark you make on the earth; like leaving some kind of legacy. Will they remember you? What difference does it make? You're dead. You could have accumulated millions, or painted a hundred masterpieces, but in the end you will still be dead. Of course, you can leave a legacy for your children, but you will still be dead. If there is nothing more, then what is the point?

By the time the service was over, Garrett was feeling quite melancholy. The last thing he wanted to do was to talk to people, but it was unavoidable. It seemed every guest wanted to catch up, although he couldn't remember the names of most of them.

As the evening was winding down, Mr. Benson walked toward the four friends as they were gathering their coats and were about to leave. There was a young man trailing behind him, looking less than pleased.

"I'm so glad you were able to come," Benson said. "I'm sure Raphael would be pleased," he added, as if their friend was watching from somewhere.

"Thanks for having us," Garrett responded.

"I don't believe either of you got the chance to meet my son, William," Benson said, turning so they could get a clear view of the young man. He was taller than his father, with dark hair and dark eyes. He looked like he couldn't be more than thirty.

Garrett and Michael, in turn, reached out and shook the young man's hand. Garrett felt a bit of chill run up and down his spine. It was as if the young man couldn't look him straight in the eye.

"Hello," Michael said. "Nice to meet you."

Garrett said nothing.

"This guy is a real up and comer. We just made him executive vice president of the entire company." Benson said.

"You must be very proud," Garrett said, without enthusiasm.

"Oh, I know what you're thinking, boss' son and all," Benson said. "But, he's earned it. William here recently landed the company a huge contract with the inventor of a new holographic imaging device that is going to revolutionize the communications industry, and without it costing hardly anything. He's a real go getter, I tell ya."

"Sounds, like it," Michael said. "You must be very proud."

"And I suppose you knew our friend Raphael?" Garrett asked purposefully as he looked William in the eyes.

"Not that well, not really. He has been helping us with the holographic project, but I didn't really have much of a chance to get to know him. I'm sorry for your loss. I'm sure it must have come as quite a shock." William said flatly, with no emotion.

Garrett didn't like the way he spoke. The way he said "quite a shock" had a little sting to it. "Yeah, quite a shock," he repeated. "Just a tragic accident, I guess, unexplainable."

"Exactly," the young man said.

"Well, Mr. Benson, William, we have to be going, it's getting a little late," Garrett said. "Thanks again for having us."

"The pleasure was all mine," Benson said. "It was so good to see you all again, especially your lovely wives," he said as he squeezed each one of their hands.

"Goodnight," they said, in turn, and then started to walk away.

As an afterthought, Garrett turned once more to his host, "I look forward to hearing more about your work, William. Perhaps we will see each other again, soon."

"Perhaps," the young man returned, his dark eyes meeting Garrett's.

As they walked to the car, Garrett slowed his pace slightly, grabbing his friend's arm. The ladies were soon far enough ahead that he couldn't be heard. "We had it all wrong," he whispered so low that only Michael could hear. "Or should I say, the wrong Mr. Benson."

"I know exactly what you mean," Michael whispered back.

———

Garrett pulled his phone from his pocket. He had been expecting a call from Katie, and was clearly disappointed when he recognized the image of Detective Beck on the video screen. It had been more than a week since the memorial service at the Benson's and almost two weeks since he had last seen the Detective.

"Hello Detective Beck," he said, looking at the screen. "What can I do for you?"

"Sorry to interrupt whatever you might be doing," Beck began. "I just thought I would let you know that we have closed up shop on your friend's case. It seems it was just some random hit and run, nothing more."

"So you found the car and driver then?" Garrett asked.

"Well, no, not exactly, but we're pretty confident that it was just some kids joy riding or something. There's not enough compelling evidence to suggest that it was premeditated. It was just a freak accident; criminal, but an accident just the same. We're keeping the file open, but I just wanted let you know that it is no longer being investigated as a homicide."

"Thanks," Garrett said. "I appreciate the call, Detective." He didn't really know what else to say. He didn't want his friend's murder to go unsolved, but there was just no way Detective Beck would believe him if he told him what had actually happened. He needed more proof.

"I'll let you know if anything changes," Beck said. "Goodbye."

Beck's image disappeared from the screen. Garrett felt a little frustrated. On the one hand he was glad that the Detective would no longer be pestering him, and that the secret of the QT project would remain just that, a secret. But, it didn't seem right. Where was the justice for Raphael? The person responsible for his death should be held accountable.

Garrett knew who was responsible, but there was no way of proving it. He had no real evidence. The rambling of his distraught friend on video was not enough. He would have to find something else. If he couldn't prove who killed Raphael, he could at least find out what the young Benson was up to, and more importantly what it had to do with his grandson, David.

It seemed incomprehensible. What could it all have to do with a baby who was but a couple weeks old? No matter how much he mulled it over in his mind, he couldn't come up with any rational explanation. He had watched the video of Raphael over and over again, trying to find an explanation, but there was none. But, it was clear that his friend had been concerned that David was in some sort of danger. Garrett was worried that he was running out of time.

———

"What do you think this is all about?' Michael asked as he and Garrett stepped onto the elevator. They were back at the institute, invited by the elder Mr. Benson.

"I have no idea," Garrett said. "He just said that he had something to show us, nothing more. Quite frankly, I'm mystified."

As they approached the secretaries desk, Sandy smiled up at both of them, "go on in gentleman," she greeted. "He's expecting you."

As they entered the office, they were surprised to find that Mr. Benson was not alone. He was joined by the younger Benson, William, and a young woman who was holding a baby.

"Ah, Garrett and Michael," Benson greeted with a smile. "Welcome, thanks for coming. You of course know my son, William, and this beautiful creature is my daughter-in-law, Lucy, and of course our pride and joy, my grandson, Jonathan."

Garrett and Michael greeted their host and his family cordially, although Garrett couldn't help feel a sort of coldness towards William. "A beautiful baby," Michael said. "He looks to be the same age as our grandson, David."

Garrett looked at the baby, and then smiled at the mother. She seemed very young, perhaps ten years younger than her husband. She smiled back. "Well, I think we should be going," she said. "It will be feeding time soon, and I should leave you men to your business." She said it in such a way that it seemed to indicate that she knew her place, which did not include the affairs of her husband.

"Yes dear," Mr. Benson said. "Thank you for bringing young Jonny by. You are always welcome. Now, don't forget that Mrs. Benson and I are expecting you for dinner tomorrow night."

Without a word, William escorted his wife to the door, closing it behind her and then returning to the group.

"You said on the phone that you had something to show us," Garrett said. "What's this all about?"

"Yes, that's right," Mr. Benson said. "I asked William to join us, I hope you don't mind. After all, it was he who found it. I thought he should show you."

"Found what?" Michael asked.

"Perhaps it would be better if we showed you," William said. "Would you follow me please?" The way he spoke put Garrett on edge.

The four men walked to the elevator and then went to the basement. Garrett thought this strange, since the IEAT occupied the sixth floor entirely, and the rest of the building was occupied by a variety of other tenants. When they reached the basement, William led them down a dark hall and then stopped in front of a door marked "Storage".

"See, the reason we didn't find it at first," Mr. Benson began, "is that we hardly use this space down here, except for storage. I haven't been down here myself, in years. The other day, William came down here looking for some equipment and he found this."

The door opened to what looked like a make shift lab. There were two beds, as well as equipment lining all the walls. It looked as if it had been used recently. However, the equipment was a mess. It had all been smashed, wires were strewn everywhere. The computers looked as if they had been hit with a sledge hammer. Despite the damage, there was no mistaking it, this was their old equipment.

"Well, what do you make of this?" Mr. Benson asked.

"It's definitely our old equipment from the old QT project," Michael said, holding some of the wires up for inspection. "But what happened to it."

"It seems Raphael was conducting some experiments on his own, unbeknownst to any of us," Mr. Benson said. "He must have completely lost it. What a mess."

"So you think he did this?" Garrett asked. "You think he destroyed all of our equipment?

"Who else?" William interjected. "Whatever he was working on, it was not sanctioned by us. We had no idea."

"Then you don't think anybody else was involved?" Garrett figured it wouldn't hurt to press William a little bit to see if he could break through that cold exterior.

"Well, there might have been, but we have no idea who. Do we father?" William said.

"Not a clue," Mr. Benson. "We've interviewed everybody in the company, to no avail. It's a complete mystery. We were hoping that you could shed some light on it. Did Raphael ever say anything to you? I mean, you were kind of curious about your old project, so I thought maybe he said something to you."

"Not really," Garrett. "We were just trying to make sense of his death. You know, grasping at straws."

"Then he never said anything at all to you?" William said in such way that they both recognized that he was fishing.

"Not a word." Michael said. "Sadly, we had sort of lost touch. We hadn't even seen him at all for two or three months. He called and said he wanted to get together for coffee, you know, the day of his death; but other than that, we hadn't heard from him in quite a while."

"He said he wanted to tell us something," Garrett said, "but he never got the chance." He hoped that this would drive home the point that they knew nothing. If they were to find out what William was up to, they would have to continue to play the part of being in the dark.

"I see," William said, pausing thoughtfully. "Do you think there's any chance of repairing any of this?"

"Do you want to repair it?" Garrett asked. "I mean, it hasn't proven to be of any use anyway. We never had any real success. It seems it is nothing but trouble, if not for us, at least for Raphael."

"Well, I suppose you're right," William said. "I was just thinking that if we repaired it, perhaps we could find some clues to what Raphael was up to."

"I don't know if there's anything we can do," Michael said, holding up the wires he still held in his hand. "Raphael did quite a number on it."

"Well, I suppose you're right," the elder Mr. Benson said. "Best to leave well enough alone, in any case, I don't think we have to mention this to anyone. Nothing would come of it. I don't see any reason why we need to involve that Detective Beck or anything. We'll just have to keep it in house, right, William."

"Yes sir," William replied, although it was clear he was not fully satisfied.

"Well, Mr. Benson, I don't think there's any more we can do here," Garrett said. "Thanks for showing it to us, but I agree, there is little we can do. It's probably best to leave it alone. After all, we can't bring Raphael back." In his heart, he knew that there was more that had to be done, but they were not about to repair the equipment and give William access to it. It was out of the question.

"I think we should be going now," Garrett said.

"Yes, of course. Thank you gentlemen, it was nice of you to stop by," Mr. Benson said.

"Yes, thank you gentlemen," William echoed.

Garrett made a point to turn and look William in the eyes. "Perhaps we will see each other again," he said.

"Perhaps," William looked away.

Once out on the street, Michael turned to Garrett, "that guy is as guilty as hell."

"There's no doubt about it now," Garrett agreed. "He's up to something and I'm afraid we are the only two that can do anything about it. The guy is evil to the core."

"Can you believe his boldness, asking us to repair the equipment?" Michael said.

"Yeah, it was bold, but it also means that he doesn't believe we have any idea of what is going on. He obviously doesn't know about the files Raphael sent us. This might be our one advantage. If he thinks we are still in the dark, and that we've dropped the whole thing, then maybe he might let his guard down. Maybe he'll make a mistake."

Chapter Five

"Happy Birthday to you..." they all sang as Rachel set the cake down in front of Katie, nineteen candles blazing. It was September 30th, a double celebration of sorts, David was a month old to the day. Katie had come home from school for the weekend and Rachel and Michael had offered to throw a little surprise birthday celebration at their home. Everyone was there; Garrett, Stephanie, Emily and David. The only one missing was Jesse, who, unfortunately, was asked to chaperone the homecoming dance at the high school where he was teaching.

Katie was all aglow, not so much because they were celebrating her birthday, but because she was surrounded by her family. She loved spending time with family, celebrating all the holidays and traditions, and Rachel, Michael and Jesse had been a part of her family for as long as she could remember. She was the perfect auntie to her young nephew, providing him with lots of attention and more than willing to lend her sister a hand in caring for him.

Garrett took his beer and walked out onto the deck. It was dark and the lights of the surrounding homes were reflecting in brilliant colors off the smooth glassy surface of Lake Union. Michael and Rachel had bought this house a few years back and it was a perfect place to host these family gatherings. It was perched on the side of the hill, with a beautiful view of the lake.

"Penny for your thoughts," Michael said as he walked up behind his friend.

"Just thinking, wondering what to do next," Garrett replied.

"You mean about the young Mr. Benson," Michael said.

"Exactly, it appeared to me that Raphael was trying to warn us that he was the one trying to change the future. The only thing that makes any sense is that if he was trying to change his own future, in other words, somehow making his future better."

"I've been going over Raphael's numbers again," Michael said. "It appears that several of the jumps were very short, into the near future, in fact the very near future. If we could pinpoint the exact moments, and more importantly the exact places, maybe we could figure out what he was up to and what got Raph killed."

"Yeah, but how do we do that, Mike? You and I know that the only way we could pinpoint the location, would be to recreate the exact conditions and make a jump ourselves. And even then there would be no guarantee. Then there's the problem of our equipment."

"Yeah, about that, maybe you should come with me," Michael said rather slyly. He then proceeded to lead Garrett back into the house.

As they reentered the dining room, the party was breaking up. "The girls are leaving, Garrett," Stephanie said. "It's past David's bedtime."

"You leaving too, Katie?" Garrett asked, noticing that she was putting on her coat.

"Yeah, Jesse's going to be late, so I'm going to spend the night at Em's," Katie replied. "Once David is put to bed, were going to watch a movie."

"Alright, we'll see you tomorrow then," Garrett said as he gave both of his daughters a kiss on the cheek. Be careful driving home Em, it's starting to drizzle out there."

After helping the girls and the baby to the car, Michael proceeded to lead Garrett down into the basement. Garrett just stood in disbelief as he reached the bottom of the stairs. Over in the corner, spread out on a table, was what looked like the QT apparatus. It wasn't exactly the same, but there was no mistaking it, visor and all.

"What's this?" he was able to say as the shock wore off.

"I know I should have told you sooner, but I never thought anything would come of it," Michael said apologetically. "After we left the institute, I started tinkering around and built a replica of the QT, with some modifications of course. I know that we had said that we were done with it, but I couldn't let it go entirely. I never really thought we would get to use it, but now I think we might have to."

"I don't know what to say," Garrett said. "I don't know if I should be mad or if I should hug you. This might be our solution."

"I thought so too, but I must admit that I'm still a little skeptical. Remember what you've always said about knowing too much about our future."

"I know what I've always said," Garrett said. "I still think it, but we may not have any choice. This time, it's not just about knowing the future. It's about correcting it, making it right."

"So you think we ought to try? You think we should retrace William's steps into the future?"

"Well, yes, I think we should try. It may be the only way."

—

The windshield wipers made a squeaking noise as they swept across the windshield. There was just enough precipitation to make visibility difficult, but not enough to fully wet the windshield. It was typical Washington weather, nothing new for Emily and Katie. They turned up Westlake Drive.

"What's up with Dad?" Katie asked. "He seems so distracted lately."

"I'm not sure," Emily replied. "He's been that way ever since Raphael died. He took it pretty hard. I don't think he has quite gotten over it."

"Yeah, I always liked Raphael. He was funny in his sort of quirky, geeky, scientist sort of way."

"Yeah, we all miss him." Emily added.

"Em! Look out!" Without warning there was a flash of headlights to Emily's left and then a horrible crashing and grating of metal as a truck collided with them broadside. Emily never saw it coming. Their car careened sideways into the guardrail that separated them from Lake Union on their right.

The air bags released and it took a moment for Katie to regain her bearings. She looked over at her sister. Emily was unconscious, blood flowing down the side of her head. She looked over her shoulder, David was crying, but his car seat was still intact and he was okay. She tried to unfasten her seat belt, but it was jammed.

There was the screeching of tires against pavement as the truck reversed itself and backed away from the car. Katie shouted, "Help, somebody help! I can't get out, my sister's hurt. Please help!"

Then without warning the truck tires screeched again and the truck came directly at the car again, hitting it from behind and pushing it against the safety rail. Katie cried out again, "Wait, what are you doing? Stop, wait!" Her voice was drowned out by the roar of the truck's engine and the squealing wheels. A second surge and the railing gave way pushing the car over the edge.

Katie felt helpless as the car teetered over edge, her mind racing. What could she do? They started to fall, she screamed, "Nooo!"

———

Michael and Garrett were still sitting and talking in the basement when Garrett's phone buzzed. It was Katie, her hair was all wet and she had a blanket wrapped around her; a red light was flashing somewhere in the background.

"Dad, it's me Katie," she was sobbing.

Garrett stood up and walked over to Michael so he could see the screen. "Katie what's wrong, what happened?"

"Dad..."still sobbing, "we were in an accident," more sobs. "Dad, Emily's hurt pretty bad, she's breathing, but unconscious. She has a bad cut on her head and she's lost a lot of blood."

"David! What about the baby?" Garrett nearly shouted into the phone.

"He's okay, thank goodness for car seats. Those things really work."

"And you...are you okay?"

"Yeah, I'm fine, a few bruises, but I'll be alright, just a little shook up."

"What happened, where are you?"

"Westlake Avenue, somewhere, I'm not exactly sure. We almost went into the lake. The car got caught up on some rocks, or…" she started sobbing again, "or we would all be dead. I think he was trying to kill us."

"What do you mean, who was trying to kill you?"

"I don't know, I've never seen him before, but I tell you he was trying to kill us. Look I'll tell you everything, but right now they have loaded Em in the ambulance. I'm taking David and going with them. They're taking us to University Hospital. You'll have to meet us there. Can't talk anymore now." The phone went dark. Michael and Garrett were already at the stairs.

———

Garrett sighed with relief as he stepped passed the curtain blocking Emily's bed from the rest of the emergency room. She was awake, a large white bandage wrapped around her temples. "Em, you okay?" Garrett asked as Stephanie stepped passed him and took her daughter's hand.

"Hi, Mom, Hi, Dad, yeah I'm fine, a bit of a headache. They say I may have a concussion. Wow, it came out of nowhere. Thankfully, David and Katie are okay. The doctors are checking David out to be sure, but he doesn't seem to be hurt at all. What a miracle? Tough little guy."

"Hey, Dad," Katie called. She was sitting on a bed in the next examination area. With everyone's attention on Emily, they had hardly noticed her when they entered.

Garrett walked over and gave his younger daughter a hug. "You okay?" he asked.

"Oh, Dad," she started crying. "I didn't know what to do. It all happened so fast. I was so scared. Why would anybody do that?"

"I kept trying to tell them that it wasn't an accident, but I don't think they believed me."

"Who didn't believe you?" Garrett asked.

"The police, they were asking me all these questions. I told them that the other driver was trying to kill us, but I think they thought I was crazy."

Just then a nurse entered the room carrying David. "Everything checks out. He's fine, not even a scratch." Moments later, Jesse arrived, he bent over and gave Emily a kiss and then caressed her cheek, there were tears welling in his eyes.

"Come on Katie, maybe we can find a place where they serve coffee." Garrett put his arm around his daughter and escorted her out of the room. They found a booth in the cafeteria.

"Now tell me what happened." Garrett said as he placed a cup of hot chocolate in front of his daughter.

"It all happened so fast, I hardly know what to say," she began. "We had started up Westlake Ave, it was raining, I remember the windshield wipers were making that irritating squeal. We were just talking. Then without warning, this truck came out of nowhere from Emily's left. I was dazed at first, but when I realized what had happened, the only thing I could think of was whether Emily and David were all right. I noticed Emily was bleeding. I tried to help her, but my seat belt wouldn't release, and I couldn't open my door, we were pressed up against a guard rail on the side of the road.

I kept calling, but then I heard the truck rev its engine. It was weird. It backed up and then accelerated toward us. When it collided with us a second time it pushed us partly through the rail. I called for help again, and then it happened again, only this time we were pushed over the edge. The only thing that kept us from going into the lake was that the car got caught up on something, rocks I think. There we were teetering over the edge.

I was screaming, thinking that at any moment, we were going to fall, but we never did. I don't know what I would've done. I don't know how any of us would have gotten out.

Then all of sudden it stopped, the truck that is. It was still there, but the engine went dead. That's when I realized I had my phone. I called 911. I didn't know what else to do."

"You did great Katie. It probably saved your sister's life. You did great."

"I was so frightened. Then when I tried explaining it all to the police, they just looked at me as if I was making it up."

"What about the driver, what happened to the truck? When the police arrived, he was still there. I saw them questioning him. He seemed pretty shook up. It just doesn't make any sense. I had never seen him before. Why would he have tried to kill us?"

"So you're convinced it was intentional?"

"Now, don't you start. Don't tell me you don't believe me either."

"No, Katie, I believe you."

At that moment, Michael arrived, a familiar face was trailing just behind him. "Look who I found wandering around emergency," Michael said as he slid into the seat next to Katie.

Garrett held out his hand, "Detective Beck, what a surprise? What brings you out on a night like this?"

"I was wondering if I could ask your daughter a few questions?" Beck asked, without as much as a by your leave.

"Is that okay with you, Katie?" Garret asked his daughter.

"Sure, what do you want to know?" Katie replied.

"Sorry to disturb you Miss, I was wondering if you could tell me what happened, the *accident* and all?" Beck directed at Katie, trying to appear cordial, despite his rather cold exterior.

"It was no accident." Katie began. She then began to relate the entire event, just has she had for her father a few moments earlier. When she was done, she gave a deep exhale. "It's like I told my Dad, I don't get it. I don't know who this guy is, and I'm sure Emily doesn't either."

"So you're convinced that the driver's intent was to push you into the lake?" Beck repeated.

"Look, like I said, Detective, the truck backed up, revved its engine and then plowed into us again and then again. I think that indicates intent, don't you." Katie placed a little extra emphasis on the word "Detective" and "intent" as if to drive home her point. It was clear that she was getting a little more than irritated by people questioning her.

"Easy Katie, the Detective here is just doing his job. I don't think he meant anything." Garrett assured. "Did you, Detective?"

"No, not at all, just trying to get to the bottom of it. You see the driver said he doesn't remember a thing. It wasn't even his truck. The thing had been hotwired, somehow. The last thing he remembered was getting off work, he was in the parking lot, and then everything went blank. When he came to, he was behind the wheel of the truck and your car was teetering at the edge of the road."

"The guy's a freaking liar," Katie said. "He was trying to kill us, and he knows it."

"Easy Katie," Garrett tried to calm his daughter. "Detective, was there any indication of alcohol or maybe drugs?"

"We're not sure," Beck said. "There doing a tox screen as we speak. I should get a report shortly. It would certainly solve the mystery. Could be the guy is schizo or something. Otherwise,

I just can't see any motive for him wanting to hurt your daughters. Wrong time and place, I'm afraid."

Garrett smiled as he realized the Detective was completely unaware of the irony of his statement. He looked over at Michael and could see that his friend was thinking the same thing.

"In any case, we'll get down to the bottom of it Miss. You can count on it. I'm just glad everyone is okay. I'll say my goodbyes now. If I need anything else, I'll let you know."

"Thanks Detective," Garrett said. "Always nice to see you."

As the Detective left, Katie said, "Delightful guy, friend of yours?"

"No, not exactly. He's the same Detective that investigated Raphael's death."

"I see. Well if you two will excuse me," Katie said, "I think I will go check in on Em again."

"Yeah, you go on ahead, Katie, Michael and I will catch up."

"Brave girl," Michael said as he watched Katie leave.

"Yeah, she never ceases to amaze me," Garrett agreed. After a momentary pause he added, "I guess you know what this means?"

"It was William, he was the driver," Michael said without hesitation. "Quantum Transference, it was one of his leaps forward. He wasn't trying to kill Emily or Katie, he was trying to kill David."

"It also means that we have to find out why." Garrett responded. "The only way we protect David is by finding out what William is up to. Fire up the machine, Michael, it looks like I'm going to have to follow him to the future."

Chapter Six

Garrett sat watching Michael as he fiddled with the dials and checked all the connections. It was getting late, and they were both a little tired and irritable. It had been years since he had been hooked up to the QT machine. He felt a little anxious. On the one hand he was wondering whether he should be doing it at all; it was a bit like playing with fire. On the other, despite Michael's modifications, he was wondering whether any of this was going to work. Were they actually capable of following someone else into the future to right place and time?

Michael had made some improvements in the software and was convinced that he had improved upon the accuracy of the jumps. But there again, Michael was always confident in his calculations. He had to be, he was a theoretical physicist; a little overconfidence came with the territory.

Any speculation concerning their success was really a moot point. It didn't really matter. They had to try, because they had no other choice. The attempt on David's life had proven this.

"Well, where do we start?" Michael asked, interrupting Garrett's thoughts.

"I've been looking over your calculations and I think I've found a pattern," Garrett explained. "See here, according to Raphael's notes, William made four different jumps to what appears to be the year 2056, twenty four years from now. At first, I didn't understand it, but now I think I know what was going on.

It occurred to me that the first jump was to determine the conditions of the future, to identify a target, so to speak. They needed to determine a way to gain an advantage. Understand, William is only 29 now, in 2056 he will be 54. It seems to me that he wanted to create a condition in the future that would best benefit him at that time."

"But why that time?" Michael asked. "And why did he keep going back?"

"I don't think there was anything particularly important about the year, it could have been completely arbitrary, I simply think he was allowing for enough time, so that he would have the opportunity to make changes to the timeline," Garrett continued.

"Yeah, I see what you're saying. If he jumped to tomorrow and he wanted to change it, he would only have the time and space of the next twenty four hours in which to make any changes to the time line. The greater the length of his first jump, the greater the opportunity for him to make changes to the timeline, by any subsequent jumps."

"Exactly," Garrett agreed, "and that explains the other jumps. See here, he made a very short jump, we now know that was to the night of the accident. Then, he returned to 2056. We only assume this was because he was checking the success in the change of the timeline."

"But what does this all have to do with David?" Michael asked. "I mean he's only a baby. How could he possibly be a threat to Benson's plans?"

"He's a baby now, but he won't be a baby in 2056. At some point, between now and the year 2056, David is a part of something important, that seems to be sure. I think that's one of the first things we have to determine. What did William find in the year 2056 that he felt he could change in such a way that he would personally benefit from it? I don't think we have any choice, the first thing we must do is travel to the year 2056. There's only one thing that bothers me."

"What's that?" Michael asked.

"If we are successful leaping ahead to the year 2056, it will be the new timeline, the one that was altered by William. As a result, it may be difficult to determine just exactly what changes were made to the old timeline."

"Old timeline, new timeline, it's all getting a bit too weird, if you ask me," Michael said, shaking his head. "You do see the irony of the situation, don't you?"

"Yeah, I know what you're thinking. If we hadn't stumbled onto this technology, invented the QT and all, then we would have never altered the timeline in the first place, and then perhaps none of this would even be happening. Don't think for one moment I haven't been considering the possibility that we have very little control of the timeline and that all that has happened was exactly what had already been predetermined, right down to my attempt to save David from his future suicide."

"It's possible, or perhaps I should say probable, that David is supposed to die, just as you observed," Michael said grimacing.

"I know, but if that's the case, then we won't succeed. But that doesn't change what we must do. Regardless of whether we can actually alter the future or not, we've got to try." Garrett looked at his phone. "It's getting late. I suggest we get some sleep. Tomorrow morning we'll make the first attempt. I'll see you bright and early."

"Goodnight Garrett," Michael said as Garrett got up and headed for the stairs. "I hope you don't mind if I don't show you out. I'm going to stay up a little longer and go over the calculations one more time. I want to make sure we get this right the first time."

"Goodnight Michael," Garrett said softly, already starting up the stairs.

———

There was a flash of light, and then he opened his eyes. It took him a moment to get his bearings. He had forgotten the feeling, the sensation that his mind was momentarily outside of his body. He didn't like it.

He looked around. He was sitting at a table in a dimly lit restaurant. He held a menu, leaning it slightly against the edge of the table in front of him. It was made of a strange plastic material and the text glowed slightly. It was digital.

There was no one else sitting at his table, he was eating alone. He was grateful.

There were only a half a dozen people in the room. It was quiet. Night had fallen outside, but without knowing what time of year it was, he had no way of knowing the exact time. To his left sat an older couple. They were enjoying some kind of soup or broth, and neither was saying a word to the other. To his right were two women, about his age (his age in the past) or perhaps a little younger. The one nearest him had her back to him, the other was facing him, but her face was partially obscured by the menu she was holding as she was giving her order to the waiter standing nearby.

He looked down at the menu. The faire didn't seem anything fancy, although the prices seemed a bit exorbitant, but then he remembered he was nearly 25 years into the future, or at least he hoped he was.

On the far side of the room was a bar and above the bar was what looked like a flat screen, although it was not like anything he had ever seen. It was as if the images were hanging in mid-air. In fact, the more he thought about it, the more he realized that it didn't seem to be attached to anything. It was as if it was entirely transparent, and the images were just hanging in the air.

He was watching some type of news broadcast. Surprisingly, he could hear the voices of the people on the screen quite clearly, even though he had to be at least thirty feet away. It took him a moment before he realized that the sound wasn't coming from the images on the other side of the room, but instead seemed to be emanating from a small square shaped object sitting on the table in front of him. He touched it and something unexpected happened. An image appeared in the air directly in front of him. It looked like some kind of control panel. Across the top of the image were the glowing words *Mobile Vid-Com Interface.* One of the controls appeared to be a volume control. He poked at it with his finger, attempting to slide the control bar down and up. It worked. He could control the volume of what he saw on the screen across the room. It was strange, he wasn't really touching anything but the air.

"Can I take your order sir," a voice said from his left.

He had been so preoccupied that he hadn't noticed the arrival of the waiter. "Uh, yeah, sure. I guess I'll have the Chicken Parmesan," he said. It was the first thing his eyes landed on.

"Yes, sir, I should mention that the price for that was just raised today, to $60 a plate," the waiter said matter of fact, without any expression. "Poultry shortages and all, I'm sure you understand."

"Yes, that'll be fine." Garrett said. He wasn't sure if he could afford it, but it didn't really matter, he wasn't sure he would even be there long enough to find out.

"Very well, one Chicken Parmesan," the waiter said, as he turned and walked away.

Garrett looked at his hands. They were kind of wrinkled, indicating age. He wondered what he looked like, but there were no mirrors nearby and he still wasn't sure why he had jumped to this particular place and moment. He looked back to his right and he could now see the face of the woman facing him, his heart jumped. It wasn't just any woman. It was Katie, his daughter, only she had grown old. Her hair was shorter and her face was starting to show wrinkles at the corner of her eyes, but there was no doubt about it. It was Katie.

Then he remembered, when he had made jumps before, it was always to a moment connected with the people closest to him, something about the similarities of brain signatures. Raphael had argued this point on more than one occasion. He should have known and he should have prepared himself better for the possibility.

He touched the device in front of him and then used his finger to slide the volume control all the way to zero. He could just hear the voices of the two women talking now. He tried not to look at them.

"How are you doing, Sis?" Katie asked.

"Oh, I suppose I'm doing alright. You know, one day at a time. I try and keep busy, but I do miss him. He's all I had left in the world."

"That's not true, you still have Stephen and I. And the girls simply adore you. We are your family too. Don't ever forget it."

"I'm sorry Katie, I know that. I love you all, and I don't know what I would do if I didn't have you as a part of my life. It's just so senseless, you know. He was so young. It just doesn't make sense to me. Why did it have to happen?

Garrett was trying to keep his emotions in check. It wasn't difficult for him to imagine what the two of them were talking about. He had to keep his adrenaline under control. He didn't want Michael to yank him back before he had come to find out what he needed to know.

"It's no use trying to make sense out of it Em. It was a senseless tragedy, that's all. And it certainly doesn't do any good to keep dwelling on it. It's done and over, in the past, and there is nothing we can do it about now. You have to let go. You must live your life."

"Yeah, I know, you're absolutely right. I'm sorry, I don't mean to be so gloomy. Let's change the subject." Emily paused a moment, playing with the food on her plate. "Of course, it would be a little easier to enjoy life if we could get a decent steak from time to time," she said dropping her fork on her plate and smiling.

"Yeah, I know what you mean." Katie laughed. "The food here is horrible. I don't know what we were thinking. Come on, let's get out of here."

At that very moment, the waiter set a plate down in front of Garrett with a piece of chicken the size of a credit card smothered in some kind of red sauce with cheese sprinkled on top. There was a vegetable on the plate as well, but Garrett could hardly make out what it was. He looked up at the girls (ladies) who were making their way to the door. As they did, they seemed to pass right through the image on the video screen without noticing it. Something on the screen caught his eye.

Standing at a podium on a stage was William Benson. Above his head was emblazoned the title Dennis Corp. Garrett touched the device in front of him and raised the volume bar.

"Executive President of the Dennis Corporation, William Benson, today announced the release of a new solar cell that will soon revolutionize the transportation industry. The Dennis Corporation, which already has what many would call a monopoly in the communications field, may just have secured similar control of the transportation industry, further increasing the financial prowess of the one of the wealthiest and most influential men in America."

That was it. That was what Garrett had come to see. It didn't answer all of his questions, but it was a starting point. He now knew William Benson's objective. What's more, it was clear that he had been successful, although it was still to be determined how he had been able to accomplish it.

Chapter Seven

Garrett sat up, rubbing his eyes and trying to clear the fog. He had forgotten the way that Quantum Transference made him feel. It was almost like his nervous system was momentarily disconnected from the rest of his body. He didn't like it. He had a headache, not at his temple or in the front of his forehead, but deep in back.

"Well," he heard Michael's voice, his eyes still closed. "Did it work?"

"Yeah it worked," Garrett finally answered, rubbing the back of his neck as he spoke. "The year 2056, just like we had hoped. Your calculations were spot on this time."

"Okay," Michael said. "But did you find out what is going on? Why William is trying to kill David?"

"No, not exactly. I did find out what his objective is, but I'm still not sure what David has to do with anything. I don't think we'll know that until we make some additional jumps."

"Well, what was his objective, then?" Michael asked. "What is this all about, anyway?"

Garrett thought for just a moment, before answering. "I'm not sure I should tell you."

"What do you mean you're not sure you should tell me? What are you talking about?"

"I've been thinking. It's not a good idea for any of us to know too much about the future. If we're going to continue on with this, I think it's better for me to leave you in the dark."

"But what if something happens to you? What if I have to finish this myself? Keep in mind, David is my grandson as well. He's just as much my responsibility as yours."

"No doubt," Garrett agreed. "David is your responsibility as well as mine. I just think we need to limit any exposure to knowledge about the future. I tell you what. I will put everything I experience down on paper, and then put it under lock and key. That way if anything happens to me, then you will still have access to it."

"That seems a little silly to me, but alright, if you think it's necessary. It's not as if I am going to be able to talk you out of it once you've made up your mind," Michael said, rolling his eyes. "So where do we go from here?"

"Well, after I get some rest, we'll try again. This time we will try to follow William to a time a little closer to our own. Then one by one we'll follow his path to the other times on the list until we have exhausted them all. Hopefully, at some point we'll be able to determine why he is or was after David, and then we will stop him."

———

A flash and he found himself in a restaurant again. There was a stack of pancakes smothered in maple syrup on the plate in front of him. He looked around the room. He knew this place, he had been here before. He closed his eyes, trying to remember. He opened them again. It was the lodge at Snoqualmie Falls, where he and Stephanie had celebrated their first anniversary. It was only an hour from Seattle. They had tried to make a trip to the falls with the girls at least once a year. It had always been one of Emily's favorite places.

The lodge sat on the river just above the falls. He looked out the window next to his table. The sky was bright and blue, but there was a light mist rising from the falls below. He closed his eyes and listened. He could hear the dull roar of the water as it crashed into the river below.

He opened his eyes again and looked around, but he didn't see anybody he recognized. A young couple was sitting a couple of tables over, but he didn't know who they were. The rest of the restaurant sat empty. He waited patiently for something to happen, something that would give him a clue as to why he was here.

While he waited, he ate the breakfast in front of him. It was a strange feeling. This body did not really belong to him, but he could feel everything, including the sweet taste of natural maple syrup and he could smell the bacon. It was almost as if he was experiencing every sensation for the very first time.

When the waiter placed the check in front of him, he reached for his wallet. As he opened it up, he noticed the driver's license. His name was John Christiansen, and he was from Marysville. He glanced at the picture; it portrayed a young man in his twenties with blonde hair and blue eyes.

He paid the check and left. Once outside, he could hear the rush of the water over the falls more distinctly. It was difficult to see the falls from the lodge, but there was a trail that led down to the river below where visitors could get an excellent view. At the entrance to the trail, he noticed a young family preparing for their hike.

Emily bent down and helped her young son as he struggled with his tiny backpack. David looked to be about six or seven years old. He was clearly excited and looking forward to their hike. Jesse had what looked like a camera-phone focused on his wife and son, recording the moment for the family memory book.

Garrett stood at a distance, trying not to be noticed, the whole time watching every movement of his daughter and grandson. It was ethereal, seeing them now, what was for him six years into the future. It left him with a mixture of confused emotions, joy over seeing them so happy and well, while at the same time a little disappointed that he had missed the previous six years of their lives.

He tried to put his emotions aside. He wasn't sure why he was here, but whatever it was, he needed his wits about him, and above all, he needed to be sure that David was kept safe.

After making all the necessary adjustments, they started down the trail, Jesse leading and Emily and David trailing, hand in hand. Garrett followed at a distance, trying his best to be inconspicuous.

The trail was fairly easy to navigate, but on occasion Jesse or Emily would have to help their son navigate some of the steeper portions. At one point, the trail turned into a man-made catwalk. It was constructed of wood, and the mist from the falls, along with recent rains, made the wood planks a little slippery, but there were no mishaps.

At the bottom, the trail opened onto the rocky edge of the river. Emerging from the trees, they were presented with a beautiful view of the falls as they cascaded some two hundred and seventy feet from the cliff face above into the river below.

David stumbled over the rocks until he was near the water's edge, his father standing just an arm's length away. The young boy began picking up rocks and throwing them in the water. After his first few attempts, his father tried to show him how to skip a rock along the water's surface.

Garrett sat on a large rock about fifty feet away watching his grandson in his futile efforts to skip a rock. He couldn't keep from smiling.

He looked around at the others who were admiring the falls, enjoying the day with family or friends. Somewhere in the crowd was William, he was sure of it, but he wondered if he would ever be able to identify him. Like himself, he had taken the body of someone else, a stranger. His only advantage was that he knew William was here somewhere, but his adversary would be completely unaware that he had followed him into the future.

Jesse and David finished playing at the water's edge and then joined Emily where she had laid a blanket down on a sandy patch of ground. They sat and ate a leisurely snack. When they were done, they packed up and headed back up the trail. Garrett followed.

Once they had reached the top of the trail, the three of them decided to go to the observation deck that over-looked the falls from above. Inside the observation deck, it was difficult for Garrett to remain unnoticed and so he simply walked to the railing and looked out at the falls, as if he were taking no notice of those he was following.

Without warning, Jesse walked directly up to him. "Excuse me, sir," Jesse said. "Would you mind taking our picture?"

Garrett was taken back, and it was everything he could to hold his emotions in check. He kept his composure enough to blurt out an answer, "Uh, yeah sure. No problem, I'd be glad to." He took Jesse's phone as it was held out to him.

Jesse picked David up in his arms and the three of them stood with their back's to the falls. Garrett tried to get a little of the falls in the background, and then said, "say cheese,-one, two, three," he snapped the picture.

"One more, just to be sure," Emily said.

Garret obliged.

As Jesse was lowering his son to the ground, he said, "Hey Em, where's David's backpack?" Together, they looked around the deck, but it was nowhere to be seen.

"Oh, my gosh," Emily said. "I think we left it down at the river, down at the bottom of the trail. He took it off when the two of you were throwing rocks."

Jesse rolled his eyes. "You're right. I can't believe we did that." He rubbed his eyes in frustration. "Well, I guess I'm going to have to go back down the trail and retrieve it."

"I'm afraid so hon, that's what dads are for." Emily said with a little bit of a smile. "We'll wait for you in the parking lot."

Jesse took off back down the trail. Garrett stayed as close to David and Emily as he could without drawing their attention. If William was going to show himself, this would be the time, when the two of them were alone. When he did, Garrett would be ready.

Emily and David had to cross over a bridge that spanned the highway to a parking lot on the other side. There was a little grassy area next to their car, so they sat down and Emily gave David something to drink. Garrett hung back near the bridge, trying to remain out of sight.

Several minutes passed, and nothing happened. Emily kept looking at her phone. Garrett assumed that this was to check on the time. Nearly thirty minutes had passed, and still no sign of Jesse.

Emily was clearly becoming agitated, worried that her husband had not returned. All of sudden it occurred to Garrett that it was possible that David was not the only one at risk. William may have more than one objective. His heart jumped, Jesse could be in danger as well. They all could be.

He jumped to his feet and ran back across the bridge. Jesse should have returned by now, he was sure of it. Something had happened; he just hoped he wasn't too late. He skipped down the trail as fast as he could go; catching himself more than once as he nearly stumbled. As he reached the cat walk, a man passed him just as he entered. They brushed arms.

Garrett paused for a moment. A strange sensation had passed over him. It was as if he had touched minds with the man. As if he could read his thoughts. It was him. It was William, he was sure of it. He turned and looked after the man, but he was already fifty feet up the trail.

Garrett turned back to the catwalk. "Jesse," he thought. He took off down the catwalk as fast as he could navigate the wet walkway. As he turned the corner he heard some voices ahead. He looked over the edge and saw there were some people gathered below. He hurried on.

As he neared the end of the catwalk a young man came running up to him. "What's happened?" Garrett asked.

"An accident," the young man said half out of breath. "I'm going to get help."

Garrett ran to the spot where the crowd had gathered. There in the middle of the crowd lay Jesse's limp body, blood flowing from a gash on his head. A young lady was kneeling beside him, crying.

"What happened?" Garrett shouted.

"We don't know, the girl here saw him fall from the walkway above." A little bald man spoke for the group. "He must have slipped or something. No one really knows. He hit his head. He's dead. Can you believe it? It's tragic, he's so young."

"Dead! Are you sure?" Garrett said as he knelt by the body.

"I felt for a pulse," the girl kneeling next to him said. "There's nothing. I tried to stop the bleeding, I'm afraid it's too late. Oh, it's so horrible." She started sobbing.

Garrett couldn't believe his ears. Dead, how could he be dead? Just moments ago he had been enjoying the day with his family. It wasn't right. How could this be happening? Poor Emily, poor David, what were they going to do?

William had done what he had come to do. He hadn't been after David, after all. He had come for Jesse, but why? It didn't make any sense. What was he up to? Garrett could feel the adrenaline surging in his body. He was angry. He wanted to chase up the trail after the villain, but what use would it do. William could already be gone, back to the past.

———

Garrett sat up in the bed, pulling off the visor with all of its electrodes. He put his face in his hands. He had failed.

"Are you alright?" Michael asked.

"Not really, no," Garrett finally said.

"Well did you figure out what William was up to?" Michael asked.

"Yeah, I'm afraid so."

"And, did you stop him?"

"No, not this time, in fact, I may have failed," Garret answered. He tried to sound calm, but it was all he could do to keep from screaming.

"And what about David, is he, I mean, was he alright? You know, when you left him."

"No, David's fine."

"Then what do you mean, you think you failed?" Michael asked.

"What I meant to say, was that I failed to stop William entirely. Our work is not done here. We're still going to have to return to the future, perhaps a few more times. I wasn't successful in finding out what he is really up to. That's what I mean." Garrett wasn't about to say anything about Jesse. What would be the point? It wouldn't make it any less painful. There wasn't anything they could do about it now. He had had his chance and missed it.

"I see," Michael said. "So we're still at square one."

"Not exactly at square one; there was one thing I was able to figure out. I now know how to recognize William in the future. Next time there won't be any surprises. Next time, I will be ready for him."

Chapter Eight

Garrett smiled, trying to keep his eyes on the road ahead. The two boys in the back seat were making quite a racket, giggling and carrying on as usual. It was all he could do to keep from turning and looking over his shoulder to see what was so funny. He decided they were just being boys, and there was no serious mischief at play.

It was David's twelfth birthday and they had been planning this trip for months. At first, it was going to be just the two of them, but David had pleaded with his grandfather to let his best friend, Jonny, come along and Garrett didn't have the heart to tell him no. Jonny's mom had been a little apprehensive, at first, but when his dad had suggested they take along his satellite phone, she finally agreed.

They had passed through Bellingham a while back and they were now on highway 542, just minutes from Deming. Garrett loved the area around Mount Baker. His father first brought him here when he was a young boy and now he was able to share it with his grandson.

Ever since David's father had been killed in a tragic accident, Garrett had made a point to take him fishing at least a couple of different times each summer. It had always been their thing to do together, and he enjoyed every minute of it.

This trip was going to be particularly unique. It was an overnighter. They were going to hike into secluded Elbow Lake. A few years back the Parks Department had constructed a hanging bridge over the middle fork of the Nooksack River so the lake could be accessed from the Ridley Creek trailhead. It was a little bit of a climb, but they would take it slow.

As was typical for August, the weather was perfect. After parking the car, they grabbed their gear and started for the lake. It was still pretty early in the day.

It was only a three and a half mile hike and most of the elevation change would be at the beginning. They would be shielded from the hot sun by the thick forest canopy, which would make the hike quite comfortable.

The bridge was a little shaky as they walked across it. The base of the bridge was constructed of wood slats that were bound together, offering a stable platform for walking on, but the safety railing on either side was constructed only of rope, causing the hikers some uneasiness when crossing. The river beneath the bridge was still very swift and imposing despite it being late summer. This was probably due to the summer storm that had recently passed through the area.

By noon they had reached an overlook that provided a beautiful view of Twin Sisters. Garrett thought it would be a perfect place for lunch. As he removed his pack, he could feel the coolness of the perspiration on his back. He was breathing heavy, but a bit relieved, knowing that they had completed the most difficult part of the hike. They would have camp set up beside the lake before the middle of the afternoon.

The boys seemed little affected by the climb. They were a bit rosy cheeked, but still full of energy. They were cackling and giggling all through lunch. Each one was boasting about who would catch the biggest fish, all between bites of peanut butter and jelly sandwiches. Garrett smiled. He was glad that Jonny had come. The two boys were obviously having a great time together.

They had a beautiful view of Twin Sisters, a pair of mountain peaks that sat to the southwest of Mount Baker, the iconic snowcapped volcano of Whatcom County. Garrett loved that his grandson had grown up to enjoy the beauty of this region. It remained a wilderness untouched for all those except the most serious outdoorsman.

He inhaled deeply. The air was crisp and clean. It was one of the benefits of a region where it rained most days. But on days like today, when the sun did emerge from behind the continuous cloud cover, it made one feel a little closer to heaven. The brilliance of the evergreens against the backdrop of the jagged Cascade Mountain Range rising straight out of the earth into the deep blue sky, tickled the eyes.

The remainder of the hike was fairly easy. They passed a young couple on the trail. It was the only other people they saw on the trail during the entire day. When they reached the lake, they were able to find some dry ground on which to set up camp. There were some rocks formed in a circle, evidence of a fire pit that had been built by previous campers.

It wasn't long before they had broken down their packs, set up the tent and established a fairly comfortable campsite. The two boys explored the perimeter of the lake, while Garrett sat beneath a tree, keeping an eye on his charges. After a few moments he found himself drifting off to sleep, a consequence of the morning hike.

When the boys had finished their exploring they returned to camp and roused Garrett from his nap. They were anxious to try their luck fishing.

One of the challenges of an overnight fishing trip was to travel light, carrying just enough food to keep from starving to death, but not more than what was needed. The goal was to catch fish for dinner, or they would find themselves eating jerky and crackers.

Fishing is a funny endeavor. Regardless of how expert the fisherman, there still seemed a great deal of chance in the outcome. For the first hour, they didn't even receive a nibble. This was more than disconcerting for two twelve year boys who had been boasting about their fishing prowess during the entire length of the hike.

Failing to have any success, Garrett suggested they move to the side of the lake where the water sat in the shadows of the trees. Once again they met with little success, and after another hour, the two boys were beginning to show their discouragement.

Then, when it seemed all hope was gone, David's pole took a nose dive down toward the water. He jerked hard on the pole, as he had done many times before, and then shouted, "Hey, I think I have something."

He started reeling it in, slowly at first, his pole bending back and forth sideways as the fish fought for its life. Then, without warning, it broke the surface.

"Wow, hold onto it, David, it's a whopper!" Garrett shouted to his grandson

David was not about to let go, working with all his might he kept drawing up his pole and then relaxing it as he reeled in. After a brief battle, the fish finally tired. David finally landed it. Garrett reached down and lifted the fish in the air, holding it by the gills.

"What a beauty!" Garrett exclaimed. "A rainbow, at least 20 inches, I'd say."

David was beaming, a smile stretched across his face from ear to ear. "It was a fighter, Gramps. I think it's the biggest fish I've ever caught."

"It could be, David," Garrett agreed. "Well let's stop admiring. They're biting now boys; let's see if we can catch a few more before dinner."

A few moments later, David landed another, just a bit smaller than the first. Jonny was not at all happy that his friend was getting the best of him, so insisted that they switch fishing spots. As if on cue, David caught another, just a few moments later from his new position.

Garrett laughed, "Well, Jonny, some people have all the luck. I guess this is just David's day."

"I guess so," Jonny said, a little irritated at his friends success.

They were just about to break it up and head back to camp when all of a sudden Jonny gave a shout, "I think I have one!"

Sure enough, his pole was dancing. Garrett coached him to be patient, not to hurry. Slowly, but surely, he was able to land the fish. Like his friend, he was now smiling from ear to ear. "I can't believe it," he said. "I did it. I actually did it. I caught one."

David laughed. "Easy, Jonny, you're sounding like it's the first fish you have ever caught."

"Well, it is," Jonny said, and then they both laughed.

Garrett smiled. Everything was as it should be.

There's nothing like eating pan fried trout, cooked over a fire, under the stars. A little flour for breading, a little butter and some salt and pepper, and you have a gourmet meal fit for a king, or at the least two young boys who felt like kings. They savored every bite.

With their stomachs full and at the end of a very full day, Jonny and David slowly began to wind down. Without any prodding, they decided to hit the sack. They would be up at sunrise again to see if they could improve upon their evening catch.

Garrett sat quietly, watching the fire slowly burn down. Somewhere in the distance he could hear the hoot of an owl. His body was a little sore from the morning hike, but he didn't much mind. He was at peace. The business of life, the daily lectures, the never ending grading of papers, all faded into non-existence. It was just him, his grandson and nature. Nothing else seemed all that important.

He was glad he could be there for David, especially since his father had died. He wondered if he would ever be able to tell David everything, about the QT and how he had stumbled on the plot to change his future. How would he ever be able to explain to his grandson that he had traveled into the future to save his life? He had already seen the results of knowing too much about the future and he didn't want David to have to carry this burden.

David was important, his life was important. It was not just about one individual life. David was part of something much bigger, something that had ramifications for the future, everyone's future. At some point Garrett would have to tell him, but when? Certainly not yet, he was still too young.

The boys were up as soon as the sun peaked over the mountains. Garrett stayed behind in camp while the two boys found their favorite fishing spots and began casting their lines. Even from where he was Garrett could see the plop of the tackle as it broke the glassy surface of the lake.

It didn't take him long to get a fire going, and to place a pot of water on a rock next to the flames. Before the water even boiled, Jonny gave out a holler, indicating he had made his first catch. By the time Garrett joined the boys on the edge of the lake, David had also made his first catch of the day. He handed each of the boys a cup containing some instant oatmeal.

"Here you go boys," he said, "a little sustenance to carry you through the morning."

"Thanks gramps," David said. "Wow, they're really biting this morning."

"Looks like it," he replied.

By mid-morning they had all caught their limit. Garrett had instructed the boys in how to catch and release the small ones. In the end, they only kept a few of the largest fish to show as trophies to the boy's moms.

As the sun started to rise in the sky, Garrett had the difficult task of informing them that it was time to go. "I promised your parents I would have you home for dinner, Jonny," he said.

"Alright Gramps, we're ready," David said, as he started reeling in his final cast. He looked over at his friend, "Hey Jonny, did you hear my grandpa? It's time to go. Jonny! Did you hear me? What's with you? Are you daydreaming?"

Jonny seemed in a bit of a daze just staring out at the lake. "Uh, yeah, right," he finally responded. "Sorry, I guess I forgot where I was for a moment. Having too much fun I suppose. I just sort of blanked out there."

"Well, come on, we have to pack up," David said.

"Right behind you," Jonny said as he pulled his line out of the water.

The return hike was much easier given that it was mostly downhill. They stopped for a brief rest at the overlook to take one last look at the view. Another hiker came upon them as they sat finishing off the last little bit of jerky.

He was young, in his mid-twenties, tall and dark. He wore a baseball cap with the University of Washington logo.

"Good morning," he greeted. "Are you headed down?'

"Good morning," Garrett replied. "Yeah, we spent the night at Elbow Lake last night, but we're headed home."

"Ah, it must have been your fire I saw last night. I was staying on the other side of the lake."

"Did you go to U o'dub?" Garrett asked.

"Uh, yes, oh you mean the hat. Yeah I graduated a couple of years ago, Biology major."

"Oh, then you must know Professor Johnson," Garrett said.

"Uh, well, yeah of course. I had him for a couple of classes; great teacher. Well, anyway it's a beautiful day isn't it? Enjoy the rest of your hike. I have to be going; think I might go up to Mirror Lake today."

"Have a safe trip," Garrett said as the stranger started off down the trail.

"I don't like that guy," Jonny said. "There's something about him that gives me the creeps."

"Yeah, I know what you mean," Garrett said. He thought it strange that the young man didn't know that Professor Johnson was a woman.

The two boys danced down the trail ahead of him as they descended the trail that led to the river. At times, they were nearly running. The steepness of the descent began to take its toll on Garrett's knees and it was all he could do to keep up with his two young companions.

Before long they could hear the rush of the river ahead. "Race you to the car," David said to Jonny. Without hesitation the two of them took off running down the trail. Garrett tried to follow, but it wasn't long before the boys were out of sight.

David reached the bridge first and as he skipped across, it swayed slightly from the impact of his feet against the wooden slats. He had to reach out for the rope railing in order to catch his balance. Without warning the rope snapped and he fell, head first into the water. Fortunately, he had the alertness to hold on to the rope. He held on with all his strength, as the water pulled at him dragging him down and toward the rapids below.

Up and down he bobbed, still clenching the rope, his only life line. As he looked up he noticed Jonny straddling the bridge just above his head. "Here!" Jonny yelled. "Grab the end of the pole with your other hand," he shouted extending his fishing pole toward the struggling David. "You can do it!" he yelled again. "A little further, there."

David pulled as hard as he could on the rope and then reached with his right hand for the pole. The water was pulling against his body, but he didn't let go. After two failed attempts, he finally was able to catch hold of the pole.

Jonny had wrapped his leg around one of the support ropes on the bridge and began to pull as hard as he could. Slowly, but surely he began to pull his friend to safety.

Just when it appeared he had exhausted all of his strength, a voice came out of nowhere. "I've got him Jonny," a strong arm reached and grabbed David by the belt and lifted him onto the bridge. It was his grandfather.

The two boys stumbled across the bridge and then collapsed onto the grassy bank on the other side.

"Everyone okay?" Garrett asked. "David, are you alright?"

"Yeah, Gramps, soakin' wet, but other than that, I'm fine, thanks to Jonny."

"Yeah, that was pretty quick thinkin', Jonny," Garrett said, but there was no answer.

"Hey, Jonny, are you okay?" David asked.

"Uh, yeah, well, I guess, so," Jonny said, hesitancy in his voice. "Where are we? What happened?"

"What d'ya mean what happened?" David exclaimed. "You just saved my life. Don't you remember?"

"Uh, I don't know," Jonny still sounding unsure. "I must have blanked out. The last thing I remember was fishing at the lake, and then everything after that is a blank."

"Well if that doesn't beat all. You save my life, and you can't remember a thing. What do you think of that Gramps?"

Garrett had walked back over to the bridge and was inspecting the rope. It had been cut, there was no doubt. "Yeah, sounds a bit strange to me too, David. You didn't hit your head or something, did you, Jonny?"

"No, I don't think so, Jonny, said. It's weird, I just don't remember."

"Well, anyway, everyone's okay, and that's all that matters. Let's get you to the car and into some dry clothing, David. Come on you two, I don't think we need to stay here any longer." He wasn't sure if someone might be watching.

Chapter Nine

Garrett opened his eyes. He tried to clear his mind of the confusion. This time he had been successful, but it left him very unsettled. For the first time, his mind had been transferred into the body of a young boy. It was a strange feeling, inhabiting a body so young. It took him a moment to get used to being so short, seeing the world from a level closer to the ground. To say it was strange or bizarre was an understatement.

To compound matters, it was the first time he had encountered himself in the future. It was strange looking at himself from outside; seeing himself older. He didn't like it. No one should see themselves older. It was disturbing. It was all he could do to remain calm, to stay focused on his task. Fortunately, he had recognized William or at least his mind when they encountered him on the trail. It made him alert, realizing that something could happen at any moment.

When David had fallen into the water, he had been quick to react. He saved him. It had worked. At least this time he was able to thwart William's attempt to harm David.

"Well?" Michael asked as Garrett tried to wipe the fog from his mind.

"It's done. I was successful. I was able to recognize William, and disrupt his plans, without him being aware of our interference."

Garrett closed eyes. The headaches caused by the QT experience were growing more pronounced. It was possible that it was doing more damage than he realized. It didn't matter. He had to continue even if it meant risking himself.

"Do you think we're making a difference, you know, actually changing the timeline?" Michael asked.

"I don't know. I'm not really sure," Garrett answered. "The more I think about it the more confusing it gets. The space time paradoxes are too numerous to imagine."

He paused, caught up in his own thoughts. Now he was faced with the problem of knowing that David would fall from the bridge and be saved at some point twelve years in the future. If he was now made aware of it, why couldn't he just stop the event altogether; by not taking his grandson on the fishing trip at all. Of course, if the fishing trip didn't happen, then he would not have needed to travel into the future, but if he had never traveled to the future he would not have the knowledge.

How was it possible that they could change the future at all? Perhaps it was all an illusion, and that none of it was really in their control. He realized that this meant that something or someone else might be in control.

"I know what you mean by paradoxes," Michael interrupted Garrett's thoughts. "It's like, how could William travel back to the past using Quantum Transference and then cause an event that was the very thing that led us to the development of time travel to begin with? It's completely illogical. And yet here we are."

"I know what you mean," Garrett agreed. "Was it possible that the invention of Quantum Transference had been predetermined so that nothing has happened as a result of chance, or, more importantly, because of our choice? Was it possible that everything had happened just as it should; that it was all a part of plan and there had been purpose behind every event."

"What do mean? Like *God* set this all in motion?" Michael asked.

"I don't know what I mean. I can't say I fully understand any of it. Regardless, I feel we must do all we can to protect David's future. Which means, we are not done; we still have more work to do."

"Agreed," Michael said.

Over the next few weeks, Garrett made three more jumps to the future, each one following the pattern set by William Benson. It was taxing, both physically and emotionally. It was all Garrett could do to keep it together. With each jump, he became privy to new knowledge about his own future and the future of his friends and family; none of which was he able to share with anyone, not even Michael. The burden was great.

There was also the problem of the headaches. They persisted, and it was becoming clear that they were the direct result of QT. He knew that he might be risking his personal health, but there was no turning back, not now.

"It's done," Garrett said, as he removed the visor and stripped the electrodes from his body for the last time. "David has been saved. There is nothing more to do. The rest will be up to him and how he makes use of the time we have given him."

"How can you be sure?" Michael asked.

"Well, that's just it. We can never really be sure. All we know is that William made no other jumps. We've done all we can."

"Yeah, well, I've been thinking about that as well. It seems to me, there is one other thing we can do."

"What's that?" Garrett asked.

"We can keep an eye on William; in this time." Michael said.

"What do you mean?"

"We will have to watch him."

"How do you propose we do that?"

"I'm not sure, but it might mean getting close to him. It makes me nauseas to think about it, but we might need to spend time with the guy; get to know the guy." Michael said.

"It might be worthwhile at that. It'll keep him in the dark. He won't be aware that we know anything. He will think his plans are still in place. If we're close to him, we might be able know what he knows, so to speak."

"That's what I was thinking," Michael said. "And I think I know how to get close. I have decided to offer my services to the Institute again, that is, if they'll have me. I figure with Raphael's death, they probably have an opening, and the way that Mr. Benson treated us the last time we saw him, I think he might be glad to have me back."

"I think your right, but are you sure you want to do this? I mean, keep in mind, you will be working alongside of someone who has attempted to take the life of your grandson? You'll have to keep your emotions in check. Any let down on your part, and you could blow our cover."

"I know, it won't be easy, but I think it's the only way. I don't think this is over. He has to be watched."

"No, it's not over," Garrett said under his breath.

—

Garrett and Michael sat alone in the gazebo at edge of the yard. Their wives were sitting on the grass with Mrs. Benson and their two grandson's David and Jonny. It was Jonny's first birthday party and the Benson's had invited the DeAngelos and Adams to come for the celebration.

Jesse, Emily, William, Lucy and the elder Mr. Benson were all sitting at a table on the patio, enjoying some refreshment.

Garrett couldn't help but realize the irony. Jonny was William's son; the same Jonny who went on the fishing trip and the same Jonny whose mind Garrett had occupied. Jonny had saved David's life, so to speak. Jonny's father had been the one who had tried to take his life. And here they all were together, one happy family. It was another paradox. If Michael hadn't suggested getting close to William, then Jonny and David may never have become friends, and then they would not have gone on the fishing trip together. It was all so confusing.

"Well, is this getting close enough?" Michael said with a smirk.

"Yes I guess it is." Garrett replied. Even now it was difficult to keep from telling Michael, everything that would happen. "It is a little unnerving, I must admit. However, it does give us a chance to know the man a little better. It might gain us an advantage, if we need it."

"Well it looks like we're gonna become fast friends. Emily said that little Jonny was going to come over for a play date. Evidently his mommy has to go to the doctor for a check-up," there was clearly a little cynicism in Michael's voice.

"Easy Michael, there's no reason to allow your disdain for the man to carry over to his wife and children. They've done nothing wrong."

Lucy Benson was eight months pregnant. She had already announced that it was going to be girl. She seemed like a nice enough person, not too much upstairs, but kind and pleasant in her own way. Garrett had a hard time figuring out what she could see in William Benson. He was an arrogant snob, and everyone around him recognized it. She was clearly ten years his junior. Of course money can cause one to look past a multitude of faults.

"Do you think he's on to us?" Michael asked, looking over at William Benson.

"No, I don't think he has a clue. At this point, I think he's just waiting for the future to unfold."

"I've been checking around at work. It doesn't appear that he has made any attempt to reconstruct the Quantum Transference apparatus, with no one to help him."

"I don't think he would know where to begin, not without Raphael's notes. He certainly can't enlist our help, not without giving himself away. No, I think he is content to wait it out. In the mean-time, you be careful. You don't want to give him even the slightest hint that we are on to him."

"Don't worry," Michael assured. "Like you said, I don't think he has a clue, and I'm not about to let on. By the time he knows anything, it'll be too late."

"I sure hope so, as well," Garrett said. "Come on, Grandpa, it looks as if the grandmothers could use a break. Let's go see if we can teach the boys to play catch."

"Uh, catch? Don't you think there a little too young?" Michael questioned.

"Okay, maybe we can teach them to roll the ball." Garrett said with a laugh.

Epilogue

Garrett sat down at the table and took a sip of his coffee. Stephanie set a plate in front of him; eggs over easy, bacon crispy and some lightly buttered toast, just the way he liked it.

"Well, this is a big day. David's sixth birthday, it's hard to believe," he said aloud. "It seemed like just yesterday that we were all at the hospital, welcoming him into the world."

"Yeah, I know what you mean," Stephanie replied as she hugged him from behind and gave him a kiss on the cheek.

"When are they coming over?" he asked.

"Oh, didn't I tell you. The birthday party has been postponed until tomorrow. They called last night."

"What do you mean postponed?" Garrett said.

"Well, school starts for Jesse next week, and so they wanted to get away for the weekend. They were going to go over to Leavenworth. They said they'd be back tomorrow afternoon and we could do the cake and presents then."

"When are they leaving?" Garrett asked.

"They left last night. They were going to stop at Snoqualmie last night, see the falls and continue on to Leavenworth today."

Garrett jumped up from his chair so rapidly that it sent it falling to the floor behind him, "Snoqualmie, are you sure?"

"Yeah, what's the problem?" Stephanie said, looking at the chair as it lay on the floor.

"I have to go," was all that Garrett could blurt out. "I'll explain later, but right now I have to leave."

"What do you mean you have to leave? What are you so worried about? At least finish your breakfast."

"Sorry, Steph, no time. I'll call you." Garrett was out the door before Stephanie had a chance to object any further.

Once in the car, he spoke aloud, "Call Michael." His phone lit up and then the sound of a phone ring filled the car. "Come on, Michael, pick up." Garrett said anxiously.

"A little early on a Saturday to be calling, isn't it Garrett," Michael's voice was finally heard.

"Michael, I am on the way to pick you up. Jesse and Emily are in Snoqualmie, just found out. My God, I hope were not too late!" Garret said.

"Snoqualmie, what? How?" Michael answered.

"I don't know exactly; last minute decision. Stephanie just told me. I'll be there in just a few minutes."

"Hurry, I'll being waiting out front." The phone connection ended.

Garrett had tried to keep what had happened at Snoqualmie a secret from Michael, but as the years passed, he became more anxious and he couldn't keep it from him any longer. When he had first told him, Michael had been furious that he hadn't been told sooner. When he had finally calmed down they talked for several days about what they were going to do about it.

They knew they couldn't travel to the future in an attempt to prevent Jesse's death without tipping off William. In the end, they decided their best course of action would be to wait. They knew approximately the time it would happen, so they would just watch and listen. If Jesse and Emily ever planned a trip to Snoqualmie, they would find a way to intervene. They figured they would always have plenty of time. The only thing was, they hadn't anticipated the unexpected; the spontaneous change in plans.

As soon as Michael was in the car, "I knew we should have told them," he blurted out.

"There's no way, and you know it. We couldn't have told them, we would have had to tell them everything. There's no telling what the ramifications would've been. We covered this already. This was the only way. I only hope we get there in time."

"I know. You're right, of course. I just feel so helpless. Hurry! We can't have much time. You said it happened in the morning."

Garrett was pushing the speed envelope already. "Try and call Jesse on the phone. Maybe we can warn him somehow."

Michael obeyed without hesitation. "No answer," he said clearly frustrated.

"Call Emily," Garrett said aloud. The phone rang and rang, but there was no answer.

"Their phones must be off. I don't get it. Whoever turns their phones off anymore?"

They were both pensive for the entire drive. It was emotionally draining. Garrett kept looking at the sky to see the height of the sun, trying to remember where it had been, but it was no use, it was all a blur.

When they finally entered the parking lot of the Lodge, both of their hearts sank at once. They were too late, much too late. There was an ambulance already sitting near the entrance to the trail. It could only mean one thing.

They sat for a moment, not sure what do to. Jesse was gone, and there was nothing they could do about it.

Michael put his head in his hands, "I don't understand. Why did this have to happen? Why couldn't we have saved him?"

Garrett placed his hand on his friend's shoulder. "I don't know. Maybe we were not meant to stop it. Maybe we really can't change the future."

"But if we had only got here a moment earlier." Michael said reaching for answers.

"Maybe we were not meant to get here a moment earlier. Remember, we're not really in control."

Garrett's phone rang. "Hello Dad, it's Emily," she was crying. "Dad...Jesse's dead. He's dead," more sobs. "I need you Dad, can you come?"

"We're on our way Emily. We got a call from the police a while ago. We'll be there in a few minutes. I'm so sorry, honey." The call ended.

"Look Michael," Garrett said, "I don't get any of this. The only thing I know is that you rescued Rachel from certain death, and as a result you rescued Jesse as well. You've been a great dad, and he grew into a fine young man. I don't know why he's gone, why it has to be this way, but it is. We won't always be able to play the guardian angel. We won't always be there. We just have to do the best we can."

He paused a moment. "I know how much you loved Jesse, but he wouldn't want you to sit here grieving. Right now his wife and son are over there, and they are in pain and the only ones here to provide them comfort are you and I. Right now we need to go do what we can for them."

"I know...of course, you're right," Michael said, tears in his eyes. "I was just hoping we could have played the Guardian again, just this once."

GUARDIAN

Part III

And I saw something else under the sun: In the place of judgment-wickedness was there, in the place of justice-wickedness was there, I thought in my heart, God will bring to judgment both the righteous and the wicked, for there will be a time for every activity and every deed...
The Teacher, *Ecclesiastes*

Chapter One

The human mind is a conundrum. This not merely a supposition, but in fact, is both an assertion and testament of its actuality. It is the ability of the mind to contrive a paradox, or to realize mystery which makes it an object of extreme curiosity. However curious it might be, it remains to be determined whether it can ever be truly comprehended. Nothing demonstrates this perplexity more than when the mind begins to falter in rational thinking due to the inevitable process of aging, or the more horrifying fate of disease. Isn't the mind the soul? Can the soul decay like the body? Then why should the mind decay with age?

David sat beside his grandfather's hospital bed, as the old man slept. The room was so silent that one could hear the faint blip on the heart monitor recording the rhythmic pattern of the patient's heartbeat.

It was strange for him to see his grandfather in this condition. He had always looked up to his grandfather in awe. He was his hero. He had stepped and filled the void left when his father had died so unexpectedly when he was still a young boy. His earliest memories were of the times he and his grandfather had shared together fishing and hiking in the Cascades. It was difficult to see him the way he was now, frail and vulnerable.

He had always believed his grandfather to be a brilliant man and nearly invincible. After all, he was a scholar; he had a Ph.D. in neuroscience and had taught at the University for as long as David could remember. He had always believed that he had inherited his own propensity for academics from his Grandpa Adams. It was hard to sit by and watch him deteriorate, seeing his life slowly slipping away.

It had been over a year since his Grandfather had first been diagnosed with an inoperable brain tumor. At first, it was hard to believe he was even sick because there was very little evidence that anything was wrong, but then, slowly, but surely the subtle changes began. Everyone started to notice the momentary lapses in memory. Not long after that, there were signs of nervous system decline as he began to lose control of simple motor function in his hands. Then the memory lapses grew worse, and before long the brief moments of mental clarity became rare.

It was difficult for David to see his grandfather like this. It was one thing to see the physical weakening of his body, but another thing altogether to watch the slow deterioration of his mind. There were occasional moments of lucidity, but they were few and far between. Often times his grandfather didn't even recognize him.

This was not one of those times. "Hello David," a voice whispered. David realized almost immediately that this would be one of those good moments for his grandfather. He could see it in his eyes. There was strength and clarity there. He was fully cognizant of where he was and who he was.

He had been caught a little off guard when his grandfather spoke, not having noticed that his grandfather's eyes had opened. He smiled, "Hello Grandfather, how are you doing today?"

"Same as always, I suppose," his grandfather replied. It seemed he didn't remember the moments of absent mindedness and confusion. "How long have you been here?"

"Just a few moments," David replied. "I didn't want to disturb your sleep. Mom wanted to be here today, but she had some kind of meeting downtown she had to be at."

"Shouldn't you be out with that pretty girlfriend of yours? You know, what's her name?"

"Come on Grandpa. You know her name is Michelle. As a matter of fact, she was going to meet me here. She should be here any minute."

Michelle and David had been dating for more than two years. They had known each other most of their lives. Michelle was the younger sister of David's best friend, Jonny Benson. They had practically grown up together. David had always had a bit of a crush on Michelle, but he could never get up the courage to ask her out until they were both in college.

Once they started dating, it seemed the most natural thing in the world. In fact, David was sure they would one day get married. He was hoping to finish grad school first. He hadn't proposed, and he wasn't really in any hurry. He liked the way it was. They were together and there was still plenty of time, after all they were still pretty young. For the moment, Michelle seemed content with the way things were, but he knew in his heart that she was beginning to lose patience.

His grandfather had talked him into attending University of Washington and he was now in graduate school, hoping to earn a Ph.D. in Chemical Engineering. He was currently working on making improvements to a rechargeable storage cell for use with solar panels. The oil industry was struggling amidst political turmoil and global unrest. It appeared as if it may never same again. Solar power was still the only viable alternative to fossil fuels and provided at least some hope for the future.

"I look forward to seeing her," his grandfather's voice interrupted his thoughts. "If I were you, I would marry that girl."

"Yeah, Grandpa, I know. You've said that before." David wasn't sure if his Grandfather was unable to remember this, because of the tumor, or if he just liked teasing his grandson.

His grandfather's tone turned serious, "I'm glad were alone, David, I've been meaning to talk to you about something. I know my health is failing, and that I am having trouble remembering things, so I had better get this off my chest while I can, that is while I can think clearly enough."

"Don't talk like that, Grandpa. I'm sure you're going to get better." David knew that this was a lie, and that his grandfather knew that it was a lie, but he had to say it just the same.

"Thank you, David, but I know the reality of my condition, and I have no qualms with the fact that I am dying. But before I go, I need to share something with you."

"Sure, grandpa, I'm listening."

"David, what do you remember about my work before I began teaching at the University?"

"Not much really. I remember once you told me you worked for the Institute for Enhanced Artificial Thought, I think. That's where you and Grandpa Mike and Raphael all met. Why? It had something to do with virtual world imaging or something."

"That's right, the Institute for Enhanced Artificial Thought." He paused. "It has been a very long time since I have even mentioned the name. We were doing some very significant things in those days, trying to change the world of virtual experience. Jonny and Michelle's grandfather was my boss in those days. I suppose that's how you kids met, at some sort of company gathering or something when you were little. The rest is history as they say."

"Yeah, I think I remember playing with Jonny at a company picnic at Woodland Park." David had a vague memory of meeting Jonny when they were only about four or five years of age. "Although, Mom said that we actually first met when we were babies."

"Yeah, those were fascinating days, working with Raphael and Michael. We had some really good times together." He paused again, as if trying to figure out what to say next. "There were good times, but there were also some very difficult moments as well. We stumbled on a discovery that would change the course of all of our lives."

"Discovery? What kind of discovery? You've never mentioned anything about it before."

"That's because we decided to keep it a quiet. It was a discovery that if used the wrong way or by the wrong person, could be very destructive. We decided it was best to put it aside, to hide it, so to speak. Well, that is until I was forced to put it to use again. "

"I don't understand. What was it?" David asked again.

"I don't know if I can explain the whole thing to you right now. It was all very complicated. I'm not sure if you would believe me, in any case. I can't be sure how much longer I will be clear in my head, so to speak. It would be better for you to learn about it on your own. That is, if you want to."

"Sure, but I don't understand. How can I learn about it on my own?"

"By reading my journals," his grandfather whispered. "I kept everything. I had thought about destroying them, several times, but I could never bring myself to do it. I was afraid. We, that is, Michael and I discovered that someone else had found out about our work and had used it foolishly and selfishly. I was always worried that somehow, someone would have to use it again to correct the problems created by this very evil individual."

"Who?" David was having a hard time believing what he was hearing. Could it be possible that his grandfather was having a moment of dementia, that he was imagining things?

"You wouldn't believe me if I told you. Besides, I have no real proof. It would be best for you to come to your own conclusions. There is no other way."

David was feeling more than a little skeptical. He had never heard his grandfather talk like this before, and given his condition, it was hard to make sense out of any part of what he was saying. "Come to my own conclusions, but how? Why?"

"Go to your mother's house. Look in the basement. On the east wall is the electric panel. Open the right panel. There is a magnetic key box in the bottom of the inside of the panel. Inside is a key. The key is to a fireproof cabinet in the corner of the basement. You won't see it at first. I covered it with a tarp and there are a bunch of storage boxes on top, labeled *old tax documents and personal records*. I figured no one would bother to disturb them. My journals are in the cabinet. Take care with them. They contain data and information that could be very dangerous in the wrong hands."

"But what am I supposed to do with them?" David asked.

"You're a bright boy, David. You'll figure it out. I'm sure you'll do the right thing."

"Hello, you two." A voice was heard at the door. A young woman entered, walked over to David and kissed him on the cheek.

"Hi, Michelle," David replied, still trying to make sense of what his grandfather had said.

Michelle was nearly as tall as David and athletic in form. She had been a pretty good volleyball player in high school and she carried herself with poise and confidence. She had blond shoulder length hair and beautiful dark brown eyes. She took after her mother, a very attractive woman in her own right. Despite the fact that she lived in Seattle, she had a tanned complexion, which suggested that she had spent a good deal of the summer out of doors.

"What were the two of you talking about?" she asked.

"Oh nothing really," David was not about to let her in on his grandfather's revelation, since he really didn't understand it all himself. "Grandpa was just telling me a story. He seems to be doing pretty well today."

"A story, I love stories." She said as she turned toward Grandpa Adams. She had always liked David's grandfather and she had a way of showing him a little special attention whenever she saw him.

"I'm sorry Miss, do I know you?" Grandpa Adams said quizzically.

"Why Grandpa, don't you recognize me? It's me, Michelle. You know, David's girlfriend."

"I'm sorry Miss, I don't think I've ever seen you before."

It appeared as if his grandfather had slipped back into an amnesiac state. However, when he looked into his grandfather's eyes he could see the clarity he had seen before; it was some sort of faint. But why, why would he try and deceive Michelle?

"It seems he doesn't remember me," Michelle turned to face David.

"It's okay, Michelle. It's nothing personal. He has his good moments and he has his bad."

"Yes, it's okay young lady. Why don't you come and sit beside me and tell me about yourself?" Grandpa Adams said with a smile.

Michelle proceeded to sit down on the bed and then began to explain to Grandfather who she was and how her and David had first met. David stood at the foot of the bed and listened to the entire dialogue, not wishing to interrupt. He could sense that his grandfather was only play-acting, but he didn't let on. He figured his grandfather had his reasons.

After several minutes, David noticed the clock and realized that visiting hours were nearly over. "It seems the time has come for us to leave," he said to Michelle, indicating the clock.

"Oh, right, I guess I lost track of the time." She replied. She stood up from the bed and then took David's hand in hers.

"It's time to say goodbye, Grandpa," David said.

"Yeah, goodbye, Grandpa. You take care. We'll be back to see you real soon," she said in a way that sounded almost patronizing, as if he was a little child.

They turned to leave. "David." Grandpa Adams said aloud before they had left the room.

"Yeah, Grandpa, what is it?" David asked.

"David, do you know what a guardian is?"

"You mean, like a guardian angel?"

"Well, sort of." He hesitated slightly. "There will come a time, after I am gone, that a man will come to you and he will call himself your guardian. You must listen to him. You must trust him."

"Okay, sure, Grandpa, whatever you say."

"David, listen to me. This is really important. You must trust him. Promise me."

"I will Grandpa, I promise. Now, you get some rest. Michelle and I will be back to see you again on Friday. Goodbye, Grandpa."

Together they turned and walked out the door. He could hear a faint "goodbye, David" as they walked down the hall.

"That was weird," Michelle said when they got on the elevator. "What was all that guardian stuff?"

"I have no idea. You know what he's like when he gets this way. Half the time he doesn't know what he was saying. It didn't mean anything. He was just rambling."

Even as he said it, he realized that he was trying to convince himself. There was something about the way his grandfather had looked when he said it, something in his eyes. He had been completely lucid. But what could he have possibly meant? Who was this Guardian?

Chapter Two

Michelle and David stood in line at the bus stop on Cherry Street. Buses were about the only motorized transportation anyone saw in the city anymore. There was of course the occasional solar powered car, or even more commonly the solar powered motorcycle, but with the way the economy was only a small percentage of the population could afford the ever inflating price tag. Cars with the conventional gasoline combustion engine sat vacant along the street, many not having been in use in more than a decade. The city had tried to have them removed, but they finally gave up. There were too many.

It had been ten years since the oil industry had first began to crumble. Heavy regulation, deepening anxiety over rapid population growth and global pollution had crippled North American oil production. The Middle Eastern and South American Alliance had completely shut off the supply to the U.S., a political maneuver intended to cripple the economy of the West. It had nearly worked. Gasoline prices soared to unimagined heights, which resulted in soaring inflation of every commodity that required transportation. This combined with the fact that nearly half of the population had become dependent upon some form of government assistance, created an environment in which the economy had nearly come to a standstill. There was a domino effect. People lost their jobs at an unprecedented rate which meant they could barely afford the essentials of food and clothing. Gasoline became a luxury, one that half the population could do without. After all, they didn't have a job to travel to. Everyone just stayed home and tried to find a way to find a place of escape.

The one industry that continued to remain profitable was information, which was in no way affected by the cost of oil or transportation. Advances in the speed and availability of nearly unlimited streams of data had provided the general population with an affordable diversion from their depressed condition. The virtual world had become a welcome relief from the pains of reality.

Michelle's father was one of the few who had been able to profit, while so many suffered. He was the CEO of the largest producer of virtual reality devices and holographic communication devices. Michelle, for her part, resisted the advantages provided by her father's wealth, empathizing with the poor and destitute. Even so, at this moment, David was kind of wishing she had borrowed one of her father's solar powered cars so they could have avoided taking the bus.

The first bus had been too full, and they were forced to remain at the stop and wait for the next one. He stared at the buildings across the street, while they waited. It was the campus of Seattle University. Even though it was September, there was no life there. Like half of the colleges and universities around the country, it had closed nearly four years earlier. When the economy became crippled, fewer and fewer students had the resources necessary to pay the tuition, especially at the expensive private institutions. The larger public universities like the U of W were able to survive, but this only due to some extreme measures by the state and federal government, and with this came heavy cost at the expense of the infrastructure of the nation. David's family didn't have a lot of money, but his

Grandfather had taught at the University and this provided him with at least some privileges.

They were able to squeeze onto the next bus, barely. David had to lean back as the electric doors closed. It was a warm day and the aroma was anything but pleasant. David thought he caught Michelle placing her hand over her nose. They didn't say anything. No one talked on the bus. No one looked at anyone else. Everyone ignored everyone. There was no connection between persons. Where was everyone going? Where had they come from? No one cared. This was the human race, literally. Each one was competing for space and resources with everyone else. It was a race for survival. It was hard and depressing. It was the way it had always been. David couldn't remember a time when it was not like this.

On the seat nearest him, next to the window, a young man sat with a VID (virtual interactive device) pulled down over his eyes. There was no movement. David wondered if he was even conscious. People were always missing their stops because they were so distracted by their fantasy experience that they would lose track of the real world. Just the other day there had been a news report of an elderly man found dead on a bus, his VID still activated.

The bus finally came to a stop on Queen Anne Avenue. It was a relief to step off the bus and breathe the fresh air again. He took Michelle by the hand and together they walked the six blocks to his mother's house.

As they turned the corner on Highland, he looked up the street to check the lines at the Market. It was still called a Market, but in reality it was merely a food distribution center. The exorbitant gasoline prices had the greatest affect and the agriculture and grocery industry. Food prices had escalated to unreasonable heights. Grocery stores were soon struggling to provide affordable products and inflation had made it difficult for the average citizen to get enough to survive. In the end, the government had to step in and take control. The Market became the place where citizens could get the basic staples to survive, things like rice and other cereals, soy and corn products, and if they were lucky, the occasional fresh produce. Beef had been particularly difficult to come by and could only be purchased on the black market. Fortunately, living in Seattle meant that fish was a little easier to come by, even though it was still very expensive.

David could smell the aroma of fish cooking when he entered the house. His mom had already begun dinner. Knowing that Michelle was coming to dinner, she had made a special effort. Michelle lived a life of opulence, and Mrs. Jacobson was always a little embarrassed by her meager existence. She must have stopped off at Pike's Street Market on her way home from work, and purchased a little cod, or perhaps red snapper. It wouldn't be much, but she would find a way to stretch it into a meal for the three of them.

"Hello, Mom," David said as he entered the kitchen.

"David! Good, I am glad your home. I was afraid you would be late. Dinner is nearly ready. Hello, Michelle. How are you?" She turned back to the stove, barely pausing long enough to look the two young people in the eyes as she greeted them. It was her way. It wasn't as if she was rude. She had a sort of shyness about her. She just didn't look people in the eyes, or if she did, it was not for very long.

"Hello, Mrs. Jacobson," Michelle returned. "Thank you for having me. Is there anything I can do to help?"

"Thank you dear, but no, I think I have everything under control. You two go ahead and have a seat at the table."

David directed Michelle to her chair and then took his place next to her. They were catching up when Mrs. Jacobson brought the food to the table. The portions were light, but it smelled good. Somehow, she was able to make the best of the circumstance.

David admired his mother, she was kind and compassionate, but also had a special strength about her. She had been especially resilient when David's father had been killed in a freak accident, years earlier. David had been devastated. He and his father had been close. Despite her own grief, his mom had been his pillar. He loved her for it, although he'd never really found the words to tell her how much.

His grandfather had also been a great friend during that time. Without fail, week in and week out, they would get together on the weekends, go to the mountains, or hang out down on the waterfront.

"Did you see Grandpa?" his mom asked as she took her seat at the table. "How was he today? Did you tell him I would be up to see him tomorrow?"

"Yeah, Mom, I told him. He seemed to be doing pretty well. In fact, at the beginning he seemed a bit like his old self. He remembered who I was, and we actually had a rational conversation. Then when Michelle arrived, he fell right back into his memory lapses."

"Oh great," Michelle jumped in. "I suppose I should have never showed up."

"That's not what I meant," David apologized. "I just meant that for a moment there, he seemed perfectly normal."

As they finished eating, David noticed that the sun was descending on the horizon. The summer months were coming to an end and with the changing of the season there would be a shortening of the days.

Music was coming from Michelle's bag. She reached in and pulled out her D4. "Sorry, it's my dad," she said as she promptly placed the device in front of her on the table. "I hope you don't mind?"

"No, go ahead," Mrs. Jacobson said. "I was just about to clear away the dishes anyway."

"Answer," Michelle said in the direction of the device. It was a flat metallic blue object, about three inches by five inches and less than half an inch thick. Immediately an image of a man's head appeared hovering just above the surface of the device.

The D4 was the fourth generation of a computing or communications device produced by The Dennis Corporation, the company owned by Michelle's father. The first generation device was called The Dennis, named after Dennis Gabor, the inventor of Holographic Imaging. The key advancement in the device was the DOHIP or Digital Optimized Holographic Imaging Processor. It had been invented by The Dennis Corporation, and to date had not been reproduced by any of the other major tech companies. As a result, Dennis had gained a near monopoly on the communications and virtual imaging industry.

At first, it hadn't been well received by the public. The holographic images were a bit unnerving, appearing out of nowhere and disappearing without leaving a trace. However, as is always the case, the younger generation soon adapted and the Dennis became a must have. Not only did it project holographic images of people you were communicating with (soon to be referred to as h-com), but it also could create a three dimensional data screen in mid-air that responded to the human touch, completely eliminating the use of hard screens for computing. It also featured voice recognition software that made each device only accessible to the owner.

"Hello, Daddy," Michelle sad, speaking to the floating head facing her.

"Michelle, where are you?" the head responded. "Are you watching the time? You know I don't like you out after dark in the city."

"Daddy, don't worry. I'm at David's. I'm perfectly safe."

"How are you getting home?"

"I thought I would take the bus," she answered. "I'll be home in no time."

"No you don't. Stay right where you are. I'm sending a car. David, are you there?" The head turned slightly as if trying to look around. The D4 only had a 180 degree peripheral vision, somewhat like humans, so David had to move a little closer to Michelle to be seen.

"I'm here, Mr. Benson," David responded.

"David, don't let her leave. I think you understand my concerns with her being out after dark. I'm sending a car. Keep her there until it arrives."

David did understand. The city was dangerous place after dark and it seemed as if it had been getting progressively worse. It was the natural consequence of increasing poverty and distress.

"I understand, Mr. Benson. I probably should not have let her stay here this late. Time kind of got away from us. I'll put her in the car myself." David was always trying to make a good impression with Mr. Benson, but he rarely felt he was successful. It wasn't as if Michelle's father hated him, but it didn't seem that he liked him much either. No matter how much he tried, he was unable to break through Mr. Benson's cold exterior. David always took it to be the demeanor of an overprotective father and left it at that.

"Thanks, David. I knew I could count on you." The head turned back to Michelle. "You come straight on home, Michelle. No side trips. I expect you home within the hour."

"Goodbye, Daddy," Michelle said with a little disdain in her voice. The head immediately disappeared. "Sorry, about that. He's a little *too* caring, if you know what I mean."

"It's okay," David returned. "I think it's great that he looks out for you. That's what fathers are supposed to do, look out for their daughters and all."

"I know he loves me, it's just that I wish he would give me a little space, you know, trust me a little more."

"Relax," David assured. "It could be a lot worse. He could have forbidden you from seeing me at all."

"Yeah, about that, sometimes I think the only reason why he lets us date is because you're a friend of Jonny's. There's something strange about the way he looks at you, as if he only tolerates you when you're in the room."

"I don't get it. What does he have against me? I mean, what's not to like?" David joked.

"Yeah, right." They both laughed.

A few moments later a car pulled up outside. There was nothing mistakable about the high pitched hum of the electric engine. As they walked down the steps, a young man stepped out of the driver's seat. "Hey you two," the young man shouted. He was tall, his blond hair catching the last bit of sun as it set on the horizon.

"Hey Jonny," David returned. "Didn't expect to see you tonight, thought you had tickets to the game."

"It was 10-0 in the fifth and so I left early. I overheard Dad say he was sending a car for you, so I offered to come. Hope you don't mind Sis."

"Why would I mind?" she replied.

"Well come on then, I promised Dad I would have you home by dark."

"Goodbye, David," Michelle turned and gave David a kiss on the cheek. "Will you come to dinner on Saturday night?"

"Are you sure it's okay with your dad?"

"Sure, he won't mind. Say six o'clock?"

"I'll be there," David said as he ushered her into the passenger seat. "Hey Jonny, are we still on for meeting up at Tony's tomorrow night?"

"Yeah, I'll be there. See ya David. Say hi to your mom for me." Jonny slid back into his seat and closed the car door.

"Goodnight Jonny, goodnight Michelle, see ya Saturday." David closed Michelle's door and stood watching as they drove away, the hum of the engine growing quieter in the distance.

Chapter Three

David decided to spend the night at his mom's. He had an apartment on campus, but it was getting late. He didn't have any classes in the morning and he wasn't due to meet with his advisor until ten. He was teaching a class at three in the afternoon, after which he planned to meet up with Jonny at Tony's, an Italian restaurant on the edge of campus. The university district was still a bustling place. The University of Washington had been able to maintain a fairly healthy student population despite the failing economy and the local businesses had benefited.

The basement was dark and musty smelling. He couldn't remember the last time he'd been down here. He pulled on a string that hung down from the light bulb that was dangling just above his head as he stepped down off of the bottom step. He was immediately flooded with memories of his boyhood. This was the only home he had ever known. He and Jonny used to play together in the basement, building forts and treating it as if it were their own private clubhouse.

Even in the dim light, it wasn't difficult for him to locate the electric panel on the far wall. He had to move several boxes in his path, and with only minor effort he was able to reach it. The panel door creaked as he opened it. He felt along the bottom edge with his fingers. It was there, a small magnetic box clinging to the base of the panel. He plied it from its perch and held it up to the light. It was slightly rusted, but he was able to slide off the cover. Inside there were two shiny keys.

He looked across the basement. The light was dim, but his eyes finally came to rest on a mound in the far corner. Just as his grandfather had described, there was some furniture and a stack of boxes piled high, sitting on top. There was just enough light for him to detect the corner of a file cabinet. He managed to move the boxes out of the way, clearing a space in front. He slid the first key in its hole and it turned easily. The lock popped open and he pulled open the top drawer. The front half of the drawer was filled with files in hanging folders. The back half of the drawer had a half a dozen green, bound notebooks. The bindings had dates written in ink across them. He calculated in his head. They covered a period of about six years, beginning just after the birth of his mom. This was what he was looking for. He took all six upstairs, and set them down on the coffee table in the living room. After pouring himself a cup of coffee from what was still warming in the pot on the kitchen counter, he plopped himself down on the couch and began to read.

David was only vaguely familiar with his grandfather's research. He knew that he had been working on some type of virtual reality visor, similar to the one he had seen on the bus earlier that evening, but he never knew whether his grandfather had had any success. The first few entries confirmed this. In fact, he'd been working with his friend Raphael, and Michael, David's paternal step-grandfather to create a more realistic virtual experience. The notebooks were full of data and charts and what looked like test results and interviews with trial subjects. There were some flash drives attached to the inside cover as well. He would have to rely on the paper copy. He wasn't sure the flash drives would still work after so long a time. It seemed all a little antiquated. It was pretty tedious to go through. It wasn't until about half-way through the first notebook that the entries started to take on a strange mood.

> *...something quite unexpected happened to me today. I was sitting at the bus stop waiting for my afternoon bus, when I witnessed an accident right in front of me. A man was hit by a car and killed instantly. What made it so strange, was that it was exactly the same thing I had experienced in my virtual experience test project; not almost the same, exactly the same. What does this mean? Was it some sort of déjà vu?*
>
> *...subject six returned to the lab today, quite shaken. She had been a trial subject two weeks earlier. She was so agitated she could barely describe what had happened to her. When we finally got her calmed down, she described that the day before she had relived her virtual dream, only this time it wasn't a dream, it was real. This confirmed my suspicions.*
>
> *It seems the combinations of the telepathic enhancing drugs and the electromagnetic stimulation had somehow opened a hole in the space time fabric enough for a person's conscious mind to be able to see forward into the future. The virtual stimulator was not creating a dream world, but instead a look into the* real *future...*

David stopped reading. He could hardly believe his eyes. He reread the previous paragraph several times to be sure he understood what he was reading. There it was, in black and white, *a look into the future.*

> *...yesterday was a success of sorts. I was able to travel more than thirty years into the future, or at least my mind was. This was significantly more than even Michael had planned for, or perhaps,*

more than any of us thought was even possible. Although a success, it came with a price; something I was entirely unprepared for.

I met my grandson, David, today. It seems strange to even think of it, for he has not even been born. He was Emily's son, but she is but a baby. There he was, right in front of me, talking to me. It was hard to believe that it was not a dream, but deep inside I knew it was real. For the first time, I began to question whether what we're doing is right. It's not a good thing to know too much about the future. I know that now. The question is, is it the future that must be or is it only the future that could be?

David set the journal down. How was this possible? Somehow, his grandfather had traveled into the future and met him, and all this happened years before he was even born. Was this real? When did this happen? Had he already met his time traveling grandfather, if so when? Or was he going to meet him sometime in the future? It all seemed so crazy, unimaginable. It had to be some kind of mistake, it couldn't be true. Perhaps his grandfather had been wrong. Maybe he was only experiencing a type of dream. Time travel just seemed so improbable. Could it possibly be true?

He came to the end of the first journal. It was approaching midnight, but he couldn't stop now. He had to know what it all meant. What had his grandfather discovered? Sleep would have to wait. He opened up the second journal.

...it appears that my passage through the time portal is not exactly random. We have the ability to somewhat control the place and time of the opening of the micro-wormhole on the other side. If this is true, we might be able to change the future, or at

least find the cause of future events. I know this a bit like playing God, but if there is a way I must find it…

David didn't fully understand the explanation for the Quantum Transference. There were a lot of calculations and records of ongoing trials. He kept turning pages, pouring over more data and interviews and then in the third journal he came across the following…

…Michael saved my life today. I was locked in my recesses of my own mind, a sort of subconscious prison. I couldn't get out, I didn't know how. It was my fault. I couldn't rest until I knew everything, and it nearly cost me reality. The strain had been too great for my mind to cope. It was what came from believing myself to be God, thinking that I can know and even control future events. My own arrogance was nearly the end of me. I now know that this research project must end, even more, the Quantum Transference device and any evidence of it must be destroyed. It is far too dangerous…

———

David felt a hand on his shoulder. "David, shouldn't you be getting up. It's nearly eight." It was his mom. He must have fallen asleep while reading his grandfather's journals.

"Uh, yeah, thanks Mom." He said, as he tried to rub the sleep from his eyes. "I guess I fell asleep… What time did you say it was?"

"Eight o'clock," she repeated.

"I need to shower and go. I have to meet Professor Kensington at ten and there is no telling if I'll be able to find a spot on the bus."

"What is all this stuff?" she asked pointing to the journals.

"Grandpa's journals from when he worked at IEAT. Haven't you seen them before?"

"No, I've never seen them. What are you doing with them? Where were they?"

"They were in the basement. Grandpa wanted me to read them. Did you know what he was doing when he worked for the institute?"

"No, I was just a little girl at the time. By the time I was old enough to know any better, he had started teaching at the University. He never talked much about those days, and I never really bothered to ask. Was it important?"

"Important? Perhaps, at the very least it was intriguing, very intriguing, but I'll have to tell you about it another time. I don't really have time right now." He stuffed the three journals he hadn't read into his back-pack, they would have to wait until later. He took a quick shower and accepted a piece of toast and some coffee at the urging of his mother. Then he was out the door, hopeful that he wouldn't have to wait very long for a bus.

When David arrived at campus, he had to wait in line at the security check point. The entire campus had been enclosed by an electrified fence ten or twelve years earlier. There were only four entry points, and they tended to get clogged each morning as students arrived for class.

When it was his turn, he stepped up to the terminal and placed his right thumb on the pad. His image promptly appeared and he was asked to confirm his identity by standing in front of camera that scanned his eyes. The light on the side of the gate turned green and he pushed his way through. It was the same procedure every day. Only faculty, students and district residents were allowed entry, no guests. Just the same, it was generally accepted that there were ways to get around the system.

By the time he had arrived at Professor Kensington's office it was nearly ten thirty. He was late, a not so uncommon occurrence. He pushed through the door and prepared to receive the Professor's rebuke for his tardiness.

The office was more laboratory than office. The windows had been completely blacked out and on the far wall was an optics bench covered with various lenses and mirrors and other devices. To David's left was a desk piled high with papers, to his right, another table covered with all manner of electronics equipment, pieces of this and that. Professor Kensington never threw anything away. "Everything is salvageable," he would always say. Next to this table, with his back to the door was the professor. He was an older gentleman. He seemed to be playing with the dials on the EM wave modulator on one end of the table. He looked up as he heard the door close.

He was a tall, thin man with reddish brown hair that showed patches of thinning on top. His chin was covered in a scraggly beard that was almost entirely gray. Perched on his nose were small round spectacles. His clothes were a little ragged, looking a bit as if he had slept in them, which he probably had. He wore blue jeans and a blue oxford shirt covered by a brown cardigan sweater that was showing heavy wear on the elbows.

He gave a slight smile in David's direction and then turned back to whatever it was he was doing. "Nice of you to come, David," the Professor said in a kind of mocking tone. "I had all but given up on you."

"Sorry, Professor," David said sheepishly. "I had to spend the night in Queen Anne, and I was forced to the take the bus in this morning. It seems the lines are getting worse every day. You know what it's like."

"Yes, I'm afraid I do. It's why I rarely leave the district anymore. It seems as if it's getting more and more difficult to get anywhere these days. I can still remember what it was like, being able to go anywhere, anytime you wanted. Who could have ever imagined that things would get this bad?"

"Yeah, yeah, the good old days," David said with a slight mocking tone in his voice. The Professor was nearly seventy years old. He'd seen a lot in his lifetime and he was part of a generation that could still remember the days when there were nearly as many automobiles on the road as there were people.

David had only vague memories of what it had been like from his childhood; it had been years since he had last ridden in a gasoline powered vehicle. A failing economy amidst complex global politics continued to create an environment of growing poverty and a populace which had grown dependent on government intervention and public transportation. Now, only the very rich were able to afford electric vehicles, and most of those were limited to just a few small wealthy districts in every city. It wasn't long after the gasoline shortages began that electric rates began to climb as well. In most cities, the public transportation had completely been converted over to electric, however, the rising costs and shrinking profits soon forced the government to step in and take control of all forms of public transport. The private companies were soon forced to close down. As with most things, the bureaucratic lack of efficiency had created an intolerable system of corruption and unpredictability.

"If only we could come up with a more efficient form of solar energy," Kensington interrupted David's thoughts. "We could then create a vehicle that was both inexpensive to own and inexpensive to operate."

"And don't forget greater range as well," David added. The aging nuclear power industry, strapped by heavy regulation, had become less profitable and unable to keep up with the demands. Wind generated electricity was highly unpredictable. Solar power still seemed to be the most likely solution to the world's energy needs; the sun wasn't going away anytime soon.

A better solar cell would certainly provide much of the solution. Electric cars that operated only on storage cells were still subject to the rising cost of electricity. The persisting problem with solar cells still lay in the need for a great deal of surface area, making them impractical for motor vehicles. Motor vehicles would have to be completely covered in solar cells to generate enough electricity to provide enough for propulsion.

To add to the problem, storage cells were unreliable and constantly failing. In fifty years of research and development, no one had been able to solve the problem of range of an electric vehicle when operating solely from the charge on the battery. Electric Vehicles were still limited to a range of 100 to 150 miles on one charge, and there was the problem of how long it took to recharge the batteries; it was all highly impractical.

The problem of the battery was similar to the problem of the solar cell. The greater the amount of energy needed, the larger the battery needed to be. The chemistry just didn't allow for anything else. Whatever the solution was, it was going to have to be something new, something unexpected, something revolutionary.

David liked working for Dr. Kensington, he was old school, part of the same generation as his grandfather. He was a bit eccentric, but he always treated David with respect. Even more than that, he was respectful of everyone. He genuinely cared for others, even strangers, and it was clear that he was driven more by the need to solve problems for humanity than any desire for prestige or fame or even money. It was why David had become a scientist. He wanted to make a difference. Looking back, he realized that this was something that had been instilled in him by his grandfather.

Research could be a frustrating endeavor. At the end of the day, after hundreds or perhaps thousands of trials, the failures far outweighed the successes. Just when you felt like it was time to throw in the towel, something would happen; a new discovery, something small, but just enough to provide the motivation to carry on. Unfortunately, there were too many rabbit holes where one started down a path that ended up leading nowhere.

David felt like he had reached the end of one these rabbit holes. He wasn't really making any progress, he was stuck and the one person who could get him turned around was Dr. Kensington. He never really came right out and told David the answers, but just kept asking him questions, leading him down the path. Every time David would come in feeling despondent, but, in the end, he would walk away feeling as if he was back on track. It wasn't as if Dr. Kensington had solved any of his problems, but he had the ability to look at the problem a different way and this would instill a new enthusiasm and confidence, and David would always come away with a new strategy on how to attack the problem. David wasn't going to solve the world's energy problems by himself, after all he was only a grad student, but he at least hoped to contribute in some small way.

After his session with Kensington, David returned to his own lab and spent the remainder of the afternoon working through some calculations and setting up a new experiment. He didn't make a whole lot of progress. He accidently broke one of the connections in the micro-circuit he was working on and spent a half an hour trying to remember where he had left the micro-soldering iron. Besides this, he was a little distracted. He couldn't stop thinking about his grandfather's work. As the afternoon wore on, he realized that he wasn't really getting anywhere, so he gave up on trying to get any real work done. He pulled his grandfather's journals from his backpack and started reading.

He still couldn't believe what he had found. His two grandfathers, with the help of Raphael, had been working on time travel experiments. It was fantastical. The very thought of it made his head swim. One hand he was still very skeptical and on the other, he could hardly contain his excitement. How could they have made such an astounding discovery and then have kept it all a secret? How was it even possible?

He had to admit, that none of the data really made any sense to him. He knew very little about quantum physics and micro-wormholes. Despite the fact that he was a scientist and was supposed to be open-minded, he couldn't let go of the lingering skepticism.

After browsing through two more journals, he reached out and touched his D3 device sitting on the table in front of him. A holographic image appeared in front of him that looked like a viewing screen. He spoke aloud to it, "search micro-wormholes." Almost immediately, the image in front of him showed a list of articles on the topic. He reached out and touched buttons in the air, selecting the one that seemed most likely to provide him with the education he needed. For the next hour he tried to acquaint himself with the concept of wormholes and of their had been any attempts at time travel.

Chapter Four

Music began to play. David spoke aloud, "Answer," and his D3 responded. Jonny's 2-D image appeared on the screen hanging in mid-air directly in front of him, "Hey, David, where are you? I've been waiting here for ten minutes," he asked.

David looked in the upper right corner of the screen, it read 6:09. "Oh, crack! Sorry Jonny. I sort of lost track of time. I'm on my way. I'll be there in five. Go ahead and order our usual." He grabbed his D3, and the journals, and then stuffed them in his pack and was out the door before Jonny had time to respond.

Tony's was not far from the lab, but it took David closer to ten minutes before he was actually sliding into the booth across from his friend. "Sorry Jonny, I was completely caught up in what I was doing," he apologized again.

Jonny tried to look like he was mad, but it was clear that he was just trying to make his friend feel guilty. "Yeah, like this is the first time you kept me waiting. What were you doing that had you so distracted; making some headway in your research?"

"Uh, no not really, same old, same old," David replied. "As a matter of fact I was doing some research into some of the work that my grandfathers had been working on when they were younger. You know, back when they were working for your grandfather. Something my grandfather said to me yesterday got me to thinking."

"Yeah, they were working on virtual reality stuff. I remember my grandfather used to talk about how disappointed he was when they left the company. I think he really liked working with them."

"Yeah, I think he said the same thing to me once or twice. Anyway, I was just curious about their work so I was trying to see if I could find anything in the Strat (short for stratosphere, the term used to describe the global network). "

"Any luck?"

"No, not really," David wasn't really ready to reveal too much to Jonny. Talking about time travel was too much like science fiction, and he wasn't sure how his friend would take it.

"Well, anyway, you were late, so you have to pick up the tab."

"Come on, it was only fifteen minutes," David objected. "Hardly seems fair."

"More like twenty, and you'll have to pay the piper for it."

At that moment, a waiter placed a large pizza on the table in front of them.

As they began eating, Jonny said, "Hey, good news...my Dad agreed to let us use the ETVs (Electric All-Terrain Three Wheeled Vehicles) for our trip next weekend. We'll have to stop in Bellingham for a charge, but they should have enough range to get us where we need to go."

"That's great." The two friends had been planning a trip to Elbow Lake near Mount Baker. The last time they had been there together was when they were in sixth grade. "What about the girls?"

"Michelle's all excited, but it took some doing to convince Sarah. She's never been camping and if Michelle hadn't worked on her a bit, I don't think I would have ever talked her into it. Anyway, it's all set." Sarah was Jonny's girlfriend. They had only been dating for about six months, which was actually a fairly long time for Jonny to be in any relationship with a girl. David was never sure if this was due to commitment issues, or Jonny's personal insecurities.

"That's great! I'm really looking forward to it. It reminds me. I still need to dig up the tents. I think they're still in my mom's basement. It's kind of ironic, I was just down there last night and I completely forgot to look for them."

David and Jonny had been planning this trip for some time. It was an opportunity to relive some of their fondest childhood memories of camping and fishing with David's grandfather. Transportation being as difficult as it was, the only way they would ever be able to make the trip was if Jonny's father agreed to loan them the vehicles. It had been a long shot. Mr. Benson was not particularly fond of David, and despite the fact that he was quick to overindulge his children, he was not usually agreeable to allow them to be too far or too long from his sight. His overprotective nature bordered on being controlling, even totalitarian.

David was a bit surprised that Mr. Benson and consented, "So your dad actually agreed."

"You didn't think he would?" Jonny asked.

"Well, don't get me wrong, I'm elated, but it just seems out of character for him. I mean, he doesn't like Michelle to be out after dark. And there are times I get the impression that he is not too keen on me."

"Yeah, I know what you mean. I have to admit I was a bit surprised. I guess he figures we'll be so far from civilization that it would be unlikely we would ever run into anybody. I had to promise to call him and check in with him, and of course he could send a helicopter in to pick us up at any moment." His immense wealth meant that Mr. Benson was never really very far from his children.

"Yeah, I'm always of the opinion that your father doesn't really trust me."

"Oh, I think it's just his way. I think he likes you. If he didn't he would have attempted to end your relationship with my sister some time ago. The reality is, he's not very cordial with anybody. Anyway, he knows you're coming to dinner on Saturday. I'm sure he plans to use the opportunity to set down some very clear ground rules."

"Great, sounds like a very pleasant evening," they both chuckled.

The two friends spent the rest of dinner making plans, compiling a list of the things they would need for the trip. The ETVs had small trailers for baggage, however, they would have to be extremely conservative in their packing, especially since they were taking the girls along and they would have to carry everything on their backs once they started up the trail.

By the time they were done eating, it was dark outside. They stood outside the restaurant for a moment, saying their goodbyes. "Are you staying on campus tonight?" Jonny asked.

"No, I thought I would go back to my mom's. I promised I would go with her to see my grandfather at the hospital tomorrow. She doesn't like going by herself. Besides, it will give me a chance to dig up the tents for our trip."

"I have my dad's car. You want me to give you a lift?"

"No. Thanks anyway. I'll just take the bus. I'll be fine."

"You sure. It's no problem, really."

"Nah, thanks anyway."

Jonny's house was just across the canal from campus, and David couldn't see any reason why he should have to drive him back to Queen Anne. Tony's was on the far side of campus from the bus stop, and David would have to pass back by his lab. He decided to stop by his office and pick up some student papers he had left. He would be able to grade them in morning before he went to the hospital.

As he left the engineering building he passed by the fountain in front. He stopped and looked back over his shoulders at his office window to be sure he had turned the lights out. It was something he did every time, just as a matter of habit. He could hear a door close on the ground floor, but when he looked in that direction there was no one there. He thought it strange, he hadn't heard anybody approach as he left the building, and it seemed logical to believe the door closed because of someone leaving the building, but there was no one there.

As he passed by Johnson, he thought he could distinctly hear footsteps behind him. He stopped, turned around to look, but there was no one there. He was starting to feel a little anxious; that feeling, when you know something is wrong, but you can't seem to put your finger on it. He felt a slight chill, and the hair on the back of his neck stood on end. The feeling was nearly overwhelming him. His heart was beginning to beat faster. There was no real explanation for it, but he knew that something was wrong, terribly wrong. He quickened his pace.

As he reached Meany, he paused and peaked around the corner of the building to see if anyone was there. There was no one. He waited, for a moment, standing just around the corner out of sight, where he could see clearly in the direction he had just come from. It was quiet, deadly still. Just as he was about to give up and continue toward the bus stop, he noticed someone in the shadows, creeping along the side of Johnson. He was sure of it, there was no mistaking it. Someone was following him.

He began running, not fast, but a sort of jog, trying to put some distance between him and his pursuer. The gate to leave campus was just two hundred yards ahead, on 15th. The bus stop was in front of the Post Office, a couple of blocks beyond. As he reached the gate, he could hear the steps of someone running behind him. He looked back as he pushed through the exit gate, but the stranger was keeping to the shadows.

What was happening? Who was it? What did they want?

As he started down 15th, out of nowhere a car pulled up beside him and the door flung open, the engine dying to a quiet purr as it braked. "Come on, get in," a voice shouted from within.

"What the heck? Who are you? And what do you want?"

"I don't have time to explain. We only have a few minutes. Get in the car!"

"I'm not getting in the car. I don't know you and don't care to. Now get out of here before I call the cops."

"Look, I'm here to help you, whether you believe it or not. The person following you is out to do you harm and I'm here to protect you. I'm your...I'm your Guardian."

David heard the gate close behind him. There was no time to think, he simply reacted instinctively as he jumped into the passenger seat and slammed the door, all in a fraction of a second. The engine roared and he was pressed back in the seat as the car accelerated. He looked back over his shoulder to see a shadow standing in the street where they had just been. And then there was a gun shot and the back window shattered into a million pieces.

"Keep your head down!" the driver yelled at him.

"Who was that?" David shouted. "What's going on? And why the heck is he shooting at us?"

"Not us, you," the driver said calmly.

"But, why? What'd I ever do to him? I mean, I 've never seen the guy before in my life."

"Maybe not, but he was after you just the same," again he spoke with a surreal kind of calm.

"How d'you know that? I mean, who are you anyway? And where'd you come from?" David was still shouting.

"Calm down. Everything is going to be alright. You're safe now; at least for the time being."

"What do you mean, for the time being?"

"David...do you believe in Providence?"

"What, you mean like fate?" David was starting to calm slightly.

"Well, sort of, it's kind of fate with a purpose. Do you believe it is possible that we are here for a reason, that we have purpose for being here?"

"What, like the human race?"

"No, not just the human race, but every individual. Is it possible that every individual has a purpose, a place in this universe?"

"I guess it's possible."

"And if that's true, do you think it is possible that there are some who have a purpose that is more significant than others; a purpose that might have ramifications for an entire community, or perhaps an entire society."

"I don't know. I suppose I do, sort of like an Abraham Lincoln. It's hard to believe that everything is just a product of chance; too many problems with the statistical improbabilities and all," David had once taken a course in Philosophy and had come to grips with the fact that science didn't have the answers to every question, and it was possible that there are things outside of the realm of human comprehension. He used to have lengthy debates with his grandfather about such things...

He realized why he had gotten in the car, "Grandfather!" he said aloud. "Were you sent by my grandfather? Are you the one he was talking about?"

"I'm not exactly sure what you mean?" the stranger said. "I'm here because I believe you are important, that you may have a purpose greater than the average person. I'm here to make sure you find that purpose and complete it."

"What purpose? I don't understand. What do I have to do that is so important?"

"I can't tell you that. You have to find your own way. The only thing I can tell you is that it's important and there are those who would try and keep you from discovering it."

"But, how do you know? How do you know me, I mean? We have never even met before. I don't know anything about you."

"It's not important, David." As he said this, the car pulled up in front of his mom's house.

"How did you know where I was going? How do you know my address? Who are you anyway?"

"Like I said David, it's not important. You'll be safe here tonight. But, remember, there will be other moments, so be alert. Keep your eyes open and be aware of those around you and you'll be alright. It's time for you to go now."

"What that's it? No explanation. Swoop in like Batman, save my life and then disappear again; just like that."

"I'm afraid so. But, David you won't be alone. There will be a Guardian there the next time you need one. It won't be me, but there will be someone watching, someone there to protect you; trust him. Now say goodbye." The stranger reached over and pushed the door open.

David was dumbfounded. He got out of the car, because he didn't know what else to do. He stood there a moment looking back at the stranger.

"Goodbye, David. And don't worry. We will keep you safe."

The car pulled away, leaving David standing alone in the dark. "Goodbye," he said. And then he whispered, "Strange fellow, but familiar somehow; something about his eyes."

Chapter Five

David was surprised with what he found in the sixth journal. The first few pages described how after much debate and uncertainty, the three friends had given up on any further use of the Quantum Transference technology. His grandfather had grown more concerned about the ramifications of playing God. Together they chose to put aside their research into time travel and decided to pursue other endeavors.

There were some blank pages, and then the journal picked up again. He looked at the date. It was fifteen years later than any of the other journal entries...

...we thought we were done with Quantum Transference altogether, but with Raphael's murder, Michael and I realized we had no choice but to revive our experiments. The future of our grandson was at stake, and perhaps even more. We had to try and stop whoever was tampering with the future, to preserve the timeline as it was supposed to be...

David paused for a moment trying to understand what he had just read. What did his grandfather mean when he said that *his future was at stake*, and who was this person who was tampering with the timeline.

The pages that followed gave an account of each of the attempts at traveling forward in time, attempting to retrace the steps of the nemesis they were trying to stop. David found himself dumfounded to discover that there had been attempts on his life, much like the one the night before. But why, what did it all mean? Why would someone want to harm him? And what did it have to do with his two grandfathers?

...with each leap into the future, I find myself once again questioning my own actions, and perhaps my motives as well. It's foolish to think that I am capable of remaining objective when confronted with knowledge about my friends and loved ones that I should never have discovered. I'm not God, and I will never really be in control. To think otherwise is only a self-deception, nothing less. I have tried to do the right thing in every circumstance, but that doesn't seem to be enough. No matter what I do, I'm unable to protect the ones I love. What will be, will be...

David's head was spinning in circles. Someone was trying to kill him and he had no idea why, or for that matter who. Somehow his grandfather had found a way to help him, but the ramifications of time travel and all the paradoxes it poses, was a little more than he was willing to deal with at the moment. Had his life been a series of events interlaced with occasional visits from individuals from the past. Was any of this even real? Had there been other moments when his life had been at risk?

———

Michael sat on a bench, eating the last of the popcorn. He smiled as he watched David, Jonny, Bethany and Sadie with their noses pressed against the glass, watching a young brown bear in the exhibit beyond. There was a pool of water that came right up to the glass, so that observers could see above and below its surface. The bear was lounging on a knoll beyond the water.

Katie and Emily were close, keeping an eye on the children, while Grandma Rachel was snapping pictures of the kids at every opportunity.

It was David's tenth birthday, and they had invited Katie, the girls, and Jonny, David's best friend, to join them at Woodland Park Zoo in celebration of the event. Emily was his daughter-in-law, and Katie her sister. They were the daughters of his best friend, and the only family he and Rachel had, ever since Jesse's death.

It had hit him pretty hard, losing the only son he had ever known, but being able to share in the lives of Emily and David, his daughter-in-law and grandson, had provided some consolation in his grief. It was hard to believe it had been four years. He and Garrett had tried to do all they could to save Jesse, but they had been too late. He'd been murdered by an evil individual, who could move through time and assume any form. They had tried to intervene, to change the fate of his son, but they had failed. It just wasn't to be, they were not meant to save him.

"Hey grandpa, do you see that?" David shouted, interrupting Michael's thoughts.

A large adult grizzly had emerged from the back of the enclosure and was now standing at the edge of the pool, sniffing the air, only water and glass separating him from the children. For a brief moment, Michael wondered if the glass was really enough to stop the bear had he wished to escape.

The children were chattering and giggling as they watched in awe as the bear stood on its hind legs. It must have been seven feet tall. Michael stood up and walked over to where David was standing next to the glass and placed a hand on his grandson's shoulder. A crowd of onlookers had gathered and everyone stood with gaping mouths.

"Look at the size of those paws," Michael said to his grandson.

David looked at his own hands as if he were making a comparison. "And look at his claws," the young boy said in response.

Michael slid next to his wife just as the bear returned to all fours. "Did you get a picture of that?" he asked.

"I think so," Rachel said. "Isn't he beautiful?"

"Beautiful, yes, but also incredibly powerful. I can only imagine what it would be like encountering something like that in the wild. I'm thinking my legs would have difficulty catching up with the rest of my body."

"I know what you mean," Rachel whispered.

"Look out!" a scream came from someone standing behind them. "He has a gun!"

The crowd divided like the parting of the red sea, everyone attempting to move toward either one of the exits of the viewing shelter. As the crowd thinned, a man was left standing in the center of the shelter, holding a hand gun in his right hand.

The children were still pressed up against the glass, their mothers instinctively standing between them and the gunman. Michael took a similar defensive position, standing in front of his wife.

The stranger looked strained, his eyes were wild and his long hair was tussled and greasy. He waved the gun in Emily's direction. "Move over there," he pointed, "away from the glass."

Slowly, Emily tried to coax David to move with her, making every effort to keep her son shielded.

"Leave the boy," the gunman said gruffly.

Emily froze. She was frightened to the point of tears, but it was clear that she was not going to expose her son. Her motherly instincts took precedence over her self-preservation.

"I said leave him!" The gunman said, a little more sternly, "Or I will shoot you where you stand."

"Why, what do you want with us?" Emily pleaded. "I don't understand!"

Michael realized that the stranger fully meant what he said and that both Emily and David were in grave danger. "Easy now mister," he said as calmly as he could. "You don't want to do this."

The gunman turned in his direction, the gun now pointing at his chest. "Stay out of it mister," the gunman growled. "This has nothing to do with you."

"Now easy, there," Michael was trying to buy some time, hopeful that help might be on its way. Surely someone had gone for a security guard. "I'm just thinking that you don't really want to do this. There's no reason anyone needs to get hurt. Maybe you should just put the gun down, before this gets out of hand."

"Like I said, it's none of your business." The gunman started to turn back toward Emily and David.

Without warning, a large man emerged from the crowd, wearing green overalls with a zoo insignia on the chest. "You heard him mister, maybe you should put the gun down."

The gunman looked at the man and then without flinching, shot him in the leg, causing the man to cry out and fall to his knees. A woman screamed and the rest of the crowd began pushing against each other in an attempt to get away.

Then he turned to face Emily, holding his hands spread wide, "now as I was saying, move to the side or I will shoot you where you stand."

"I'm not going anywhere without my son," Emily said through clenched teeth.

"Okay, have it your way," the gunman raised the gun once again.

What happened next happened so quickly, that it was a blur to those who were still watching. A man emerged from the crowd and leaped toward the gunman. In the same moment, Michael jumped toward Emily in an attempt to place himself between her and the gunman. The gun discharged.

Emily fell back against the glass, knocked aside by Michael. When she gained her bearing she could see the gunman pinned to the ground by two men, while the man who had intervened stood over him, now holding the gun. She grabbed David and held him close to her body. Looking past him she noticed Michael was lying on the ground, blood staining the front of his shirt.

"Michael!" Rachel screamed, as she hurried to his side, kneeling down beside him.

The stranger who had tackled the gunman knelt down next to Rachel. He tore off a section of his t-shirt. "Here," he said to Rachel, "take this and hold it against the wound. We have to try and control the bleeding. Someone, call for an ambulance!" he shouted.

He then proceeded to place his fingers against Michael's neck, checking his pulse. Michael stirred, opening his eyes. "Hang in there, Michael, you're going to be all right," the stranger said.

"I...I can't feel anything," Michael whispered.

"Easy, don't talk," the stranger continued. "Help is on its way. Just hang in there. Don't you die on us."

Michael looked into the strangers eyes. "I couldn't let him harm Emily," he whispered. "I just couldn't. He had already lost his father. He couldn't lose his mother too."

"I know," the stranger said. "You did good. Look she's fine," turning his head toward Emily. "Look, you saved her life, now just hang in there."

Michael turned his head slightly toward Emily and David and smiled. Emily smiled back. He turned back to face the stranger one more time. "I'm cold…" He turned to look at Rachel who still held her hand tight against the wound, tears streaming down her face. "I love you Rachel, I have always loved you."

"I love you too," Rachel replied. "Now be quiet, you need to conserve your energy. Everything is going to be alright, you'll see. Now just hang in there, help is coming." She looked up as if hoping to see paramedics coming, but all she could see were the faces of strangers staring at her from the crowd.

"I'm cold," Michael said again, and then he closed his eyes.

Chapter Six

David stood on the front walk for a moment, not sure if he wanted to go in. As much as he loved Michelle, he was completely mortified at the thought of having to sit through an entire dinner with her father.

He had wondered about whether he should tell Jonny what happened after they had parted the other night. The more he thought about it, the more he realized he couldn't. He wouldn't even know where to begin. Jonny would end up thinking he was crazy.

He had hoped to talk about it with his grandfather, but the visit to the hospital was unfulfilling. His grandfather had sunk back into a state of amnesia. It was the worst David had ever seen him.

Talking to his mother was out of the question. She wouldn't understand and it would only serve to make her worry.

He knocked on the door. When it opened, he was greeted by the butler. He was tall and broad shouldered, with chiseled features that complimented his crew cut. He wasn't really a butler, but that was what Mr. Benson called him. In reality, he was a body guard, hired to protect Mr. Benson from the riff raff who were always trying to get a piece of his money. Where ever he went, Mr. Benson was always shadowed by two body guards, the other acting the part of chauffeur.

"Hello, Danny," David greeted. "Am I on time?"

There was no response, just a stare which gave David the feeling that he was being visually inspected. After a brief pause,

Danny turned and held out is hand as if directing David to pass. David didn't question or hesitate. He simply entered and made his way directly to the receiving room. He didn't look back at his escort.

As he entered, Michelle rose from a chair which was positioned in such a way that she could see whoever entered the room. She walked over to David and gave him a gentle kiss on the cheek. "About time you got here," she whispered in his ear.

Jonny and Sarah were sitting on a couch, the arm of the former around the shoulders of the latter. David was relieved to discover that he would not be the only one under the magnifying glass. Mr. Benson was standing at the back window, his back to the group, as if he didn't care to acknowledge the arrival of the new guest. Mrs. Benson was standing near the bar, holding what David assumed was a martini. David had always liked Mrs. Benson, but in recent years, every time he saw her it seemed she had a drink her hand. David wondered if it had anything to do with her husband.

David's impression of Mr. Benson was that he was a little too self-absorbed, and a hardened man. He was driven by wealth and would do anything to advance his position in the world. Most of these opinions were a result of conversations he'd had with Jonny, and not necessarily from any personal observations. Regardless, it was clear to everyone that Mr. Benson had little respect or affection for his wife. Despite the dysfunction of this relationship, both Jonny and Michelle seemed to be pretty well adjusted. This was most likely due to a very loving and devoted mother.

"Hey, David," Jonny greeted.

"Hi, Jonny, hi, Sarah," David replied.

"Hello David, can I pour you a drink?" Mrs. Benson said.

"No thanks, Mrs. B., I'm fine."

"Danny, please let Margie know that Mr. Jacobson has arrived and that we are ready for dinner," Mrs. Benson directed.

"I hope I haven't kept you waiting, Mrs. B," David apologized.

"No, not at all, you're right on time."

Dinner was a little surreal. Mr. Benson didn't say a word. Sarah and Michelle carried most of the conversation, with Mrs. Benson occasionally interjecting stories from Jonny and Michelle's childhood. Her eyes sparkled as she reminisced, almost as if she was reliving every moment.

"I understand your grandfather is ill," Mr. Benson said abruptly, causing everyone to stop talking and turn to the head of the table where he sat. It was the first words he had uttered during the entire dinner.

"Uh, yes that's right. He has an inoperable tumor, there is very little they can do. The doctors say he may only have another month," David replied.

Everyone else sat quietly as if in shock, wondering if Mr. Benson really cared, and waiting to see if he would say anything else.

"That's too bad," the way Mr. Benson spoke gave no hint of emotion. It gave David the creeps.

"Thanks," David said, somewhat under his breath.

"I understand you plan to go on this camping trip...to the Mount Baker area."

"That's right," David answered, still feeling unnerved that the conversation had shifted to him and Mr. Benson.

"I hope you'll be careful. I am placing the welfare of my son and daughter in your hands. I wouldn't want anyone getting hurt."

David was convinced that he was being threatened in some way. It was eerie.

"Oh, Daddy, relax," Michelle jumped in. "We'll be fine. David has been there a hundred times, isn't that right?"

"Well maybe not a hundred, but we've never had a problem." David looked over at Jonny. There had in fact been an incident, the only time Jonny joined him on one of his trips with his grandfather, but they had determined not to tell Mr. Benson. Neither of them had been hurt and they saw no point in saying anything. It suddenly struck David, maybe it hadn't been an accident after all.

Jonny smiled at David as if he were thinking about the incident as well. "Yeah Dad, we'll be fine. These days no one has the means to travel into the cascades. We probably won't see another living soul the entire time we're there."

"I just don't see why we have to sleep on the ground," Sarah chimed in. Unlike David, Sarah was from a very affluent family. This was probably why she was considered an agreeable match for Jonny.

"It wouldn't be camping if we stayed in a hotel," Jonny said mockingly. "Besides you'll be fine as long as the snakes don't get you."

"Snakes!" Sarah shrieked. "You didn't say there would be snakes."

"Relax, Sarah," Michelle came to the rescue. "He's just kidding. You'll be fine, really. We're going to have fun, isn't that right, David?"

"Yeah, it will be great. Besides, if we do come across any snakes, I'm sure Jonny will take care of 'em. Isn't that right?" He looked over and Jonny. Truth was that Jonny hated snakes as much as anyone.

"Uh, yeah, right," Jonny said, a little color filling his cheeks.

Mr. Benson didn't say another word. It was as if he had decided that his part in the conversation was over. Everyone else complied.

"Oh look, here comes dessert," Mrs. Benson said.

Margie proceeded to place a healthy slab of chocolate cheesecake smothered in a raspberry sauce in front of each one. David wondered how much the raspberries must have cost. The one thing he could count on when visiting the Benson's was that the food was always first class.

During the entire dinner, Danny stood in the shadows, just a few feet from where Mr. Benson sat. David thought it strange. Why would he need a body guard here in his own home? Certainly he had nothing to fear from within. If anything, the danger would be more likely to come from outside, beyond the fence surrounding the house. He wondered if Danny wouldn't better serve his master by remaining outside. Besides, he didn't like him. There was a darkness that seemed to hover around him, similar to the one that surrounded Mr. Benson.

Chapter Seven

David liked the feel of the wind against his face. They were starting to head into the mountains and it wouldn't be long before they reached the Ridley Creek trailhead. He had grown so accustomed to the whine of the ETV engine that it was barely noticeable.

The afternoon was growing late and he was a little concerned that they had spent too long in Bellingham recharging the batteries of the ETV. As he turned off the main road, the tires skidded slightly as they hit the gravel. Michelle tightened her grip around his waist. He could feel her leaning against him, her chin on his shoulder. He looked in his mirror. Jonny and Sarah were still right behind them.

Jonny had been right about the sparse population of the mountain communities. Since passing through Deming, they hadn't encountered another vehicle on the road. This had once been the gateway to the Mount Baker National Forest, but no more. The general population was forced to remain near urban centers for lack of affordable transportation. The small communities in the mountains, which had once serviced the tourists, had now all become ghost towns, unable to survive without any viable industry. David threw caution to wind as he sped up the road. It was unlikely they would meet anybody coming in the other direction. They had left civilization behind.

When they reached the end of road, David chose a small clearing where they could park the ETVs. At one end of the clearing was a dilapidated sign with letters that spelled the name "Ridley" barely still visible. They unpacked the gear, placed some broken branches over the ETVs in an attempt to provide some concealment, and in minutes they were on the trail.

As they crossed over the bridge, David hesitated slightly. It had been more than ten years since the last time he had been on this trail, and the memories of that fateful day came flooding back all at once. The slight rocking of the bridge made him tremble slightly. He was surprised by his feelings and felt relieved when he stepped onto solid ground on the other side.

They made good time and reached Elbow Lake just as the sun was beginning its final approach to the western horizon. Sara had been surprisingly quiet on the trail. She had barely uttered a word, refraining from any form of complaining; it was quite unexpected. "Okay, so I have to admit, this is really beautiful," she said as she sat down on a log at the edge of their campsite.

"Yeah, I know what you mean," Michelle said. "It's so peaceful."

"Hopefully it will stay that way," Jonny said, giving David a wink.

"What do you mean, hopefully?" Sarah asked.

"Well, I wouldn't want you to worry or anything, but there are bears in these woods," Jonny said.

"Bears! What do you mean bears?" Sarah shouted.

"Don't listen to him Sarah, he's just trying to scare you." Michelle said.

"Don't worry, honey, I'm here. I'll protect you," Jonny said as he sat down next to Sarah and put his arm around her.

"Hey who's going to help with dinner?" David asked.

"What are we havin'?" the girls asked in unison.

"I'm afraid all we have is franks and beans," David replied. "Tomorrow we'll have to try and catch some fish."

"Franks and beans! Are you serious?" Sarah said.

"Come on Sarah, it'll be fine. Come with me and I'll show you how to build a fire," Michelle offered. The girls started off into the trees in search of some firewood. David and Jonny proceeded to set up the tents.

It was a bright clear night. The stars seemed so close. It was as if you could reach out and touch them. Dinner had gone off without a hitch. Sarah was making every effort to keep a positive attitude. No doubt it was the first time she had made a meal of franks and beans, but she didn't complain a bit. Despite her opulent upbringing, Michelle was able to adjust to any circumstance, never complaining, always content. She was the eternal optimist.

The four friends lay back against the log, staring up at the night sky. The fire, just beyond their feet, had died down to nothing more than glowing red coals.

"Can you see the Bear?" David asked of no one in particular.

"Bear, what bear?" Sarah exclaimed.

"Not a real bear, silly," Jonny chimed in. "He's talking about the stars."

"The Big Bear, Ursa Major, some people call it the big dipper," David explained. "See that large star there," he pointed. "That is Polaris, the north star. Now move a little south, there, that is the edge of the Big Dipper. See how the four stars form what looks like a cup at the end of a handle."

"Oh, yeah, I see it!" Sarah exclaimed. "Do you know of any other constellations?"

"Well, yeah, over there," he pointed, "is Ursa Minor, the little bear." He went on to point out every constellation he could remember.

"What's that?" Michelle said pointing. A bright light appeared, streaking across the sky, growing larger, and then falling to the earth in a huge explosion of water, just on the other side of the lake."

"Oh, my gosh!" Jonny yelled, "What was that?"

All four friends stood to their feet in unison. "Wow, I've never seen anything like it. It might have been a meteor or something, or maybe a piece of space junk." David suggested.

"Space junk?" Michelle asked.

"Part of an old satellite that has just been sitting up there until its orbit decayed enough for it to fall back to earth," David explained.

"It could have killed somebody," Sarah said.

"Yeah, whatever it was, I'd like to have a look," David said.

"Look," Jonny pointed. Just at the water's edge there was a blue glow. "Do you think we should go check it out?"

"Not tonight," David said. "There's no moon and it's too dark out there. It's not going anywhere. It'll still be there in the morning." He made a mental note of the direction using a tree at the edge of the lake as a reference point. They wouldn't have any difficulty finding it in the morning. "Let's get some sleep."

Jonny was stirring the fire as Michelle emerged from the tent the next morning. "Good morning," he greeted. "I have some water boiling. Would you like some tea?"

"That would be great," she said rubbing her arms as if trying to get them warm.

"How's Sarah doing?" he asked as he handed her a cup.

"I think she's doing fine, but maybe we should let her sleep, her first night in the wild and all."

"I heard that and I'm up," a voice came from the tent. "I just can't seem to find my socks." She emerged from the tent, her hair sticking up in all directions. "Oh, my aching back," she said rubbing her back and sides. "I don't know how you guys do this, sleeping on the ground and all. I'm not sure I slept at all."

"You slept alright, I could hear you snoring," Michelle said.

"I don't snore."

"Here, Sarah," Jonny said chuckling to himself, "drink this, it will get your blood stirring."

"Where's David?" Michelle said, looking out at the lake.

"He was up at dawn, got the fire going and then took off. Said he was going to check out that thing that fell from the sky last night. I guess it kept him awake all night. He said we could catch up to him once we had breakfast."

"Where is it? How will we know where to find him?" Michelle asked.

"See that dead tree on the far side of the lake. He figured in went down pretty near the edge of the lake just to the right of that tree. I figure he should just about be getting there by now."

"What's for breakfast?" Sarah asked.

"Well, we have a little instant oatmeal, or you can have a bagel, no cream cheese, and we have some trail mix."

"Ah, yummy," Sarah murmured.

They made quick work of the meager breakfast, threw some trail mix in a back pack and began the trek toward the other side of the lake. It was going to be a beautiful day, typical for this time of year. By midmorning they emerged from the trees to find David standing knee deep in the lake.

"Good morning," David said as he saw his three friends arrive.

"Any luck," Jonny asked.

"Yeah, it seems to be some kind of meteorite. Not very big, about the size of a basketball I would say. It's all covered in mud from the bottom of the lake. I don't think I can lift it myself, I'm going to need some help." He stepped out of the water onto the shore as he spoke.

"I think it might be best to take some of those small logs over there and use them as a sort of ramp to roll it up on, to get it out of the water." He was pointing at some small dead pine trees that were down and lying on the shore of the lake. The branches were all broken off and they were nearly stripped of bark. "Come on Jonny, give me a hand. You're going to want to take your shoes off. You too girls, were going to need your help."

After laying the logs down at the edge of the water, David and Jonny were able to tie them together with some rope that David had in his pack. They placed one end of there make shift ramp down in the water near the object in question. Michelle stood on the end of the logs to keep them beneath the surface, while Sarah held the other end still at the edge of the lake. It took every bit of strength that David and Jonny could muster, but they were able to roll the meteorite onto the ramp and then carefully roll it to the edge of the lake, while Michelle and Sarah coaxed them along.

When they finally had accomplished the task, the two of them sat down at the water's edge admiring their discovery. It didn't look like much, still covered in patches of mud, but they were still satisfied that they had been able to extract it from the lake.

Michelle took one of her socks, soaked it with water and began wiping some of the mud away. "Look at this, there seems to be some sort of crystals embedded in the rock." The four friends gathered around and stared. Michelle's attempts to clean the surface of the object had revealed glassy crystals all over the surface of the rock interspersed between patches of what looked like lava rock. They glassy material was slightly blue and almost appeared to glow in the sunlight.

Together, Michelle and David cleaned the entire surface as best they could so they have a better look. Jonny reached out and ran his fingers across the surface of one of the larger crystals. Then in surprise, he pulled back his hand, "Ouch!" he screamed.

"What's wrong?" David asked.

"I think that thing just shocked me," Jonny said.

"Shocked you? What do mean shocked you? It couldn't have." David replied.

"I'm telling you, that thing shocked me!" Jonny exclaimed.

David ran his fingers across the rough stone, but then as his finger approached the glassy objects, he drew it back rapidly. "It's the crystals. They seem to be producing a small electrical charge, very curious."

"Do you think it could be from passing through the atmosphere, some sort of static build-up or something?" Jonny asked.

"No, that's unlikely. It would have dissipated as soon it hit the water. It's strange, whatever the cause." David responded with a slight shake of his head. .

"Well what do you propose we do with it now that we have this thing out of the water? It's a sure bet we are not going to be able to carry it all the way back to the road." Jonny said, still rubbing his hand.

"I think you're right," David replied. "It must weigh at least a couple hundred pounds. I'm curious about these crystals though. There more like glass than anything else, no identifiable facets to speak of."

He took is knife and hatchet from his backpack and then using his hatchet as a hammer, he began chipping away at the rock surface. The rock around the glassy material was relatively soft and brittle and gave way underneath the point of the carbon steel knife. After several minutes he was able to chip enough of the stone away that he nearly freed one of the crystals.

"Michelle, give me one of your socks," David requested.

Michelle rinsed the sock in the lake and then handed it to him.

David placed the sock on his left hand and then gently held the crystal with it as he used the knife as a lever. With a fairly gentle effort he was able to extract the crystal without breaking it. He held it up to the light. It was three to four inches in length, and when held up to the light it had a transparency to it. It glistened with a light blue color that was reminiscent of the sky. He turned the sock inside out and gently placed the wrapped crystal into his pack. He then repeated the procedure and after several minutes he was able to free two other large samples, each of which he placed carefully wrapped into his pack.

"That will have to do for now," he finally said. "Help me move the meteorite over there." He pointed to a place next to an old stump about thirty feet from the shore of the lake.

After a lengthy struggle, the four friends were able to half roll half carry the meteorite and place it behind the stump. David found some old pine boughs to place over it, shielding it from sight of anyone who might pass by.

"That should keep it safe, until we can figure out a way to transport it to the road," David said.

"Why couldn't we just use one of the trailers?" Michelle asked. "I'm sure between the four of us, we could get it up the trail."

"Not a bad idea," David said. "It's just the problem of getting the trailer across the river, and then back again. I'm not sure we could get it across the bridge."

"Yeah, I think it's too wide," Jonny said. "We would need something to float it across the river, some kind of raft or something. And then we would have to find a different place in the river, where it is not quite so swift."

"I agree," David said. "In any case we're not going to be able to solve the problem now. I suggest we get some lunch and think on it."

Chapter Eight

David lay awake, not able to sleep. There was no real reason for it other than the fact that his mind was still at work. He carefully climbed from his sleeping bag, trying not to disturb his friend lying next to him.

He sat down on the ground and stirred the last remaining coals of the fire which were nearly burned out, emitting a soft red glow; the only remaining source of light. The moon was barely visible as a sliver. He reached into his pack and withdrew one of the crystals, still wrapped in a dirty sock. He carefully removed it from the sock, being careful not to drop it or damage it.

To his surprise the crystal was glowing, emitting a soft blue light. He touched it with the end of his finger. There was no static charge this time. Whatever had been the source of the charge had dissipated. He couldn't figure out, Why had it given off an electrical charge to begin with? The residual charge could not have been the result of static build-up. It would have dissipated when it became grounded. .

He sat there staring at the crystal, trying to unravel its mystery. He was so absorbed in thought that he was completely unaware of the passage of time. At some point, his weariness took over and he drifted off to sleep.

Somewhere in the trees an owl hooted and woke him from his slumber. He was chilled from the night air. The fire had completely died. He placed the crystal back in his pack and returned to the tent.

Everyone was up bright and early. After a quick breakfast, they packed up camp and headed down the trail. They hoped to be back on the road again by noon. It was decided that the meteorite would have to wait until David and Jonny were able to make a return trip. It wasn't going anywhere, and with time they could come up with a better plan to get it off the mountain. Jonny was confident that Mr. Benson would offer any help they needed.

Michelle and Sarah had been good sports, but two days without a shower was about as much as they could handle and they were anxious to get back to civilization. They were all looking forward to a nice hot meal in Bellingham.

Their first rest stop was at the Twin Sisters overlook. David smiled at the girls as they sat next to one another on an old log. "You two have been real troopers," he said, "it has been hours since we have heard a complaint from either of you."

"We can hold our own," Michelle said as she gave Sarah a slight elbow. "Don't be thinking that just because we're girls, that we're soft." She smiled.

"Just don't ask us on another adventure like this any time soon," Sarah added.

"Here Sarah, you look like you could use something to drink," David said as he handed her his water bottle.

Just before it reached her hand, it slipped from his grasp and fell to the ground. He promptly bent over to pick it up. As he did so, there was a loud bang followed by an equally loud crack as the bark of the tree over his shoulders splintered.

"What was that?" Jonny exclaimed. "It sounded like a gunshot."

"Everybody down!" David yelled.

The girls knelt down behind the log as David and Jonny stood behind the nearest trees.

"Do you think it was an accident?" Jonny asked. "Maybe a stray bullet from a hunter or something..." Almost before he completed the sentence another gunshot sounded and a branch on the tree he was standing behind exploded into pieces.

"Run!" David yelled. "Quick, everyone down the trail!"

Without hesitation all four friends took off down the trail, the girls leading and the boys on their heels. There was another shot. They ran on. Then, just as they were about to turn a bend and enter the trees beyond, there was another shot and Jonny cried out and tumbled to the ground.

David stopped to help his friend, the girls continued on into the trees. David knelt next to Jonny. "Are you hit!" he shouted.

"Yeah, it's my shoulder. Damn it hurts." Jonny answered.

"Can you walk?" David asked.

"Yeah, I think so."

David helped Jonny to his feet and half carried him into the trees where the girls had found a place to hide behind a large rock. David looked back up the trail, but there was no sign of their assailant.

Michelle was already tearing away Jonny's T-shirt to determine the damage. Without hesitating she rummaged through her pack and found some gauze in the first aid kit they had packed, and then began applying pressure to the wound.

"I don't get it!" Sarah cried out. "Who would want to shoot us? What do they want? What did we do to them?"

"I don't know," David said. "It doesn't make any sense, but clearly those bullets were intended for us." He looked over at Michelle. She had a grim look on her face. "How's he doing?"

"He's lost a lot of blood. I think he's going to be alright, but he is not going to be able to run much further." She had already begun to wrap the wound.

David was impressed with how calm she was. There was no indication of panic. He paused for a moment, trying to assess their situation, trying to find a solution to their predicament.

There was only one course of action. "Okay, here's what we are going to do. We can't stay here, and with Jonny being injured, we can't all outrun whoever it is that's out there. I need for you all to remain hidden here. I'm going to go back to the trail and try and draw them away from you. Once I know they are following me, I'll take them north up along the river. That will give you the time to get down the trail and back to the ETVs.

I'll then try and double back and get back to you. But don't wait long. If I'm not there in half an hour, then go on without me. Go to Deming and try and find some help."

"We're not going without you." Michelle said with determination in her voice.

"Look, you have to get Jonny to a hospital. I will be alright. Trust me. You have to do this. I'll be alright. Do you understand!"

"Yes, okay, but only...be careful," Michelle said, and then she kissed him. "Don't get yourself killed."

"I won't."

David ran to the trail and then looked back to see if he could see if anyone was following. There was a solitary man kneeling down where they had stopped at the overlook. He was holding a rifle and inspecting the ground, as if he was looking for evidence that his first attempts had met with some success. David didn't recognize who the man was, but he was relieved to discover that he was alone. He was hopeful. If it was only one pursuer; they might still have a chance; they might still escape.

The stranger looked down the trail and his gaze met David's. The rifle was brought to his shoulder. David didn't hesitate. He was off bounding down the trail before the shot rang out. The bullet strayed helplessly into the trees behind him.

David continued a hundred yards down the trail, and then veered to his right leaving the trail. As he did so, he stopped a moment. His pursuer was shielded from view by the trees. He removed his sleeping bag and tent from is pack and placed them on the ground next to a small bush, as if to make it look like they were hidden. This was partly to lighten his load, but mostly to leave a sign that he had left the trail and was now going north. He had to be sure that he drew the shooter away from his friends so they could find their way to safety. He had to leave signs of his trail, without making it look like he was leaving signs.

Through the trees he ran, occasionally changing direction in an attempt to make a difficult target. After another two hundred yards he stopped, kneeling down behind a tree, he tried to catch his breath. He could hear his heart beating in his ears. He was beginning to wonder if he had been too good in his escape and that he was no longer being followed. Then, all of a sudden, the man appeared again, just a hundred yards back. It had worked. He now had to lead him further north until he could find his opportunity to double back.

He began running again, keeping to the trees as much as possible. After what must have been a quarter of a mile, he could hear the rush of water off to his left. He was approaching the river. He stopped again, trying to catch his bearings. He knew he couldn't keep up this pace much longer. For a moment, he thought of abandoning the rest of his pack, but then he thought better of it. There was no telling how long this would go on, and he wasn't about to give up the only thing he had left that provided him with the tools for survival.

Another two hundred yards and he reached the river. He was on a ridge that dropped straight down in front of him to the water below. There was no way of getting down to the water. His only option was to follow a narrow path that seemed to follow the edge of the precipice. He had no time to stop and ponder his circumstances, time was of the essence. He would have to either find a place to cross the river, or double back.

He had gone another two hundred yards before he realized his mistake. The trail came to an abrupt end. In front and to his left was a sharp drop to the water fifty feet below. To his right was a cliff face that climbed straight up and impossible to traverse. He was trapped. His only course of action was to go back down the trail and find another way around.

His only hope was that the stranger in pursuit had not followed him on this path. He returned down the trail, walking as quickly and as quietly as he was capable. As he returned to the trees, he stepped cautiously, not knowing if he was still alone.

His heart sank. Just as he began to look for another route, the stranger stepped from behind a tree, just thirty yards from where he stood.

"A valiant attempt, young man, but I'm afraid there is no escape this time," the stranger said. He had a full beard and was wearing jeans and a heavy flannel shirt. He looked like someone who was accustomed to the forest.

"I don't understand," David said. "Who are you and what do you want with me?"

"Haven't you figured it out? I'm here to kill you."

"But why, what did I ever do to you?"

"It's a little hard to explain. It's not so much what you've done, but what you are going to do. I'm sorry I just can't let it happen."

"What does that mean? I don't understand. I'm sure we can work something out. I don't think you really want to kill me."

"Sorry kid, it is nothing personal," the stranger said, as he started to raise the rifle and point it in David's direction.

"Wait, don't!" David shouted, closing his eyes as a reflex action.

A shot rang out, but nothing happened. David didn't feel a thing. He opened his eyes.

The stranger was slumped over on the ground. He couldn't believe his eyes. He looked up and there stood a ranger, holding a revolver in his hand.

"Wha...who are you?" David stammered. Where did you come from?"

The ranger knelt down behind the man on the ground. He felt his neck for a pulse, and then looked up. "It seems he's dead. Very unfortunate, but I couldn't very well let him shoot you."

"Yeah, thanks," David managed to utter, still not sure what had just happened.

"You were warned, to be alert, to keep your eyes open," the ranger said as he stood to his feet.

"Then you're a Guardian," David said, hardly believing it was happening again.

"Yes, you may call me that," the ranger said.

"Why me? Why was he after me?"

"We don't always know why things happen the way they do. However, it's not by chance. There is a purpose, and there is a reason for everything. In time you will understand this. In time you will understand your purpose. But right now, you must rejoin your friends."

"Oh my gosh! I almost forgot. Jonny is hurt. We need to get him to the hospital."

"Yes you do, and quickly. Take this path along the river. It will take you to the bridge, but hurry now, for time is of the essence."

"What about him?" David asked pointing to the body.

"That's for me to deal with."

"Will I see you again?"

"You never know, if I'm needed I will be there. Just remember, you have a strength all your own. You are a survivor and you will know what to do when the time comes. Now go."

David didn't wait around. He knew the conversation was over and he didn't need to prolong it any longer. He also knew that his friend's life might hang in the balance. He sprinted down the path, his mind racing, trying to comprehend all that had happened. The trees flew by on either side, as if it was all a blur. It was all he could do to stay on his feet and to keep from stumbling.

When he reached the bridge he skipped across it as if his feet were only touching the air. As he stepped onto the far shore he stopped for just a moment, looking back at the bridge and remembering; remembering another time like this one.

When he reached the place where they had parked the ETVs, the others were waiting. Michelle ran to him and gave him a hug. Jonny was sitting on the ground propped against one of the ETVs, Sarah was holding a bottle of water to his lips, trying to get him to drink.

"How's he doing?" David asked.

"He's pretty weak, but still breathing. I'm worried. We got him to drink as much water as he can hold, so he is at least hydrated, and I think we have controlled the bleeding. What about the shooter? We thought we heard a shot."

"It's okay, he won't be following. Come on let's get Jonny some help."

"What do you mean he won't be following? What happened?"

"I'll have to explain later. Now's not the time. Right now we have to see to your brother."

David proceeded to help Jonny onto the ETV and then climbed on after, joining his friend. Michelle and Sarah tied the two of them together with a rope. If Jonny passed out, he would not fall off. Michelle would have to drive the other vehicle.

David went as fast as he could without agitating his passenger's wound. It was less than a half an hour to Deming. The town was almost a ghost town, but they were able to find a market where they were directed to the only doctor in town. He was an old codger, but seemed to know what he was doing. With Michelle assisting, he was able to able to remove the bullet and stop the bleeding altogether.

"He's stable, I think he'll be okay," the doctor said when he was finished. We should try and get him to a hospital though. Is there anybody we should call?"

"Oh, my God, Father!" Michelle exclaimed. "I need to call him right away. He'll be furious."

She set her D4 on the table and said, "Call Father." In moments Mr. Benson's holographic form appeared.

"Hi honey, how did it go?" Mr. Benson asked.

"Hi Daddy, we're all okay, but...Daddy, Jonny's been hurt. He's going to be okay. We're at the doctor's now. He was shot."

"Shot! What do you mean shot?" Mr. Benson was clearly angry and alarmed.

"I don't know, exactly. Someone shot at us. We don't know who or why. I'll tell you the whole story later. Right now we need to get Jonny to the hospital."

"Where are you?"

"We're at a doctor's office in Deming."

"I'm sending a helicopter to get you. Stay where you are. Was anyone else hurt? What about David."

"No, everyone else is fine. Just Jonny."

"Oh, I see," Mr. Benson said. "I'm glad."

David got the impression that he wasn't really all that glad. Perhaps Mr. Benson was wishing it had been him instead of Jonny.

Chapter Nine

It was only a week before Jonny was up and around, almost his old self. If Mr. Benson had been over protective before, he was ten times worse now. It was almost as if Jonny and Michelle were made prisoners in their own home. If they left the house, it was with a body guard. This made dating a little awkward.

Investigators were unable to discover who had shot Jonny. It was believed to be a recluse who lived in a cabin just outside of Deming, but they found no trace of him. He had disappeared and no one had seen him for more the two weeks. In the meantime, none of the rangers in the area admitted to knowing anything about the incident. It was left as a mystery.

His contact with Jonny and Michelle having been highly restricted, David found himself completely preoccupied with solving the mystery of the crystals. Professor Kensington was beside himself when David first unveiled his discovery. Together they spent every waking moment trying to decipher the source of the strange electric charge.

It turned out that the charge build-up was due to exposure to sunlight. It wasn't actually static electricity, but instead it seemed to be the consequence of some sort of a photovoltaic effect, the same phenomenon that occurs in solar cells.

The professor subjected the crystals to a variety of light sources, measuring the amount of electric charge produced at varying intensities and different wavelengths. Although UV provided the best results, the photoelectrons were also produced in a range of blue and green wavelengths of visible light.

"It's seems to be a very efficient photovoltaic process," the Professor explained. "The transparency may allow for an increase in photoelectron emissions. From my initial calculations, it appears that this material could be 1000s times more efficient than any known solar cell with a similar amount of surface area."

"Wow, really!!" David said, excitement rising in his voice.. "If that's true there would be countless applications. It might be the stepping stone to solving the solar power problem."

"Yes, the implications are limitless," the professor said. "It's only left to us to find out what the composition is and to find a way to reproduce the conditions in which it was formed."

"Can't we send it to the lab for analysis?" David asked.

"I'm afraid not, David. I'm not sure we should trust the lab with this. This is a highly unusual find, and there are those who would want to get their hands on it, no matter the cost. I think we must keep this between us."

The professor had never been much to trust his fellow colleagues, probably due to the number of times he had seen research results stolen by others for their own personal gain. He had always been a particularly good judge of character and shortly after David had chosen him as an advisor, he had shown him a hidden wall safe where he kept his research, his biggest secrets, so to speak. It was where he would keep the crystals and any documentation of their work.

The next day they were able to schedule some time in the lab to do the spectral analysis on their own. The professor was a little eccentric and had made similar requests in the past and so the lab technician didn't question this one, especially since it was during his lunch hour and would not keep him from his work.

As soon as the technician went to lunch, they went right to work. When the analysis was complete, David noticed a sparkle in the Professor's eyes. "It makes perfect sense," he said as they made their way back to their own lab.

It turned out the crystals were not crystals at all, but a kind of glassy metal. The results showed that they were primarily an amorphous alloy of Aluminum, Zirconium and Silicon. However, the spectral analysis also showed fair concentrations of two rare earth metals, Actinium and Dysprosium. The glassy nature of the alloy must have been due to the extreme temperatures created when the meteor entered the atmosphere and then the rapid cooling when it hit the water. There had been many attempts to create glassy metals with some level of transparency, but up until now it had met with very little success. To discover an alloy of this type with the photovoltaic properties it exhibited was a brilliant stroke of luck.

The professor kept stroking his chin as he poured over the results of the analysis. He was clearly pleased, but as always there was a subtle look of skepticism in his eyes.

"Do you think they can be reproduced?" David finally asked after allowing for as much silence as he could stand.

"It's possible..." the Professor stroked his chin. "Dysprosium and Actinium are not easy to get your hands on, but the good news is that there was a report about a decade ago that someone had discovered a unique form of pitchblende that had an unusually high concentration of Actinium, somewhere in Alberta, I think. In any case, we have to try. This is an amazing find, simply amazing." The professor stroked his chin again, a slight smile crossing his lips.

It was the first time all four friends had been together since the incident at Elbow Lake. Mr. Benson had begrudgingly agreed to let Michelle and Jonny out of their cage. David could see Leonard the chauffeur through the front window. He was never very far away.

They had all agreed to meet up at Tony's. Since it was within the boundaries of the University district, Mr. Benson considered it somewhat safe. In any case they would try to make the best of the opportunity.

"How's your shoulder?" David asked Jonny.

"It's okay, a little sore when I get up in the morning, but I think it's mostly healed."

"It's about time," Michelle chimed in. "I was getting a little tired of playing nursemaid."

"Come on Sis, I wasn't that bad," Jonny said looking a little hurt.

"We're all just glad you're alright," David said. "It seemed like a bit of a close call there for a minute."

"Yeah, it was kind of weird, someone shooting at us like that, and all," Jonny said. "And Dad says they never caught the guy, no sign of him."

"It was a nightmare," Sarah added. "The whole thing was like a bad dream; the entire time I kept saying to myself that *this isn't real.* I kept thinking that at any minute I was going to wake up and it would be all over."

"Yeah, I know what you mean," Michelle said. "I was afraid, but it was as if everything was going in slow motion. I was reacting, but I didn't really have time to think. It all happened so fast. And then there was the waiting…waiting to see if David would ever come back."

"Yeah, about that," Jonny interjected. "You never did tell us how you got away."

David hesitated, not sure he wanted to tell his friends everything. They would never believe him, he wasn't exactly sure he believed it himself. Someone was trying to kill him, and that was why Jonny got hurt. What was more troubling was that he still didn't know why, or what it had to with his grandfather. "I was just lucky I guess, someone must have been watching out for me."

"Well I for one am glad, luck or not. I don't know what we would have done if you hadn't returned. I was this close to going after you." Michelle smiled and squeezed his hand.

"And you would have, too," David said, with a little reprimand in his voice. "After I had expressly told you to leave without me."

"It wasn't going to happen," Michelle snapped back, "you know, all for one, and all."

David knew in his heart that Michelle would've never left without him. That was her nature. She was courageous, but also stubborn to a fault. They were all fortunate that someone had been watching out for him, or the outcome might have been much different.

"I, for one, thought we were all gonna die," Sarah interjected. "I've never been so scared. I'm just glad the whole thing is over." She looked at the clock on the image projected screen over the bar. "Oh, shoot, look at the time. I told my parents I would be home half an hour ago. I need to go. They've been a little paranoid, ever since the riot downtown last week.

They don't want me out after dark. Do you think Leonard could give me a ride home?"

"Sure, no problem," Jonny replied. "Come on Sis, we better be going as well."

"Oh come on, Jonny, I want to stay here a while longer. David and I have barely seen each other the past couple of weeks. Besides you have to come by here on your way home anyway."

"I'm okay with it, but I don't know if Leonard will go for it."

"Look, it's going to take you at least a half an hour to get Sarah home and then get back here. David and I will be waiting right here for you when you get back."

"Alright, I'll try and take it up with Leonard, but I can't guarantee he'll go for it."

Jonny and Sarah went outside and a lengthy discussion ensued between Jonny and the chauffeur. In the end it appeared Jonny won the battle. The chauffeur was clearly not happy and there was concern etched on his face, but he finally relented. The three got in the car and departed, leaving David and Michelle alone.

"Do you mind taking a little walk?" David asked. "I need to grab a couple things from the lab before I head home tonight. We should be there and back in twenty minutes, long before Jonny and Leonard return."

"I'd love to," Michelle responded with a smile. "It's getting a little noisy in here anyway."

David took Michelle's hand in his and they walked at a leisurely pace through campus. The night was pleasant. There were no clouds and the stars were bright in the sky above.

"Michelle, there is something I've wanted to tell you, but I haven't been sure how to start. It's a little weird."

"What do you mean? What is it?"

"Well, it's going to sound a little crazy. I'm not exactly sure I believe it myself. When I mentioned before that someone must have been watching over me when we were up at Elbow Lake, I wasn't just making an allusion. It turns out, someone was in fact watching out for me, and it wasn't the first time."

"What do you mean? I don't understand. Who was watching over you?"

"I would have been killed, except someone intervened. He stopped the person who was shooting at us before he had a chance to kill me. He calls himself the Guardian. It wasn't the first time. I've encountered him before...or at least I think I have."

"What do you mean, before?"

"Well, you see, I think the shooter was after me. He was trying to kill me, just me. Jonny just got in the way. It wasn't the first time. There was at least one other time, but now I wonder if there may have been more. Somehow it has to do with my grandfather's research...I know this is going to sound a little strange, I don't know if I believe it myself, but I think my grandfather figured out a way to travel into the future, or maybe I should say look into the future...it's all a little confusing. Somehow he became aware that I was in danger, and he traveled into the future to protect me. I'm not sure, but I think my grandfather is somehow this Guardian. He doesn't look like my grandfather, but it's him just the same, or at least I think it is. It is the only explanation I have been able to come up with."

"Wait a second," Michelle stopped walking and turned and faced him, a look of concern stretched across her face. "You're saying your grandfather is a *time traveler*."

"Yeah, sort of. I know it sounds a little like science fiction, but somehow he, with help from Grandpa Mike, and their friend Raphael, was able to transfer his consciousness through some kind of quantum crack into the future. It all sounds a little crazy, but the more I think about it, the more I think it must be true. It's the only thing that makes any sense."

"Makes sense, in what way does it make any sense?" Michelle was still skeptical. "It sounds ridiculous to me."

"Yeah, I know. I don't really expect you to believe it, at least not right away, but the truth is, I would be dead if the Guardian had not intervened. He saved my life." David looked past the fountain toward the G-Lab. "It looks like the professor is working a little late. The light is on in our lab."

"Now don't try and change the subject," Michelle said with a little irritation in her voice.

David spent the rest of the way trying to convince Michelle of what he was saying. He told her about is first contact with the Guardian, and everything he had discovered in his grandfather's journals. Slowly but surely she started to accept what he was saying.

When they left the stairwell and entered the fourth floor hallway, he hesitated for a moment. "That's strange," he said, looking down the hallway. "The lab door is open." There was something wrong, he could sense it, but he didn't know why.

As they got to the door of the lab, he turned around and looked back down the hallway. Someone was there, he could sense it; someone was lurking in the shadows. He could see the outline of a form, it was familiar, but he didn't know why. He stepped through the door of the lab, Michelle right behind him, still jabbering away. He put his finger to his lips as a way of letting her know that she should stop talking. He closed the door and placed his thumb on the lock pad. Nothing happened.

Without warning, Michelle screamed, causing David to jump. She was completely white and pointing to the back wall of the lab. The Professor's body lay on the floor. There was a dark red pool beneath his head. David ran over to the body and placed his fingers against the Professor's neck. He was dead. There was a bullet hole in the back of his head.

David looked up at Michelle, tears were streaming down her cheeks and she held her hands over her mouth as if trying to refrain herself from screaming again.

"He's dead," David said. "He's been shot."

"Shot, you mean murdered!" Michelle sobbed. "Who would want to kill the Professor?"

"I don't know, but whoever did it is still here. I think I caught a glimpse of him in the hallway. I can't get the door to lock. We need to get out of here, right now."

As soon as the words left his mouth, the lights went out and they were left standing in the dark.

"What are we going to do?" Michelle whispered, a little more composed.

"We only have one chance. There's a small maintenance elevator on the other side of the building, rarely used. Maybe our friend out there doesn't know about it. If we can get to it, without being noticed, we might have a chance to get away unnoticed."

He led Michelle to the back of the lab where there was a door that connected to the lab next door. He tried the knob, it wasn't locked, as he expected. He slowly opened the door, trying to avoid making even the slightest noise. He peered inside, it was empty. He coaxed Michelle through the door and then closed it gently behind them.

They crept along the wall toward the hallway door. He motioned to her to stay low, below the level of the counters so they could not be seen through the windows that looked out onto the hallway. The door had a frosted glass window and there was a light green glow, revealing that the exit sign in the hallway was still lit. They knelt down beside the door, listening intently for a sign that they were not alone. David could feel his heart racing, the adrenaline coursing through his veins. He looked over at Michelle. He could see the strain on her face, but her eyes were clear, and he could see that she was determined and she was trying to be brave.

She grabbed his arm and pointed to the door. A shadow passed across the window. They were not alone. He was here.

They remained quiet and still, listening for any hint of movement. The door to the neighboring lab, where the Professor's cold body still lay, opened with a squeak. David carefully opened the door they were kneeling at and peered around the corner. Now was their chance. He pointed down the hall and Michelle obeyed without hesitation. They left their hiding placed and moved as quickly and quietly as they could down the hall.

Just as they rounded the corner into the next hall, they heard a door bang, they had been found out. They started running. It would take a moment before their pursuer realized that they had not taken the stairs. They rounded another corner and David directed Michelle to the end of the hall.

When they reached the elevator, David pushed the button, it lit up, but the doors didn't move. The lift was on a lower floor. They waited, breathing hard, knowing that at any minute they would be found out. It seemed an eternity.

The door opened and as quick as they could, they both stepped inside. David turned to look back down the hallway, a shadow appeared. It was coming toward them. He pressed the button to close the doors, there was a slight hesitation and then they slowly began to close. A whistling sound was heard and a bullet hole appeared on the back wall of the elevator just before the doors clamped shut.

David leaned back against the wall as the elevator started its descent. "That was a close call." He looked over at Michelle. She was as white as a sheet. "Michelle we made it."

"Did you see..." she stammered. "That was...that was Danny!"

Chapter Ten

"I'm telling you, I saw his face. That was Danny," she said again. "But I don't understand. Why would he want to harm the Professor? I don't get it."

"I don't know Michelle. It doesn't make any sense to me, but we can't wait around here to find out. I need to get you out of here and then we need to find some help."

The elevator reached the ground floor. David peaked out. There was no one in sight, not a sound to be heard. It was dark. He could see the soft glow of a street light through the glass doors at the entrance. They would have to risk it.

They sprinted for the door, David stopped, allowing Michelle to pass through the doors as he looked back, anticipating that their pursuer could appear at any moment. Michelle squealed as soon as she was outside. She had run right into Jonny who was about to enter the building.

"Hey!" Jonny exclaimed as he half stumbled backwards. "What's going on?"

"Jonny!" Michelle said in a tense whisper. "We have to get out here. There is someone following us."

"Following you, what do mean?"

"No time to explain," David said, still looking back. "The professor has been murdered, and his murderer is right behind us. We need to get out of here right now."

"Leonard has the car parked over on Mountlake."

"I don't think that's a good idea. Come on, I'll have to explain later. We can catch a bus near the canal bridge."

Jonny tried to put up an argument, but realized it was no use, as both David and Michelle took off in the direction of bridge. The three ran across the campus, staying close to the buildings so they could remain hidden in the shadows. Occasionally, David would stop to see if anyone was following, but there was no sign of their pursuer. By the time they had reached the bus stop, they were feeling confident that they had lost him.

"I don't understand," Jonny began, "you said the professor has been murdered. Why? Who would want to murder him?"

"We don't know. All we know is that he is dead, shot in the back of the head," David said, breathing hard, still trying to come to grips with the grief of losing his friend and mentor.

"That's not all," Michelle added, "the murderer...I think the murderer is Danny."

"Danny? What? Are you crazy? What makes you think it was Danny? I mean, he doesn't even know the Professor." Jonny was incredulous.

"I know it sounds crazy, but I saw his face, just for a moment. It was dark, but I'm almost positive it was Danny," Michelle insisted.

"I didn't get a clear look, but I think she might be right. It was the way he moved. It was all too familiar."

"But I don't get it," Jonny said. "Why would Danny want to kill the professor? It's just ridiculous."

"That might be, but what we have to ask ourselves, is that if Danny is in fact the murderer, is there anyone else involved. In other words, is Leonard involved, or..." David hesitated not sure whether he should utter what he was thinking.

"Wait a second, Father? Are you thinking our *father* had something to do with this?" Jonny asked.

Michelle was dumbfounded and the look on her face was one of horror, suggesting that the thought had not already crossed her mind.

"I don't know. I'm not trying to imply anything. I'm just asking the question." David tried to be diplomatic. "Danny works for your father. It doesn't make any sense, but maybe, just maybe, Danny was acting on your father's orders."

"That's crazy," Michelle emerged from her initial shock. "Why would father want to hurt the Professor? It's crazy I tell ya. I have never liked Danny. There has always been something weird about him, something dark. Perhaps he was just acting on his own."

David looked at Jonny, he was clearly pondering something. No one spoke. They sat quietly, each of them dealing with their own thoughts.

"Oh my gosh," Jonny broke the silence. "The other day, Dad was asking me all these questions about the crystals we found. He wanted to know if the Professor had been able to solve the mystery of their strange properties. At the time I didn't think anything about it. Is it possible they were after the crystals?" He hesitated, David and Michelle said nothing. "Is it actually possible that *he is* involved?"

"I hope not," David said. "It doesn't do any good for us to sit here and speculate. I suppose first things first." He removed his phone from his pocket. "Dial 911," he said aloud. His phone immediately responded.

"Wait! What are you doing?" Michelle asked anxiously.

"I have to let the police know about the professor. We can't just ignore what has happened."

"Please state the nature of your emergency," a voice said.

"I want to report a murder at the Guggenheim building at the university, fourth floor. The victim is a Professor Kensington."

"Are you there with the victim now?"

"No, I had to leave. The murderer may still be in the building. Tell whoever you need to, they may want to investigate a Danny..." he hesitated.

"Morgan," Jonny added. "His last name is Morgan."

"Morgan, Danny Morgan," David repeated.

"And your name," the operator asked.

"Can't talk now, hang up." The phone sounded a musical tone as it turned off.

A bus arrived. "I think we should pay your father a visit," David said. "It's the only way to get to the bottom of this. I hope he's innocent, but one way or the other we need to find out."

———

As they walked up the driveway to the Benson home, David felt a wave of anxiety wash over him. He was afraid. It felt as if he was walking into a trap. There was no sign of the car, or Leonard for that matter, but that didn't mean anything. It could be parked in the garage. If Danny and Leonard were working together, they would have had plenty of time to return, well ahead of the bus.

David stopped the others before they entered the front door. "Whatever happens," he said in a low voice, "know that I hope with all my heart that your father is innocent. Regardless, I don't think we are in any danger here. I don't believe he would ever harm either of the two of you, and I am counting on him to realize that he can't really do anything to me with you in the room. But we have to find out what the crack is going on, and whether he is involved. What's more, we'll have to be alert, because if Danny is anywhere near, he knows that we are witnesses to the Professor's murder. If your father is not involved, then he doesn't know the danger that Danny poses. We must be careful."

The others nodded their heads indicating they understood. Jonny led the way into the house. No one was in the entryway, but they could see a light on in the living room. Mr. Benson was sitting at the bar. He looked up as they entered.

"Where have you been? I have been worried sick. Leonard called more than a half an hour ago and said that you had disappeared. I told you that you are not to go anywhere without Leonard or Danny."

David was trying to get a sense of the sincerity of his words. Was he really worried? Or was it all an act? He couldn't really tell. The only thing he could tell for sure was that Mr. Benson still held him in disdain. He could see it in his eyes. It wasn't hatred, exactly. It was more like disinterest, as if Mr. Benson felt nothing for David, neither like nor dislike; nothing.

"Sorry Dad," Jonny jumped in first. "It wasn't really our fault. It seemed David and Michelle ran into a little trouble."

"*Trouble?* What kind of trouble?" He spoke with his usual coldness.

"Oh Daddy, it was horrible," Michelle blurted out. "Professor Kensington was murdered. We were just visiting the lab, to pick up some things for David, when we found him. And then we thought the murderer was still there, so we had to get out of there. I saw..." David gently squeezed her arm in an attempt to stop her from saying too much. She looked at him as

Justice

if she understood. "I...I was so afraid. If it wasn't for David... well, who knows what might have happened."

"Who would want to kill Professor Kensington," Mr. Benson directed toward David. "I mean, was he involved with someone, you know, someone who would want to hurt him? Did he say anything? Was there anything missing from the lab?"

"Not that I know of," David said. "He never said anything to me. I mean all we ever talked about was our research."

"And what were you working on? Was it anything important? You know, important enough that someone would want it bad enough to shoot your professor in the back of the head over it."

David began to feel the hair stick up on the back of his neck. It was the same feeling he had at the lab. Something was wrong, terribly wrong. He looked Mr. Benson directly in the eyes. That was it, he knew that look. He had seen it before. "Who said he was shot in back of the head?"

"Well... what do you mean?" Mr. Benson said, apprehensively. "Michelle just said it a moment ago."

"No," David said. "She said the Professor had been murdered. She didn't say how. How did you know he was shot in the back of the head?"

"Hey, that's right," Jonny said, looking concerned.

"*Daddy?*" Michelle blurted out. "Daddy, what have you done?"

As if on cue, Danny stepped out from the shadows of the darkened corner of the room where he had been hiding until that very moment. Leonard came through the door behind them, they were both holding guns.

"It was you all along," David said. "Danny here was only acting on your orders. It has always been you. It was you at the river, at the zoo, and the bridge."

"David, what do you mean?" Michelle was growing agitated, Jonny looked completely confused.

"I'm sorry Michelle, but your father has been trying to kill me. Somehow he was able to steal my grandfather's research. He used the Quantum Transference to jump into the future, with the intent of killing me. Isn't that right Mr. Benson?"

Mr. Benson didn't respond right away. He kept looking at his two children, first one then the other. "You always were a bright young man, David. I suppose you got that from your grandfather. You have to understand, it wasn't personal. It was business."

"But Daddy, why?"

"I'm sorry, sweetie. I never meant to hurt you. How was I to know that you would fall in love with him? That was just a stupid act of fate. You have to understand, this all started long before you were even born. There was no way I could have known." He turned back to David. "I guess your grandfather somehow discovered what I was doing." David nodded his head in affirmation. "I should have known. I should have guessed it the first time you survived. I just thought it was bad luck. You have to understand David, this was never really about you, not really."

"That's a little hard for me to accept. I mean after all, you were trying to kill me."

"I don't understand," Jonny interjected looking even more confused. "What's this all about? Dad, why did you want to kill David, what did he ever do to you?"

"It was all about the crystals. Isn't that right, Mr. Benson?" David said.

Mr. Benson nodded. "My first attempt at looking into the future revealed your discovery of the crystals. It was then that I realized that I had to change the timeline, change it in such a way that I could gain control of the technology. It was too valuable. I had to have it. It would insure that I would have complete control of the most important energy source of our lifetime. I had to have it."

"That's what this is all about, money?" Michelle said, exasperation ringing in her voice. "What do you need more money for? We have everything we could ever need."

"It wasn't just about the money, Michelle," David said. "It was also about the power, about the control."

"Michelle, you don't understand," Mr. Benson said, pleading for her understanding. "This was all for you, for you and your brother."

"Please stop! Don't bring us into this!" Michelle was nearly yelling. "This had nothing to do with us. My God, you murdered the Professor. And for what, just so you could have a little more money. Don't try and make this about Jonny and me. This is all about you, your ego. You are nothing more than a villain."

"You don't understand. We're talking about a three dimensional photovoltaic cell that would be thousands time more efficient than anything ever imagined. It would mean billions, not to mention, complete control of an energy source which has unlimited applications. There would be no telling where it could take us. Kensington was the fool. All he had to do was sell me the technology and everything would have been alright. But no, he wanted to *give* it away. Make it available to everyone. Damn fool, I had no choice."

"And what about my father?" David asked somewhat hesitantly, not sure he wanted to know the truth. "Why did you have to kill him?"

"At first I thought I could just change the timeline, first by eliminating your grandfather, then, maybe your father would never even meet your mother. When that didn't work, your father seemed the next logical choice. I thought it would change the course of your life, put you on a different path, so to speak, but it didn't work. I didn't count on Garrett and Michael finding out, and then intervening."

"The perfect crime, impossible to trace, because it wasn't really you, it was merely your consciousness inhabiting another person's body."

"I think you have the whole picture," Mr. Benson said.

"Wait a second," Michelle interjected. "Are you saying it was you in the mountains? You were the one shooting at us. You shot Jonny...you shot your own son."

"Michelle, Jonny," Mr. Benson looked at one and then the other, strain etched on his face. "You have to understand, it wasn't me from now, it was me in the past, from the distant past. Jonny was barely a baby, and you had not been born yet when I began using the Quantum Transference. There was no way I could have recognized you. I couldn't possibly have known that you and David would have become friends. It was an accident. I would never want to hurt Jonny." He looked Jonny in the eyes. It was becoming clear that he was losing all respect in the eyes of his children.

"And what about now?" David asked. "What are your plans? Are you going to kill me? And what about them?" He indicated Jonny and Michelle. "What are you going to do with them?"

"I'm thinking we can still come to some kind of arrangement," Mr. Benson said, regaining some of his composure. "You don't have to die. You hand over the crystals and all your research and promise to keep quiet about this whole matter, and we can leave it at that."

"You expect me trust you then," David said. "I mean, you killed my father, and a grandfather I never knew. How do you expect me to stand idly by and let you get away with it? How do you expect me to stay silent?"

"Well that's just it, isn't it? Power is an interesting thing. You have to realize that I can reach out to any corner of your life, for example, your mother, or what about your two cousins, delightful girls, I'm told. I'm sure you wouldn't want any harm to come to them. After all, there's nothing connecting me to Kensington, and as far as the other incidents, you have already put it very eloquently, it wasn't *really* me. The only people who really know what happened are right here in this room. And then again, there really isn't any proof."

David didn't like the sound of that. He knew what Mr. Benson was capable of and he wasn't bluffing. However, he also didn't know that David had his grandfather's journals. Then there was the 911 call, he had already called the police and there would have to be some explaining to do. He looked at Michelle and Jonny, he sensed they were conflicted, a mixture of rage and confusion. Then he caught something in Jonny's eyes. It was a message of sorts, something that could only be understood between the best of friends.

In a flash, Jonny grabbed the poker next to the fire place and swung it as hard as he could, dislodging the gun from

Danny's hand. In the same instant, Michelle tried to grab the arm of Leonard, only to find herself knocked to the floor with one swipe of his arm. It was all the distraction that David needed. He jumped at Leonard, grabbing the arm that held the gun. There was a horrible struggle, and the gun discharged. As chance would have it, the bullet struck a surprised Danny in the chest knocking him to the floor and killing him instantly. Just as it appeared that Leonard was about to get the upper hand, there was a large crash and his body went limp.

David pulled himself to his feet. Standing over Leonard's unconscious body stood Michelle holding the remnants of a broken Chinese vase. David turned to face Mr. Benson, but he was too slow. Mr. Benson had picked up Danny's gun and was now pointing it at David.

"A very unfortunate chain of events," Mr. Benson said. "I'm afraid you leave me little choice."

"No, father," Jonny said as he stepped between David and Mr. Benson, blocking his father's view of his intended victim. "No more. I can't let you do it."

"Step aside son! Don't be a fool. You wouldn't betray your own father?"

Michelle stepped forward taking her place at her brother's side. "Give me the gun father," Michelle said, holding out her hand. "We can't let you kill him. It's over. This ends now."

As fate would have it, Mr. Benson was never given the opportunity to respond. Two men in blue entered the room and shouted, "Drop the weapon!"

Mr. Benson, hesitated slightly, and then slowly lowered the gun. The police officers stepped forward and removed the weapon from his hand and then proceeded to cuff him. Michelle turned and placed her arms around David. "I'm so sorry," she whispered.

A gray haired man with a long trench coat entered the library. "Detective Beck," he said flashing a badge. "I guess we got here just in the nick of time."

"Well not exactly in the nick of time," David said, indicating Danny's limp body on the floor.

"Uh, yeah, well, I guess you're right."

"Who are you and where did you come from?" Jonny asked.

"Well, it was your friend here, the 911 call. We were able to trace his phone. And then when we discovered Morgan here was employed by your father, we knew we had the right place. Hmph, kind of a shame we couldn't have got here a bit sooner, though." He looked down at Danny again.

"David Jacobson, I believe," he said. "Seems this isn't the first time I have crossed paths with you."

"What do you mean?" David asked. "Have we met?"

"Well sort of. It's a long story. I know your grandfather. It seems you have some explaining to do."

Epilogue

David put his arm around the shoulders of his mother. There were tears on her cheeks. She had loved her father very much and it was difficult to say goodbye. Grandpa Adams had died, finally succumbing to the tumor that had invaded his brain. It was better this way. David wanted to remember him as he had been. It had been too painful to see his mind slowly slip away. He had been a loving father and grandfather and they would miss him.

Time moves forward, a natural thing. There is no controlling it. With time comes change, and with change comes age and eventually death. And the question remains, is there any real meaning to it all? Is there a purpose? His grandfather believed there was. And even if his body was now reduced to dust and ashes, his life had been a real thing, and it had meant something. The platitudes offered by the minister were nice, but his grandfather's life was more than cliché. He had made a difference, and David knew it to be true.

He gently squeezed Michelle's hand. She turned her head slightly toward him and smiled. He was glad she was there. He was glad that she had known his grandfather, and she could share this moment with him, to help him say goodbye.

When the service was completed he noticed a solitary figure sitting in a wheelchair looking out over the lake, it was his Grandpa Mike. He had been paralyzed from the waist down from a bullet that lodged in his spine. David was only ten at the time, but he remembered the moment clearly. He now knew that the bullet had been meant for him. Grandpa Mike had saved his life. It seemed as if he had had two guardian angels.

He sat down on the bench next to him. "How ya doin' Gramps?" David asked.

"I will miss him, David. It wasn't just that we shared you as our grandson, he was my best friend. I will miss him a great deal."

"It was the Quantum Transference, wasn't it?"

"You figured that out on your own, did you?" Michael looked at David and smiled. "Yes, Garrett started experiencing those headaches early on. With each jump into the future they became more pronounced. He knew that something was wrong, but he never let on, not until it was too late. How did you know?"

"He gave me his journals, warned me about Mr. Benson. He wanted me to know."

"Is that so? I thought he destroyed those long ago. He never really liked that contraption."

"Do you think Mr. Benson will be convicted?" David asked.

"I don't know son, I don't know. I suppose they will at least get him on conspiracy in the death of Dr. Kensington, although with Mr. Morgan dead, there's no way to show he is absolutely guilty. He's a very powerful man. I'm sure his lawyers have a plan."

"But what about the others, I mean, after all, he killed my father."

"Yes he did David, but there's no real way to prove it. Even if you told the police about the Quantum Transference and if they believed you, there would be no way of proving any connection. It would just be your word against his."

"It doesn't quite seem fair."

"Maybe not, but I think you will have your justice in the end. His plans have been disrupted. Not only that, but now even his own children have abandoned him. Whether he is in prison or not, he will live out his life a broken and lonely man, which is prison enough. Not only that, he will eventually pay the price for using the Quantum Transference machine as well, just like Garrett. He will get what he deserves in the end, regardless of what we think or do. That is justice, and it is far more rewarding than revenge."

"I suppose you're right." David paused, thinking about all that had happened, all that had brought him to this moment. "Why did he do it?"

"What, you mean Mr. Benson?" Michael asked.

"No, I'm fully aware that power corrupts and all and that Mr. Benson is a narcissist. No, I meant Grandpa Adams. He had to know that the Quantum Transference was beginning to pose a health risk. He had to know that it was injuring his brain."

"Yes, David, he did. The headaches came and went, but I'm sure he always knew. But you see, he really didn't have choice. He had to continue. It was all about the promises he had made. He had to see them through even if it meant putting himself at risk."

"Promises, what promises?"

"It started with your grandmother. He had promised he would love and care for her no matter what. There was a moment when he almost forgot this promise, and it nearly ended in tragedy. But then, he remembered how much he loved your grandmother and your mother and that was when everything changed. He knew no matter what, they were the only thing of real importance to him. You see, the promise he made to your grandmother was a part of a series of promises. It came with a promise to love and care for his two daughters, and in turn, to provide the same love and care for their children, you and your two cousins. He loved you all and would do anything for you. When he became aware that you were in danger, he had to do everything in his power to protect you, to become your Guardian, regardless of the danger it posed to himself."

"I just wish he wouldn't have had to pay for it with his life. I wish he could still be here now."

"I don't think he would have it any other way. He knew that by saving you, he would be risking some of the time he would be able to spend with you and your cousins, but he felt it was worth the risk. He had to do it; he had no other choice. This to, is justice. He knew that you didn't have the ability to protect yourself, you were too young. When we make personal sacrifice in order to protect and care for the innocent and defenseless, this is the highest form of justice."

"I'm going to miss him," David said.

"We are all going to miss him. But he's not really gone. Every time I look at you, I see him. You have more of him in you than you realize. It's now up to you to carry with you everything you have learned from him, to make a difference in this world, just as he did. He knew he couldn't live forever, but he had come to realize that there was purpose and meaning in all that we do. We are not always in control, and when we get off track, Providence has a way of bringing us back. The only question that is left before us is: If we in have the opportunity to make choices, the ability to determine even the smallest things, then, will we choose to do what is right and good and honorable? Will we try to make this world a better place? Your grandfather grew to understand this, and I think he made a difference. Now, it's up to you, to find your purpose and to do what is right."

About the Author

Michael Rea was born in Eugene, Oregon and spent his entire youth living in the Pacific Northwest, where he enjoyed many moments camping, hiking and fishing in the Cascade Mountains of Washington and Oregon. He attended Westmont College in Santa Barbara, CA where he earned a B.A. in Chemistry and upon graduation, enrolled in a graduate program in Chemistry at the University of Illinois. Although expecting to complete his Ph.D. and begin a career as a research scientist, he unexpectedly fell in love with teaching, completed a M.S. in Teaching Chemistry and embarked on a career in secondary education.

Aside from his love for science, and his newly discovered passion for writing, Michael is also an artist, specializing in landscape and wildlife paintings in oil. He and his wife, Janet, love to travel and they make an effort to visit at least one national park every summer. These trips have greatly contributed many of the subjects for his paintings, while at the same time providing him with a time to get away to write. Together, he and his wife share a love for literature. A list of his favorite authors suggests a diverse influence on his writing: Isaac Asimov, C.S. Lewis, J.R.R Tolkien, Sir Walter Scott, Alexander Dumas and Charles Dickens.

With over thirty years of experience in education, he has taught courses in all levels of mathematics and science, art, philosophy and religious studies. Science and the arts don't always mix well, but Michael's proficiency in both makes for an interesting combination, as does his eclectic background in coaching, teaching, and high school administration. He currently divides his time between his love of teaching chemistry and physics to his students and his love of oil painting and writing.

Today, Michael and his wife live in Temecula, CA. They have three children and three grandchildren.

www.ingramcontent.com/pod-product-compliance
Lightning Source LLC
Chambersburg PA
CBHW060544180626
46817CB00002B/717